PEOPLE OF THE BLACK SUN

ALSO BY W. MICHAEL GEAR AND KATHLEEN O'NEAL GEAR

Big Horn Legacy

Dark Inheritance

The Foundation

Fracture Event

Long Ride Home

The Mourning War

Raising Abel

Rebel Hearts Anthology

Sand in the Wind

Thin Moon and Cold Mist

Black Falcon Nation Series

Flight of the Hawk Series

The Moundville Duology

Saga of a Mountain Sage Series

The Wyoming Chronicles

The Anasazi Mysteries

PEOPLE OF THE BLACK SUN

THE PEACEMAKER'S TALE
BOOK SEVEN

W. MICHAEL GEAR
KATHLEEN O'NEAL GEAR

People of the Black Sun
Paperback Edition
Copyright © 2024 (As Revised) W. Michael Gear and Kathleen O'Neal Gear

Wolfpack Publishing
1707 E. Diana Street
Tampa, Florida 33609

wolfpackpublishing.com

All rights reserved. No part of this book may be reproduced by any means without the prior written consent of the publisher, other than brief quotes for reviews.

This book is a work of fiction. Any references to historical events, real people or real places are used fictitiously. Other names, characters, places and events are products of the author's imagination, and any resemblance to actual events, places or persons, living or dead, is entirely coincidental.

Illustrations by Ellisa Mitchel.

Paperback ISBN 978-1-63977-588-0
eBook ISBN 978-1-63977-587-3

To Jake and Shannon, our faithful muses for Gitchi

A.D.

| 0 | 200 | 1,000 | 1,100 | 1,300 | 1,400 |

PEOPLE of the LAKES
East-Central Woodlands
& Great Lakes

PEOPLE of the WEEPING EYE
Mississippi Valley
& Tennessee

PEOPLE of the MASKS
Ontario & Upstate New York

PEOPLE of the THUNDER
Alabama & Mississippi

PEOPLE of the RIVER
Mississippi Valley

PEOPLE of the LONGHOUSE
New York
& New England

PEOPLE of the SILENCE
Southwest Anasazi

PEOPLE of the MOON
Northwest New Mexico
& Southwest Colorado

PEOPLE of the MIST
Chesapeake Bay

B.C.

13,000	10,000	6,000	3,000	1,500

PEOPLE of the WOLF
Alaska & Canadian Northwest

PEOPLE of the EARTH
Northern Plains & Basins

PEOPLE of the NIGHTLAND
Ontario & New York & Pennsylvania

PEOPLE of the OWL
Lower Mississippi Valley

PEOPLE of the SEA
Pacific Coast & Arizona

PEOPLE of the RAVEN
Pacific Northwest & British Columbia

PEOPLE of the LIGHTNING
Florida

PEOPLE of the FIRE
Central Rockies & Great Plains

Museum in Howes Cave, New York—www.iroquoismuseum.org—which was established by the state of New York in 1891.

We encourage you to take a trip to see these fragile, beautiful pieces of American history. Each is a story worth seeing.

is always only a generation away. History has demonstrated many times that causing the death of a culture is a relatively easy process: First, destroy a people's written records. Second, destroy their language. When there's no one left who can recite the stories of the people, and no documents to tell the young about them, assimilation into the dominant culture is virtually inevitable. Why? Because when a people's words are lost, they must re-story their world from the traditions of alien nations.

Imagine, for a moment, what it must have been like for Henan Scrogg and Solon Skye, the last two people in the twentieth century able to read the original wampum of the Code of Handsome Lake, knotted by the Prophet himself in the early 1800s —Johansen and Mann, 2000, p. 328. Now imagine what it would be like today to lose the last two people who could read the Declaration of Independence and the Bill of Rights. Certainly Faithkeepers would keep both documents alive as long as possible through oral history, but the truth is that oral traditions are mutable. They change with the failing memories of the elders struggling to preserve them—especially if the young no longer care about such "fables."

The People of the Longhouse, the Haudenosaunee, managed to save some of the most critical wampum belts. They can be seen today in excellent repositories like the Iroquois Indian and Schmitt, pp. 223-225. We wrote about Adena and Hopewell cultures in *People of the Lakes*.

The term "wampum belt" is slightly misleading. In our culture, a belt is something that encircles the waist. Depending upon how much information was being recorded, Iroquoian belts could be four or five feet long and just as wide. Prehistorically, they may have been even larger.

Because wampum belts faithfully recorded the details of treaties, they presented both the original thirteen colonies, and later the United States government, with a problem. Wampum belts were evidentiary—they had a legal status in courts. It is perhaps no surprise that Indian Agents, traders, state authorities, and anyone else who had access to purchasing wampum belts were hired by the government to acquire these belts so that they could be destroyed. The resulting loss of information can be likened to the destruction of the Mayan codices by Bishop Diego de Landa in A.D. 1562, or the destruction of the Library of Alexandria by Patriarch Theophilus around A.D. 391. The destruction of a people's history is always the first step of conquerors.

Keep in mind that human beings are storytellers. Our cultures are founded upon stories, interpreted through them, and survive because of them. Destroying a civilization doesn't require warfare or plague or starvation. Cultural midnight

Wampum could be "read" by anyone who'd been trained.

The earliest European historical records corroborate that each bead, row, or character had a definite meaning, and further state that both sides of the belt were read. Lengthy documents, for example, the minutes of meetings, the details of treaties, the Constitution of the League of the Iroquois, and much more, were recorded on belts so completely that they could still be read centuries later. In the 1700s, Moravian missionary John Heckewelder reported that wampum readers had the ability "to point out the exact place on a belt which is to answer each particular sentence, the same as we can point out a passage in a book"—Heckewelder, p. 108—and added that a great deal depended on the "*turning* of the belt," saying that "it may be as well known by it how far the speaker has advanced in his speech, as with us on taking a glance at the pages of a book or pamphlet while reading."

Knotting wampum, tying the shells in place, was considered to be a spiritual activity in which writers "talked" their messages into the shells, which sounds very much like they were recording words or phrases. And this was apparently an ancient tradition. Archaeologists have found wampum beads that date back more than two thousand years to the Adena Culture in Ohio—Slotkin might have believed, but we know that Iroquoian peoples thought that burying weapons would submerge them in the river of Great Grandmother Earth's blood that ran beneath the surface of the earth. Her blood purified the weapons, cleansing them of the hatred and despair associated with warfare.

The earliest reference to Iroquoian peoples burying weapons is found in the rich oral history of the Peacemaker tale.

We say "oral" history, because it's generally believed that North American's native cultures had no written languages. Many archaeologists have suspected for a long time that such an assumption is false, but it's been very hard to prove that the symbols we find in the archaeological record represent a written language. Wampum—more correctly called "otekoa"—may be the exception. At least a "protolanguage," a precursor, it may have been much more.

The problem arises because of definitions of what constitutes "writing." Wampum consists of a set of blackish-purple and white symbols, recorded most often with shell beads. However, the Iroquois believe that before shell wampum existed, wampum was created with black and white painted pieces of wood. The Mohawk say that the first wampum was made using different colors of eagle quills—Tehanetorens, 1999, p. 12.

ACKNOWLEDGMENTS

There is a magical word in the Seneca language, usually stated at the beginning of the story, and by which a story may be told as a serial: *ensegaha'a*.

It has taken us around a half million words, and eight books, to convey a semblance of the richness and complexity of the Peacemaker tale. We hope you enjoy this epic tale.

NONFICTION INTRODUCTION

The term "bury the hatchet" dates to around four hundred years ago, just after European colonists arrived in northeastern North America and became acquainted with the traditions of the native peoples, but the practice of ending violence by burying weapons has a much older history.

Archaeologists debate the origins of the tradition, but one thing is probably certain: the elite members of Cahokian society practiced this rite. Cahokia, a World Heritage Site just outside of St. Louis, Illinois, is truly one of the world's magnificent archaeological sites. Cahokia was a part of the Mississippian moundbuilder tradition. We wrote about this culture in *People of the River* in 1992. In twenty years, we have learned so much more about their astounding empire, which flourished from around A.D. 700-1550. Peoples who belonged to this cultural tradition covered the eastern half of the United States with mound cities and were master architects, builders, astronomers, surgeons, as well as shell, stone, copper, and fabric artisans. Cahokian traders plied their wares across the North American continent. And they, like Iroquoian peoples five hundred years later, also "buried the hatchet."

At a unique hilltop site in the American Bottoms region of Illinois, the Grossman Site, archaeologists discovered a large collection of buried weapons—Pauketat, 2009. The site contains more than one hundred houses and was occupied by the Cahokian elite. Near one of the council houses, archaeologists excavated a cache of seventy buried ax heads. The largest, which had been deliberately placed on top of the cache, weighed around twenty pounds and was twenty inches long. Interestingly, the axe heads had been laid into the pit in discrete sets, as though each clan, or family, had taken turns. Usually they were placed in the pit in pairs, but one set contained twelve axe heads.

From an archaeological perspective, this is clearly a symbolic act. In our modern culture, it would be like finding a collection of buried swords with Excalibur on top. Lest you've forgotten, Excalibur was King Arthur's legendary sword.

We can only speculate about what Cahokians

ENSEGAHA'A...

PEOPLE OF THE BLACK SUN

1

As Sonon strode through the evening forest, his black cape parted the sea of frigid air, leaving ice crystals swirling behind him. Every twig on the maples and giant sycamores was sheathed in white. Far out in the trees, owls watched him with their feathers fluffed out for warmth, their eyes shining.

Deep cold was a quiet monster. It slithered into clothing, stiffened leather, and afflicted bones with agony. Its unnaturally silent voice made ears crave even the slightest sound. The sheer vastness of the frozen land pressed down upon him tonight.

What is my offering? What can I give him to help him?

When he crested the hill and gazed out across the valley where hundreds of campfires glittered, he took a few moments to contemplate the next few days. He suspected they would be some of the most difficult of his existence.

He inhaled a deep breath and started down the hill toward the warriors who had waged the battle. Frozen flowers hid amid the shriveled leaves on the sides of the trail, dead, folded in upon themselves.

As he neared Yellowtail Village, smoke flowed upward from the charred longhouses and obliterated the glittering Path of Souls that painted a white swath across the night sky. His People, the People of the Hills, believed that each person had two souls. One remained with the bones forever. The other, the afterlife soul, stayed on earth for ten days. Then, if it were lucky enough to be properly prepared, it followed the Path of Souls to a long bridge that spanned a dark abyss. On this side of the bridge were all the animals a person had ever known in his life. The animals who had loved him helped him across. Those that he had mistreated chased him, trying to force him to fall off the bridge into eternal darkness. If his animal helpers were strong enough and he made it to the other side, he would be greeted by his ancestors in the Land of the Dead.

Some people, however, had trouble finding the Path of Souls. Especially those who died violently.

His eyes narrowed. On the battlefield below, dead bodies lay contorting as they froze. There must be thousands of glistening soul lights, lost souls, out there bobbing and swaying in confusion, searching for loved ones to take care of them. If Sonon closed his eyes, he could hear their spectral cries rising.

He folded his arms beneath his cape, trying to stay warm while he continued thinking.

Yes, maybe...

Perhaps the single greatest truth of life was that the dead were not dead. Their shadows lived. They wandered the forests, slept in crackling fires and ancient sycamores, and they huddled in grass that wept and stones that whimpered. They were the painted prayer sticks that Great Grandmother Earth used to dance life in and out of this world. If humans could only learn to watch shadows pass like a mountain did, they would understand that death was just a whisper.

"Is that my offering?"

War songs lilted through the sparkling air, mixing eerily with the sobs and moans coming from the destroyed villages.

"Yes," he said softly, deciding. "A glimpse from inside the mountain."

2

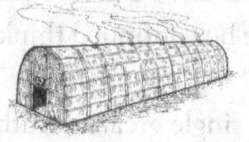

As Grandmother Moon edged above the rocky valley rim, her gleam flecked the bare tips of the trees, and the cold night took on a blazing opalescence.

Where she stood on the catwalk of Bur Oak Village, Matron Jigonsaseh spread her feet and tucked short gray-streaked black hair behind her ear. An unusually tall woman, she had seen thirty-nine summers pass. She had large black eyes, a small nose, and full lips. Her belted cape, woven from twisted strips of fox hide, hung to her knees. The only weapon she carried was her war club, CorpseEye, shoved into her belt. Only a few days ago, she had been called War Chief Koracoo. When she had accepted the position of village matron, she had undergone the Requickening ritual. Her dead mother's soul had been raised up and placed in her body, along with her name: Jigonsaseh. Koracoo hadn't grown accustomed to either the position or the name yet. When people called her Matron Jigonsaseh, she often didn't realize for an instant that they were speaking to her.

She gazed out across the battlefield. The bulk of her army had been destroyed in that gently rolling part of the bowl-shaped valley to the west, just beyond Reed Marsh. In the silvered gleam, she could see the dead. Bodies froze at different rates. Those still warm created black spots upon the frosty grass. Thousands of black spots. How many? She tried to estimate. Perhaps four thousand out there, and another eight or nine hundred in the meadow to the east of the villages?

She braced her forearms on the palisade, and squinted.

Evening carried the pungent scents of smoldering longhouses and old blood.

She concentrated on the war songs that filled the winter night. She longed to be out there in the camps with the men and women who'd waged the battle today. She missed that companionship...and the solace of friends who understood what the fight had cost her.

She bowed her head for a long moment, staring at the tangle of bodies encircling the palisade, enemy warriors who'd tried to assail the walls and failed. Here and there, the ladders they'd thrust against the forty-hand-tall palisade lay like disorganized lattices, the rungs frosted and shining.

All night long, her souls had kept repeating the battle, forcing her to live through it over and over... *six thousand enemy warriors flow swiftly, steadily, across the rolling valley swathed in mist, their clan flags fluttering. They come on like waves, dying all the while, flooding forward to engage my two thousand archers stationed in the maples...volleys of arrows piercing the fog, rising above it, and arcing down in iridescent streams...*

Only a warrior could understand the unspeakable beauty. The battle had writhed and roared, shimmered with a thousand crystal eyes. Magnificent. Terrifying beyond words.

As though to remind her of her duties, sobs of grief and the delirious cries of the wounded rang out in the plaza below. One man in the Wolf Clan longhouse kept coughing wetly, gasping. Lung wound. She had tended many such wounds. If he and his family were very lucky, it would be over soon.

She licked her chapped lips and tasted bitterness. A fine, deep-gray powder of ash continued to rise from the smoldering walls. She had ash in her hair and eyes and ash in her throat. For the rest of her life, she would remember the gritty flavor that pervaded this cold night...and the miracle that had ended the attack...*my son lifts his hands, and a monstrous storm swells above the eastern horizon and crashes down upon the battlefield in shrieking, whirling blackness...warriors scatter like brittle old leaves.*

She laced her fingers and squeezed them together in a stranglehold, desperate to keep her emotions at bay. When the next few days had passed, and she'd done the things that needed to be done, then she would grant herself time to make sense of it.

She still had things to do. *I must go see Cord.* She owed the Chief of the People of the Flint more than she could ever thank him for. Without his help today, the Standing Stone nation would have been wiped from the face of Great Grandmother Earth. Cord's help, and the support of the three Hills People villages that had turned on Chief Atotarho and fought on her side, had made the difference between life and stark oblivion. She had already gone to the Hills matrons and chiefs. She'd left Cord for the last because seeing him was the most difficult.

...on the river twelve summers ago...staring at me with such longing...the black roach of hair bristling down the middle of his skull shining with new-fallen snow...his deep voice like velvet..."If things were different...if our nations were not at war..."

She studied her village, Yellowtail Village,

thirty paces away. It was the smaller sister village of Bur Oak Village. Numerous charred holes gaped in the three concentric rings of palisades that encircled the village. All three longhouses had sustained damage. Roofs had burned through and flaming bark walls had toppled to the ground in smoking heaps. For the night, her villagers had torn down the intact bark walls that separated their interior chambers and tried to fill the gaps in the exterior longhouse walls. Firelight streamed around the mismatched squares. The central plaza bonfire blazed, flickering over the dark shapes of dozens of people who tended the dead, laid out in rows. Oddly, the feet were all even, the toes pointing upward like short stubby posts. It would have been foolish to waste the warm space inside the crowded houses on them. Their afterlife souls were not in their bodies, but roaming around the village in the form of glistening soul lights, eating the dregs in the cooking pots, and trying to speak with their loved ones. Jigonsaseh's own daughter, Tutelo, would be there tending the bodies, probably working through the night, despite the fact that her own husband had been killed yesterday afternoon, and grief must have swallowed her world.

Jigonsaseh let out a slow breath. As it condensed in the icy air, Wind Woman gently swirled it into firelit spirals. Tomorrow, the bodies would be prepared. The strongest souls would be requickened in living bodies, their confusion and agony ended. They would live again. Then, ten days from now, the main burial feast would be held. When completed, the souls that had not been requickened could be on their way to the Path of Souls in the sky, and the bridge that led to the Land of the Dead beyond.

I must see Chief Cord.

She shoved away from the palisade and headed for the closest ladder, where she climbed down, and tiredly walked toward the wooden plank gates.

The guard, short and burly, swung them open. "Matron Jigonsaseh, you should not be out alone. Shall I assign you guards?"

"I appreciate your concern, but it's not necessary. Return to your duties." Her hand, however, instinctively dropped to CorpseEye where he rested in her belt.

"As you wish, Matron."

The gates swung closed behind her without another word.

She walked eastward across the battlefield, weaving through the corpses, and down the long slope toward the Flint People's camp. Dropped bows, water bags, weapons belts torn free by desperate hands, and severed body parts lay tumbled across the ground. All around her, people with torches wandered through the blowing smoke, searching faces, clothing, jewelry, trying to recognize bodies. Their expressions were haunted. The shock was just setting in, turning their hands shaky.

Jigonsaseh rubbed her burning eyes.

Before war cries had split the day, it had been a splendid, clean morning, filled with the laughter of children dashing across the plaza, and the happy barking of dogs. It was hard to believe that their world had been obliterated in such a short time.

She marched out of the killing field and straight for the sentries who ringed Chief Cord's camp. Any other chief would have placed his camp in the middle of his warriors, where he'd be better protected, but Cord had been a war chief for most of his life. He preferred to have his back against a small moonlit pond. The water glittered and cast reflections over the faces of the five people seated on logs around his fire. On the far side of the circle, she could see him clearly. Tall and muscular, he had a long, pointed nose and piercing brown eyes. He'd seen forty-one summers pass. A black roach of hair ran down the middle of his shaved head. Turtle shell carvings decorated his black cape. The snake tattoos on his cheeks seemed to coil and strike as he spoke.

"Halt!" one of the sentries shouted at her. "Identify yourself."

He boldly stepped in front of her.

Jigonsaseh tiredly braced her feet. "I am Jigonsaseh, Village Matron of Yellowtail Village, and a friend to Chief Cord. I request a meeting with him, if he is not too tired."

At the sound of her deep voice, Cord instantly rose and walked toward her, his long legs stretching out, covering the distance in mere heartbeats.

She called, "May I speak with you?"

"Of course. Let her pass, Deputy War Chief," he ordered.

The sentry leaped to obey, and Jigonsaseh walked to meet Cord. They stood eye-to-eye for what seemed like an eternity.

...reflections of snow dancing over his tattooed face...the strength in his dark eyes enough to convince me we could achieve anything...slim rations eaten at the same fire...his closeness a physical torment...

Cord said, "Will you join me?"

"I would, thank you."

As she neared the fire, the other warriors rose and bowed to her.

Cord said, "That will be all for tonight. We will reconvene tomorrow morning when War Chief Baji is better."

Men wandered away, muttering to one another, casting glances over their shoulders at Jigonsaseh.

"Baji is hurt?"

"Nothing dramatic. Her left arm is swollen. A glancing blow from a war club."

Jigonsaseh relaxed a little. She'd known Baji since she was a girl of barely twelve summers. The tie between them went beyond clans or nations. "Please tell her I am concerned about her."

"I will."

Cord gestured to the log where he'd been sitting. "Please, sit. May I dip you a cup of tea?"

"No, but I thank you for the offer."

She lowered herself to the log, pulled CorpseEye from her belt, and rested him across her lap. Unconsciously, her hands smoothed the well-oiled wooden shaft. The club had been in her family for generations, passed from warrior to warrior. He had an ancient presence, like a great old war chief who has seen too much, and longs only to rest until the next battle begins. The carvings on the shaft added to his presence. The antlered wolves seemed to be trotting after the winged tortoises, who were in turn, being hunted by prancing buffalo. The red quartzite cobble tied to the club's head glinted in the firelight. It had two black spots that resembled staring eyes. She had no idea how much blood the club had absorbed over the long summers, but more than she could imagine.

Cord sat beside her, four hands away, and shifted to face her. His black roach glittered with firelight.

She began, "I don't know what to say to you."

He smiled. "Then tell me what you think of this strange alliance between the Flint, Hills, and Standing Stone nations. Will it last?"

"It must," she said firmly. "For all our sakes. I plan to work very hard to ensure that it does."

She looked at the superb snake tattoos in the frame of his oval face and noticed for the first time how deeply the lines cut his forehead. Others ran down his cheeks like careless chisel scratches, broken only by the prominent knife scar that slashed across his square jaw. When she lifted her gaze, his mouth tightened slightly. While she'd been studying his face, his gaze had been locked on her eyes, probably assessing the emotions he saw there.

Very softly, he asked, "Are you well? I know this was a terrible day for the Standing Stone nation. You lost so many."

She jerked a nod. "Ninety percent of our army."

"How many trained warriors do you have left?"

"We will count tomorrow, but my guess is around three hundred. Plus, another forty-one warriors from Atotarho's army that joined our side this afternoon, including War Chief Sindak."

His face slackened. "Three hundred out of how many?"

"When the morning began, we had over three thousand."

He seemed to be holding his breath, then slowly exhaled the words: "What will you do?"

"One thing is certain: Atotarho will be back. High Matron Kittle is still in council with the other elders. It's an informal meeting. Tomorrow, the Ruling Council will officially meet to decide our course of action."

He hesitated, opened his mouth as if to speak, then closed it for several moments, before he finally said, "May I be so bold as to offer you advice?"

"I have always greatly valued your advice."

He dipped his head respectfully and shifted to stare at the flames dancing around the logs in the fire. As always, the attraction between them was like lightning about to strike, almost unbearable.

"I would like to suggest that the Standing Stone nation abandon these last two villages and come with us to the Flint nation. We will adopt every member of your clans. We are stronger as one nation, than as two."

Stunned, she didn't respond.

More softly, he added, "Last summer, when your son thought he would wed Baji, he allowed himself to be adopted into the Flint People. We Requickened in him the soul of one of our greatest ancestors, Dekanawida. Is it so hard to imagine being adopted by us?"

She gave him a faint smile. "Well, Cord, I think maybe my son, whom we still call Sky Messenger, belongs to all clans and all peoples. My nation, however, that is something else."

"Believe me, I know the import of my suggestion, but if you do not accept, I greatly fear—"

"Cord..." She gripped his hand where it rested on the log between them. "You are very generous to offer, but I can't recommend that to the Ruling Council. You're talking about the death of the Standing Stone nation."

He flipped his hand over, twined his fingers with hers, and matched her grip. "Listen to me. You have three hundred trained warriors left, plus another forty-one that you don't know if you can trust, and you do not know that Chief Atotarho is gone."

"No, but it seems—"

"Yes, he and his faction of the Hills People fled the battlefield in the monster storm today, but by now, they are regrouping, assessing damage, and making decisions that may wipe the Standing Stone nation from the earth anyway. Please"—he lowered his voice—"consider fleeing to join another nation. It doesn't have to be the Flint People. If you'd prefer, I suspect the People of the Landing would take you. They've been hit hard by the Mountain People in recent moons. They would probably be glad to renew the spiritual strength of the clans by adopting—"

"I can't," she repeated, and the lines at the

corners of his brown eyes deepened. "We're desperate, old friend, but not that desperate. Not yet."

With trepidation, he disentangled his hand from hers before gently stroking her hair and anxiously studying her face. "When the time comes...if the time comes...remember my offer."

She had the overwhelming urge to hold him. But that would complicate both of their lives. "Thank you. I..." Her voice dwindled when she noted how attentively his warriors were watching them. She scanned the closest fires. Warriors either stared blatantly, or pretended to be looking into their supper bowls and water cups, while casting furtive glances their way. An awkward silence had descended. "My visit seems to have caused a disruption."

"Well, frankly, it isn't every day that a member of the Ruling Council of the Standing Stone nation appears, walking alone, in the middle of a Flint war camp. You startled them."

"If so, they are exceptionally well trained. Not a single one attempted to bash my brains out before he checked with you."

"Fortunately for him." Cord smiled and removed his hand from her hair.

Conversations instantly began to return to normal, and were eventually replaced by laughter and war songs.

Jigonsaseh said, "Cord, as you well know, I'm not given to small talk. I must thank you for what you did today. I don't know how, but—".

"It's not necessary. Truly."

"It is for me. You are an old ally, but you were under no obligation to come to our aid. Our Peoples have been at war, off and on, for generations. It could not have been easy for you to convince your Ruling Council to send warriors to support us, and I have no words for the gratitude in my heart."

His handsome face showed no emotion, but his dark eyes probed hers. "I'm just sorry it took so long. If we'd arrived a few hands of time earlier, more of your people would have survived."

"Would they?" Jigonsaseh tilted her head uncertainly. "It seems to me you arrived at exactly the instant Power demanded."

"Yes," he mused, his eyes suddenly distant, seeing the battle again. "That was odd, wasn't it? We had been in the fight for only a short time when the freak storm swept over the horizon. I've never witnessed anything like it before."

"Nor have I."

On the fabric of her souls, she saw Sky Messenger turn to face Elder Brother Sun, lift his hands, and felt the air sucked from the battlefield. A deep-throated rumble echoed to the east, then a black wall of clouds roared over the horizon. Only

Sky Messenger dared to face the storm. He'd clutched his best friend's, War Chief Hiyawento's, daughter to his chest, protecting her...and the storm had passed over them, leaving them untouched.

Cord said, "Dekanawida has become a living legend." He gestured to something behind her. "I noticed he has spent the past hand of time walking the battlefield alone. Is he as stunned as everyone else by the rumors racing through the war camps?"

She glanced over her shoulder and spotted her son, Sky Messenger, on the far eastern edge of the forest with his head down. He must be lonely and she suspected, confused, trying to make sense of the day. "I suspect so."

"Has he said anything to you about the miracle?"

"What could he say, Cord? I don't think he knows yet how to interpret the storm."

Cord made an airy gesture with his hand. "I'm sure my warriors add to his difficulty. They are awestruck. They believe he called the storm, and say he is the legendary human False Face prophesied to don the cape of white clouds and ride the winds of destruction at the end of the world." He looked back at her with slightly narrowed eyes, as though it hurt to look at her. "Do you believe it?"

She hesitated. "I believe his Dream. As to the source of the storm, I fear to offer an opinion. The implications..."

Blood-scented wind swept over them, flapping Cord's black cape around his long legs, and jingling the turtle shell ornaments. For two old war chiefs, bloody wind was as familiar as the feel of a war club in their hands. Nonetheless, she saw his fingers clench, and she knew he was holding on to life, cherishing the breath moving in his lungs.

Unwisely, she reached out to place a hand upon his shoulder. Something about the softness of his expression built a warmth in her heart. She longed to stay, to sip a cup of tea and talk of old times with him, but feared where it would lead. "I have duties to attend to. I must go, Cord. I thank you for your kindness."

As she rose to her feet, she tucked CorpseEye back into her belt.

His jaw clamped, as though making some decision.

"Wait. Please?" he said.

He stood up and swiftly pulled her into his embrace. For a time, she let herself drown in the sensation of being held. It had been a long time since she'd allowed a man to hold her. She was aware of the softness of his worn cape and the rhythmic pulse of his breath against her throat.

She slipped her arms around his waist and pulled him hard against her. They stood like that, clutching each other for long enough that Corpse-

Eye's quartzite cobblehead felt like it might break her ribs. The camp went silent again.

Finally, she pushed away, and said, "Very dangerous, Chief Cord. There are those among your own People who would consider this consorting with the enemy."

"I've faced danger before. I'll risk it."

As they gazed at each other, a connection grew between them. Like a rope being stretched tight, the fibers strained, about to fray and break loose. As his smile faded, conflicting emotions danced across his handsome face.

"Cord, I'm sorry that we can't—"

"It's *not* impossible." He clenched his fists at his sides, as though struggling against his own impotence. "Join my people. Please present the possibility to your Ruling Council. Let them decide. That way, no one could ever accuse you of suggesting it as a way to further your personal interests." He paused. "That is, providing you think it would be in your personal interest to share your life with me."

She lowered her eyes and watched the brassy splashes of light cast over the hearthstones by the flames. They fell irregularly, like leaf-shaped puzzle pieces cut from a golden sunset.

Smiling ironically, she said, "Actually, it would be far more in my interest if you moved to my village. That is the tradition of our peoples. When men marry, they move to the wife's village. That would suit me even better."

His brows lifted. "I hardly think that's a good idea. Your village may well be doomed."

She laughed. Warriors' humor. Bizarre, given the circumstances.

She touched him one last time, squeezing his hand. "Sleep well, my friend."

She turned and headed back across the freezing battlefield.

3

J ust a shred of sound, an exhale from a human throat.

Twenty paces ahead, a small sparkling cloud of frosted breath formed in the darkness.

The most feared witch in the land, Ohsinoh, watched it drift through the maple trunks. He'd finally located his enemy, the man they called Sky Messenger. Ohsinoh continued easing his leg through the frozen ferns, his movements barely hissing through the winter forest.

Just beyond the maples, Sky Messenger aimlessly wandered among the dead. A tall man, and muscular, Sky Messenger had a round face and slender nose. Straight black hair brushed his shoulders. Following behind Sky Messenger was his pet wolf, Gitchi.

Ohsinoh frowned. That could complicate matters. The bond between Sky Messenger and the old gray-faced wolf smacked of the supernatural. The wolf would die protecting him. Which meant Ohsinoh would have to kill the wolf first.

In the distance, the half-burned villages of Bur Oak and Yellowtail nestled together. The three rings of palisades that surrounded each village—constructed of upright logs—had been burned through in so many places they resembled mouths of rotted teeth. Smoke continued to rise from the charred areas. Even at this late hour, firelight gleamed through the gaps. Though men and women still stood on the rickety catwalks, keeping watch should the enemy return, they looked exhausted. Many heads nodded, trying to stay awake.

Ohsinoh silently inhaled and let his breath out slowly. Somewhere in the trees behind him, a Flint warrior paralleled his course. A hired murderer. A traitor to Chief Cord. To enlist his skills tonight, Ohsinoh had been forced to pay the man enough to ransom a small village.

Sky Messenger leaned over to peer into the eyes of a dead woman warrior. His lips moved, speaking to her, saying something soft that Ohsinoh couldn't hear. How convenient that he was completely alone, except for Gitchi. Where,

Ohsinoh wondered, was Sky Messenger's avowed friend and protector, War Chief Hiyawento?

Ohsinoh's gaze shifted to the south where Hiyawento's camp nestled on the hilltop.

Dark figures moved around the fire. Hiyawento was probably there, still grieving over the murder of his two baby daughters. Was he remembering their smiling faces? It must grow harder every day to teeter around the edges of the emptiness that had grown inside him. By now, Hiyawento's souls must be dark open chasms that dropped away forever, as though all the light in the world had been obliterated in a single stroke when his little girls died.

Ohsinoh barely stifled a delighted chuckle. That had been too easy. Not even a challenge for his witchery.

Sky Messenger lifted his face and seemed to be studying the campfires of the dead that sprinkled the night sky, perhaps speaking with the Blessed Ancestors who lived along the Path of Souls that led to the Land of the Dead.

As Ohsinoh watched him, his sense of triumph dwindled, returning to a hatred so potent it left him feeling slightly ill. He'd first met Odion—Sky Messenger's boyhood name—when he'd seen eleven summers. Odion had been a pathetic, whimpering little fool, terrified of everything. Ohsinoh had hated him for it.

As he pursued his prey, Ohsinoh clutched the

evil-looking charm he carried in his right hand—a tortoiseshell covered with animal fur. Two white eyes, carved of shell, stared out from the center of the fur. It was unnerving, even to him. The charm reminded him of the old stories of half-human beasts that had wandered the land just after Tarachiawagon, the Good-Minded Twin, created the world. He'd found the charm among his mother's things, cached beneath a dead red cedar tree in the faraway country of the People of the Dawnland. His mother, Gannajero, had been dead for twelve summers—but her death still devastated him. The violent manner of her murder had doomed her afterlife soul to wander the earth forever. At the age of thirteen summers, he'd been lost, starving, without hope...until her soul had stalked from the darkness and crouched before his fire. *"You young idiot. Get up! I've come to share all my secrets with you. If you've the sense to obey me, you are about to be rich and powerful."*

Her fierce words had given him back his purpose in life. He'd changed his name from Hehaka to Ohsinoh. She'd told him every place she'd cached rare Trade goods, and witch's charms. Since that night, he'd often caught glimpses of her wandering soul light as it slipped through the shadowy forest.

His gaze returned to his enemy. Sky Messenger and his filthy friends had killed her.

Ohsinoh had been struggling for summers to avenge her. All of his life, he had worked and scraped to find every bit of knowledge he could about Power...and he had. His abilities had become the stuff of legend. People said that if anyone dared kill him, he would rise from the dead and torment his murderer for eternity. He'd become the most-feared man in the world...until today's freak storm had turned Sky Messenger into an ethereal figure of awe, no longer quite human. Ohsinoh had heard warriors muttering that Sky Messenger was the long-awaited prophet, the reborn Spirit of Tarachiawagon. Sky Messenger's newfound fame ate at Ohsinoh's vitals like a fanged beast.

Tonight, old enemy, I will avenge my mother and show these fools that you are mere flesh and blood...

He inhaled a soothing breath, and the scent of the marsh penetrated the battlefield stench.

His eyes slowly panned to the west. Like a crescent moon, Reed Marsh curved around the charred villages, protecting them on the north and west sides. Its wet fragrance mixed oddly with the stenches of blood and smoke, turning it poignant and velvet. Birds perched on the tallest cattails, their eyes glowing.

A gust of wind fluttered his bluebird-feather cape. Ohsinoh pulled his hood forward to shield his face from the bitter cold.

Sky Messenger continued on his way, stopping often, apparently to gaze down into the eyes of the dead, now frozen in their skulls and sheathed in frost. As the dead bodies stiffened, they thumped and gurgled, teeth gnashed, and gasses hissed.

The old gray-faced wolf never left Sky Messenger. Gitchi kept scanning the tree line, his eyes shining in the brilliant light cast by the campfires of the dead. Tonight, the sky was a conflagration. The wolf stared directly at Ohsinoh and went rigid. He lifted his muzzle to sniff the air. Assessing the danger.

Ohsinoh went stone still.

Sky Messenger suddenly noticed his wolf's gaze and stared out at where Ohsinoh stood.

Ohsinoh called, "It's Odion, the boy who was always afraid."

Sky Messenger responded with Ohsinoh's boyhood name. "I'm still afraid, Hehaka."

"But why? You are the great man now. Elder Brother Sun obeys Sky Messenger's commands." He vented a low, mocking laugh. "Isn't it enough?"

Sky Messenger appeared to be thinking about the question. After what seemed a long time, he answered, "I know where it is."

Confused, Ohsinoh tilted his head. "Where what is?"

"Her pot."

Ohsinoh took a quick step toward Sky Messenger, breathless, unable to believe his ears. A gust of wind flapped his feathered hood around his face. He had to be sure. "Which pot?"

"You know the pot, I mean. Her soul pot."

As though Ohsinoh was suddenly back in that terrible meadow, he could hear his own pathetic voice whisper, *"She sucked out my soul...she sucked it out with that eagle-bone sucking tube and blew it into the little pot that she carries in her pack...she told me that when she kills me, my afterlife soul will never be able to find its way home. I'll be chased through the forests forever by enemy ghosts."*

Gannajero had been the greatest witch who had ever lived. She'd stolen hundreds of souls—including his.

Losing your afterlife soul caused insanity. Before Ohsinoh realized it, tears leaked from the corners of his eyes, blurring his vision. Finding that pot and releasing his soul so that it could return and take its place in his body again had been one of his lifelong goals.

Suspiciously, he asked, "Why do you tell me this?"

"You've been searching for it for a long time, haven't you? If I'd known, I would have told you sooner. Do you remember our last camp on the river where she ambushed us?"

"I do."

"Walk due northeast about one thousand

paces, and you will see a small oval clearing on a hillside surrounded by maples. There are three rocks in the middle of the clearing. That's where she died. Just before Mother found us, Zateri took the soul pot from the old woman's pack and buried it between the rocks." Sky Messenger stared hard at Ohsinoh. "Do you want me to go with you?"

Ohsinoh didn't answer for a time. He was thinking about the old woman's death. He hadn't been there, but the story had moved up and down the trails for many summers afterward. He'd heard it so often it was engraved on his soul. Baji, Odion, Zateri, and some other children he didn't know, had killed Gannajero, axed and stabbed her to death like small rabid animals.

"No," he said, and backed away, moving deeper into the trees. Even though he'd been searching for that pot for more than half his life, he would accept no help from this man.

Sky Messenger must have assumed he was gone, for he petted Gitchi's head and slowly made his way to a high point overlooking the Flint People's camp. He gazed longingly at the warriors wrapped in blankets and hides. Beyond the camp, forested hills rolled endlessly to the northern horizon.

Ohsinoh eased through the trees, continuing to watch Sky Messenger. Why had the man offered to help him find the precious pot? They had never been friends.

Sky Messenger bowed his head, heaved a sigh, and seemed to be staring at the ground.

Was he thinking about Baji? Only a few moons ago, she and Sky Messenger had been lovers. Everyone had expected them to marry. For reasons Ohsinoh didn't understand, it hadn't happened. Sky Messenger was now betrothed to a fourteen-summers-old woman named Taya. An arranged marriage. Nothing more. Sky Messenger's sense of honor had to be vying with his need for a woman he'd loved since childhood. Perhaps he was trying to dream a new future—one that could never be.

Ohsinoh silently laughed, his heart returning to the task at hand.

Sky Messenger turned away from the Flint camp and headed back for the firelit stillness of Bur Oak Village, probably seeking shelter from the icy darkness and the soul-rending sounds of the battlefield. Perhaps from his memories of Baji.

If Ohsinoh didn't hurry, he would miss his chance.

A foot crunched the frost, too close to believe. Finally, the Flint warrior...

"You're a fool, Ohsinoh."

Hiyawento's voice came from his right, less than ten paces away. Panic seared Ohsinoh's veins.

He gripped his evil charm, spread his arms, and slowly turned.

War Chief Hiyawento carried a war club, but had no guards. He stood alone, unmoving, as though a block of sculpted darkness. He was tall, with a narrow-beaked face and burning eyes. Black hair blew around his shoulders. Dressed in a worn, knee-length, buckskin cape, he might have been any ordinary warrior, were it not for his stunning presence. It was like a tingling heaviness in the air—the sense a man gets before a cougar leaps upon him from a ledge above. No one who had ever stood before Hiyawento had doubted either his will or his abilities to crush his enemy.

"I'm going to kill you, Hehaka."

Ohsinoh's laugh was a little too high-pitched. "Have you become a miracle worker, too? Like your demented friend Sky Messenger?"

"He just showed you kindness, and you call him demented?"

"He's just feeling magnanimous. After all, everyone is whispering his name with reverence. He has become a Spirit creature."

Hiyawento boldly walked to stand less than three paces from Ohsinoh.

Hiyawento towered over him.

"You gave my daughters the poisoned cornhusk doll, didn't you?"

Ohsinoh's chest vibrated with a soundless chuckle. "It wasn't my idea, you know."

"Dear gods! They had only seen three and five summers. You coward! Why didn't you kill me?"

"Were it a personal matter, I would have, Wrass. Unfortunately, it was just a hired task. My instructions were to kill your heart, to take the fire from your words. I did."

"Was it your father's idea?" Hiyawento's grief filled his taut voice.

"Of course. Chief Atotarho fears you. I don't know why. You're a pathetic excuse for a war chief. Always sniveling, always voting for peace. Do you know your own warriors despise you?"

Hiyawento's feet crunched frost as he took another step toward Ohsinoh. "After I kill you, I'm going to kill your father."

Ohsinoh laughed out loud. "But he has thousands of warriors to protect him, and he's coming back, you know. You don't really believe he ran away today, do you?"

"He and his entire army ran off like scared rabbits. I saw him being carried away on a litter."

Ohsinoh casually propped his fists on his hips. The shell eyes of the charm flashed in the moonlight. "Well, I'm sure Father needed to re-group, to take stock of how many of his forces had survived the battle and to plan his next move. You and your friends are overwhelmingly outnumbered. By the way, how many warriors did you leave at Coldspring Village?"

Hiyawento seemed to freeze.

"My guess is that you left only perhaps one hundred men and women to defend the walls. After all, you had little to fear. At the time, you and your wife, Zateri, were fighting on my father's side. He's going to punish you, you know. Treason—"

"We'll be home soon."

"Not soon enough."

Hiyawento shifted his weight to his other foot. "Why would you care?"

Ohsinoh's teeth flashed. He shook the tortoiseshell charm. As it uttered its menacing snakelike rattle, he glimpsed a shadow emerge from behind a broad sycamore trunk, only three paces from Hiyawento. The soft sound of a skillfully placed moccasin carried.

Hiyawento's shoulder muscles suddenly tensed. But he did not turn.

A contemptuous laugh escaped Ohsinoh's lips. "You should have killed me when you had the chance, Wrass. Now, it's too..."

Hiyawento leaped and swung. His war club cut the air like lightning, crushing Ohsinoh's ribcage. Before Ohsinoh had even fallen to the ground, Hiyawento spun on his toes and lunged for the Flint warrior behind him. The rapidity of Hiyawento's response had momentarily shocked the tall, gangly man. He had his war club up, but he was off-balance, in the process of stepping forward. Hiyawento's club slammed into his enemy's, knocking him backward a step, leaving an opening. Hiyawento sprang forward, broke the man's neck, and danced away. When he was sure it had been a killing blow, he took a deep breath, searched the forest for other foes, and again turned to look at Ohsinoh. His eyes gleamed.

Pain like lightning blasted through Ohsinoh's chest. He lay curled on his side in the frost-sheathed ferns, his arms wrapped around his crushed chest, groaning. Frothy blood leaked from the corner of his mouth. Gannajero's hideous charm lay at his side, within reach, but he hadn't the strength to reach for it. Shock possessed his senses. He could only cough in agony and stare. With each breath, his broken ribs grated against one another.

Hiyawento walked to stand over Ohsinoh like a dark, avenging Earth Spirit.

As Hiyawento lifted his war club to finish the job, Ohsinoh gasped, "Sky Messenger's vision...is false...the storm was...a coincidence."

Hiyawento's face betrayed no emotion. He regripped his war club and let it hang in the darkness, stationary, the polished wood gleaming with an edge of moonlit fire.

Ohsinoh chuckled. "You know it...don't you?"

After what seemed forever, Hiyawento's deep voice punctured the quiet. "This is for my daughters, witch."

Hiyawento brought his club down with all the strength in his muscular arms.

Ovhsinoh's skull cracked open like a ripe melon dashed upon a rock. Hiyawento hit him again, and again, until the soulless witch's face was unrecognizable. When he finally stumbled back, his fists ached so badly that he had to pry the fingers of his right hand loose from the club's shaft.

He slipped the club into his weapons belt and rubbed his mouth with the back of his hand. His gaze immediately sought Sky Messenger's position. His friend had made it unharmed across the battlefield and stood talking with the guards at the gates of Bur Oak Village. The firelight seeping from the village reflected from his round face, giving it a sunlike glow.

Hiyawento nodded in relief.

After the ferocious events of the day, he'd feared someone would wish to kill Sky Messenger. Especially given the whisperings that he was no longer human, but an immortal Spirit. Such claims tempted small men with delusions of grandeur.

It would have never occurred to him that he'd be fortunate enough to find Ohsinoh, his daughters' murderer, dogging Sky Messenger's path. The Faces of the Forest must have heard his prayers.

Hiyawento waited until Sky Messenger disappeared inside the Bur Oak gates, then he turned.

On the far southern hilltop, campfires gleamed. His wife, Zateri, the Matron of Coldspring Village, would still be awake, worried, wondering where he was. She'd be holding their last daughter, eight-summers-old Kahn Tineta, in her arms, grieving, as he was, for all they had lost in the past few days—and no doubt terrified of what the future would bring.

Hiyawento bent down, used the dead witch's feathered cape to wipe the blood off his war club, and took one last hard look at the body. How strange that he had to reassure himself that the man was, indeed, dead.

The white eyes in the middle of the tortoiseshell charm glinted in the grass beside the witch. They seemed to be filled with deadly promise and staring right at Hiyawento.

A chill went through him. He shook it off, and glared at the charm. "Before this night is through, I will have cut your master's body to pieces and scattered them far and wide. None of his followers will ever be able to recognize him and Requicken his soul in another body."

Hiyawento lifted his club, and paused, studying the gigantic sycamores that dotted the forest. Each was a lost warrior. They would be watching him now, judging his worthiness.

He bashed the charm to splinters. Chunks of tortoiseshell cartwheeled away, clacking as they struck frozen rocks.

When he straightened up, somewhere out on the battlefield, a foot began to tap. Rhythmic. Haunting. A percussion backdrop to the eerie symphony created by the other stiffening bodies.

He listened.

Though the night was filled with sound, a silence too great to be born lived inside him. His daughters were gone. The spaces their voices had carved in his souls boomed like finely crafted drums, hollow, empty, filled with faint circling echoes.

Grief and rage were twins, forever linked, both born in a wounded heart. Where one ended and the other began, he no longer knew.

He was certain of only one thing. Destroying Ohsinoh had not even dimmed his need to kill.

Ohsinoh had just been a hired murderer. The real culprit was the evil cannibal-sorcerer, Chief Atotarho.

Hiyawento unlaced and removed a chert knife from his belt pouch, then bent down, and began cutting Hehaka's body apart, condemning his afterlife soul to wander the earth alone forever. He would not even dignify the corpse by thinking of its witch's name.

4

Chief Atotarho drew his black cape more tightly around him and scowled out at the old leaves gusting by. Wind Woman's breath scoured the highlands, sucking away any warmth his fire radiated, and leaving his twisted body in agony. Every joint in his body ached, and each time he shifted position, sharp pains lanced down his arms and legs. They made a powerful accompaniment to the sheer rage that ate at him.

My forces ran away today!

He glowered out across the land. They'd made camp on a high rocky ridge three hands run to the north of Bur Oak Village. Slabs of rock made stair-step patterns around them, descending into valleys on either side of the ridge. From this height, Atotarho could see all the way across the rolling hills of the Standing Stone nation and to lands of the People of the Hills, his home.

He shoved another branch in his fire, and waited for the leader of his personal guards, Negano, to return from speaking with the other deputy war chiefs who stood talking twenty paces away in a grove of wind-whipped pines.

"I asked a simple question. What's taking so long?"

Could it be that without War Chief Sindak, none of his deputy war chiefs knew how to lead? Or maybe Sindak's treachery had caused irreparable rifts among his warriors? The dominance struggles, warriors seeking opportunities to climb in the ranks, had already begun. He'd had to put down three fights tonight.

Given the day's events, he wondered what was happening back in his village. Was High Matron Kelek adjusting to her new position? He prayed the runner he'd sent, the fastest man in the Hills nation, would reach her tomorrow afternoon.

Gods! His own daughter, the matron of Coldspring Village, had turned against him today. Worse, she'd taken two other Hills People matrons with her. He tried to imagine how it had happened. Had Zateri spent days or weeks convincing matrons Kwahseti and Gwinodje to betray him? Their disloyalty might have even gone on for moons without his knowledge.

She had ruined his plans.

He had intended to destroy the Standing Stone nation, and immediately proceed westward with his army to wipe out the Landing People. He'd even hoped that the weather would hold out long enough for him to attack the starving villages of the People of the Mountain.

Now, none of that will happen...

He roughly massaged the fingers of his left hand. Like knobby sticks, he could no longer fully straighten them. They remained slightly clenched in hawklike talons.

One man—he couldn't identify the voice—shouted, "I saw it, Negano! He called the storm. Don't tell me what I did or did not see today!"

It irked him that this same discussion must be going on all over his camp. His warriors must be whispering about the events of the day with awe in their voices, even longing.

The ten deputy war chiefs quieted. He glared at them. Were they casting their voices to decide who would be the new war chief? Well, they could do all the voice counts they wished. When out on the war trail, it was his decision to make.

Another powerful gust blasted the ridge top, and his fire sputtered wildly. One instant he was smothered in warm smoke and the next submerged in icy air.

Finally, Negano broke away from the gathering

and walked toward Atotarho through the firelit darkness. A tall man who'd seen thirty-two summers pass, Negano had long black hair. He'd tied it back with a cord, but it still whipped around his oval face. He had his brown eyes squinted against the onslaught.

When he stood on the opposite side of the fire, he bowed deeply. "My Chief, we are divided in our assessments as to the best route to track down our enemies. It will be difficult, given that we must carry litters filled with the wounded and dead from today's battle, and we cannot take the main trails. That's the point of contention. Most of our warriors wish to go home first to care for their relatives before we engage in any other attacks."

"Did you cast your voices for a new war chief?"

Negano seemed slightly confused by the change of topic. "No, we decided that our warriors need the night to calm down and be able to consider their choice."

"Since we are on the war trail, it is within my rights as Chief to appoint that position, is it not?"

"Of course." Negano nodded. "Your warriors may not be happy about that, but—"

"I could care less what makes them happy. They are warriors. It's their duty to obey me. How many wounded and dead do we have to slow us down?"

Negano braced his hands on his hips and

seemed to be thinking about it. "We don't have an exact number yet, but I would say around two hundred wounded, and we're carrying around one hundred dead. At your order, we left the rest of our dead relatives on the battlefield to become homeless ghosts."

The resentment in Negano's voice was clear. Atotarho ignored it and tucked his hands beneath his cape to keep them warm. "What is your personal opinion of the trail we should take to hunt down our enemies?"

Negano blinked and hesitated. "Most of us agree that if we must do this, we should follow the trail that runs on the north side of the Forks River."

"Why the north side?"

"Because, my Chief, our enemies are smart enough to correctly fear that you have already dispatched thousands of warriors to destroy their home villages in punishment for their actions today. They will try to get home as quickly as they can—that means running the trail on the south side of the Forks River."

Negano crouched down and extended his hands to the flames. Wind flipped his long hair around his face. "For part of the way—at least for tomorrow—the trail runs just below the northern river bluff, which means they won't be able to see us as we get into position to ambush them."

"Where will we cross back to the south side?"

"The Seagull Shallows. The river narrows there, and Traders from a variety of nations cache canoes at the narrows. The last time I was there more than fifty canoes were hidden in the brush, but I have seen as many as one hundred there."

"Let us assume there will be fifty canoes. If we can average six warriors in each canoe, that's three hundred warriors crossing each trip—"

"Not exactly," Negano interrupted, and looked as though he instantly regretted it—which he should have. Interrupting a chief was a killing offense. Nervously, he licked his lips. "Forgive me, my Chief, I only wished to say that the canoes are of different sizes. I think we can average six in each canoe, but two will need to row back to pick up more warriors. That means really only four crossing at a time."

"Then that's two hundred crossing at once. That means it will take ten trips to cross our army of two thousand. Three hands of time at most."

"Yes, but..." Negano shifted, pulling his cape closed beneath his chin. "We must also transport the litters filled with wounded and dead, and they are—"

"How long will that take?"

Negano gestured uncertainly. "It's hard to guess. They are unwieldy. Perhaps another one hand of time."

"Four hands of time total."

Behind Negano, the deputy war chiefs moved around their fire, trying to keep their backs to the icy gusts. Their low voices carried a dark, hostile timbre.

Atotarho tipped his chin to the deputies. "What are they most worried about?"

"Hmm?" Negano turned to look and heaved a sigh. "Almost everyone lost a friend or loved one today. As I said, while they, too, wish to punish those who fought against us, they wish to go home first, to lick their wounds, and care for their injured or dead relatives. If we engage in another battle before returning home, they fear the cost will—"

Atotarho broke in, "I don't wish to hear any more on the subject."

Softly, Negano responded, "Yes, my Chief."

"We are currently on the south side of the Forks River. That means we will have to cross it twice, once to get to the north side and once to get back. Eight hands of time. Is that your assessment, as well?"

"Yes, my Chief."

"Very well. That means we do not have the luxury of resting tonight. Roust our warriors from their blankets and get them on the trail as soon as possible." Atotarho reached for his walking stick, and grunted as he shoved to his feet.

Negano's eyes went wide. "But, my Chief, our

warriors are exhausted. They must rest or they will never be able to fight—"

"Do it now, *War Chief*."

Almost too stunned to speak, Negano stammered, "W-War Chief? You are appointing me? My chief, I do not think I am the right person—"

Atotarho turned and careened down the ridge toward where his own personal guards waited by his litter.

He did not see Negano rise, but when he looked back over his shoulder, his new War Chief was tramping through the darkness toward the assembled deputies.

A short time later, cries of indignation rose... but quickly died down, followed by the rapid steps of men and women scurrying to ready their forces to move.

5

As dawn approached, windblown veils of snow wavered across the pale blue valley. From her position on the Bur Oak Village palisade, Jigonsaseh could see the warriors beginning to stir. Campfires winked as hundreds of men and women passed before them.

Up and down the Bur Oak catwalks, her forces stood with bows nocked, waiting for the return of Atotarho's army. She'd dispatched scouts to track him, but none had returned—which meant they were probably dead. Atotarho could attack them again at any time. Villagers rushed around the plaza, trying to get the walls repaired before the attack came. The dank scent of fear hung like a pall in the frigid air.

She leaned against the frosty palisade and tiredly studied Yellowtail Village; it sat like a rotted husk. At her order, the entire exterior palisade had been torn down and stockpiled to repair the Bur Oak palisades, but the two inner palisades remained. Through the charred holes in them, she saw that the most badly burned of the three longhouses had, during the night, been stripped bare of bark, the pole frames dismantled, and everything usable piled in enormous heaps around the plaza. Between the palisades, where the makeshift refugee housing had been, piles of debris smoldered and probably would for a long time. In the next two days, everything would have been carried to Bur Oak Village to fortify it. They didn't have enough warriors left to guard two villages.

The rest of Yellowtail Village needed to be completely dismantled, and soon. She didn't wish to leave it for the use of attackers who could capture it and attack Bur Oak Village from within her own walls. She'd discuss it with High Matron Kittle as soon as the exhausted High Matron rose from her bedding hides.

Jigonsaseh looked behind her. Every possible space in Bur Oak Village, including the narrow lanes between the palisades and the rear of the longhouses, now contained makeshift housing for refugees. In the plaza below, construction continued. They had piled some of the building supplies around the circumference of the Council House and, as workers came and went, carrying wood or bark, or heavy coils of rope to lash poles together, clatters sounded. Large stew pots hung on tripods at the edges of the central bonfire, available for workers to fill bowls when they had a spare moment. Though each person was allowed only one bowlful, there were no guards on the pots. Every warrior was needed for other duties. People crowded the plaza. Some laughed and talked. Others sobbed for lost loved ones. Still others uttered dire speculations of what tomorrow would bring—and ate far more than their allotted share. She'd witnessed one man go back four times and come away with a heaping bowl.

The worst part for her was the lilting strain of triumphant joy that twined through the groans and cries of the wounded. Many fools believed they had won yesterday's battle.

She knew better.

Her gaze searched the plaza. On the western side, near the Hawk Clan Longhouse, forty-one Hills warriors, men and women who had defected to her side yesterday afternoon, stood in a tight knot, their uneasy eyes scanning their new compatriots. Atotarho's former War Chief, Sindak, stood among them, speaking in a low voice. His warriors' heads nodded and, as though satisfied that they understood what he wanted, Sindak turned away. His attention lifted to the palisades, surveying the

Standing Stone warriors on the catwalks. When he caught Jigonsaseh's gaze, he stopped and stared.

Her eyes narrowed.

Once, a long time ago, he had been a trusted friend, one of the men who had valiantly fought to help her rescue her captive children. After that, however, he'd returned to Atotarho Village where he'd gradually risen through the ranks to War Chief. Despite the fact that she understood a warrior's overwhelming desire to protect his own people, she did not understand Sindak's willingness to serve a mad chief, a man he knew to be a monster. It was a failing she found hard to forgive. Not only that, as War Chief, he had slaughtered Standing Stone villages filled with innocent people, and that was impossible to forgive.

What was he doing here? She hadn't had time to assess his motives yet. At a critical instant during the next attack, was he supposed to rally his warriors and start killing people inside the palisade?

Sindak excused himself from the knot of warriors, and stalked through the bustling crowd to the closest ladder that led to the catwalks. A small commotion broke out as he shouldered past the Standing Stone guards and made his way toward her, crossing the bridges that connected the palisade rings. The guards had orders to treat the Hills warriors as friends, within reason. After all, they'd risked their lives when they'd turned against Chief Atotarho.

Sindak gave her a tight smile as he approached. He had seen thirty-one summers pass, and had a lean face with deeply sunken brown eyes. Short black hair clung to his cheeks. His tan cape swayed, flashing the white geometric designs that decorated the bottom.

As he leaned against the palisade beside her, he bluntly said, "You've forgotten that I know that look. You think we're spies, don't you?"

"The possibility has occurred to me."

Wind fanned the central bonfire, and a fog of blue wood smoke blew around them. Sindak waited for it to pass, before he said, "We're not."

"That's good to hear. However, your word is just not good enough, War Chief. You and your people worry me."

His lips pressed into a hard line. "Until yesterday, I had never led an attack against Yellowtail Village. No matter how hard I had to argue in war councils, or what I had to do to bribe warriors to side with me, I did it. The last thing in the world that I wanted was to—"

"'Until yesterday,' those are the important words. Just a few hands of time ago, you led warriors in an attempt to destroy the Standing Stone nation." Jigonsaseh extended her palm to the dead bodies stacked along the base of the palisade, then moved it across the decimated villages. The predawn shadows devoured the horrors, but he understood.

Sindak expelled a breath. "I was overruled in council and given specific orders from High Matron Tila herself. If your Ruling Council had ordered an attack upon my village, Atotarho Village, would you have followed those orders?"

"I would. Without an instant's hesitation."

Sindak's muscular shoulders relaxed a little, though his face retained its taut expression. "We are warriors. We all do our duty, Matron."

She watched him flip up his hood against the falling snow, and tried to fathom what he must be thinking. If their positions had been reversed, she'd be desperately worried whether or not she'd made the right decision. "Statements about duty sound curious coming from a War Chief who abandoned his army and fled to the enemy."

Sindak seemed to freeze for a heartbeat, then he turned and gave her a level stare. "Our duties changed when our nation split in two and three Hills villages joined your side. We had to choose where our allegiance lay. We did."

Jigonsaseh grunted softly and let her gaze roam the snowy hillside to the west. Dark forms slinked across the white background—wolves feasting upon her relatives. Snarls and growls carried as they competed for corpses.

"Tomorrow, if you allow it," Sindak said, "my warriors and I will help gather the dead bodies of your people and Sing them to the afterlife. Perhaps that will forge some trust."

"Trust is not so easily purchased, Sindak. Hundreds of the refugees in the plaza below are from your most recent attack on White Dog Village. They hate you, War Chief."

"I understand that. I only pray they give us a chance to prove..." His voice faded when he noticed Jigonsaseh's grip tighten on the shaft of her belted war club. CorpseEye was cold tonight. Stone cold. As though the Spirit of the club had sailed far away, to another place and time.

Anxiety widened Sindak's dark eyes. "What's he telling you?" He pointed to CorpseEye.

"Nothing. We're safe. For now."

In relief, Sindak sagged against the palisade and exhaled hard. "Don't do that to me. If my good friend Towa had been here, he would have run screaming."

A half-smile turned her lips. "I'd forgotten you once held CorpseEye." *The night you saved my life by throwing me my club. The night you and your best friend fought on my side with great bravery.* "How is Towa?"

"He is well. He married eight summers ago and moved to Riverbank Village. He's spent most of the past twelve summers off on some wild Trading expedition. In fact, a Flint Trader came through Atotarho Village two moons ago and said he'd seen Towa carrying a pack of buffalo horn sheaths he'd gotten in the far west. He was headed to the Mountain People villages to Trade them for corn." He paused and his brows knitted. "However, about one-half moon ago, when the violence intensified, Towa returned home to Riverbank Village."

"I doubt he found much corn in the Mountain villages, but if he did, he's a wealthy man now. Most villages have already eaten their seed corn, which means they have nothing to plant next spring."

Desperation and despair seemed everywhere. She briefly closed her tired eyes and rubbed them. When she opened her eyes, she found Sindak looking at her solemnly.

"We are not spies, Matron," he repeated. "I give you my oath."

"Will you and your warriors swear an oath of loyalty to the Standing Stone nation?"

He glanced down at his people. Many of them were staring at him, talking in low voices. "That, Matron, would be treason. Of course not."

"Your warriors do not consider themselves traitors already? I'm fairly certain the Hills Ruling Council does."

"Which Hills Ruling Council?" he countered.

She tilted her head. "Ah. I see."

"Do you? Let me explain so that I'm certain we understand each other. We did not turn against our nation. We turned against Atotarho. So far as we are concerned, we follow the rightful leader of the People of the Hills, his daughter, High Matron Zateri."

Down in the plaza five people started a round dance, their arms around each other's waists. As though nothing was wrong in the world, their voices rose in song. One man kept stumbling, laughing.

The sight left her hollow. Were they still so flushed from yesterday's "victory" that they thought themselves invincible?

As though reading the tracks of her souls, Sindak said, "I'm sure you've heard the same things I have, but just in case you haven't, your villagers are saying that it doesn't matter if Atotarho attacks again because Sky Messenger will protect the Standing Stone nation."

"I've heard that foolishness, yes."

"Is it foolishness?" Sindak propped an elbow on the palisade and searched her face.

"You can't believe that. He's just one man."

"True, but I was there when he called the storm. I saw it crash down over the hill, sweeping my army from the battlefield—"

"And every other army," she added.

Curiosity lit Sindak's eyes. "You don't believe he called the storm?"

"What I believe is that he is right about this Peace Alliance. That is enough for me."

A confused smile creased his lean face. "I wouldn't let that get around, if I were you. If his own mother does not believe—"

"I believe in peace, Sindak," she replied in a firm voice.

The breeze tousled his hood around his face. "I remember the loathsome tone in your former husband's voice when he used to call you a Peacemaker. It still turns my blood cold."

"Well, Gonda has changed."

"Haven't we all?" Sindak frowned at the dancers. As the firelight fluttered in the wind, it cast the shadow of his beaked nose across his cheek. "If we were traitors, why would we have volunteered to stay and help protect your villages? That doesn't make any sense."

"It does if Atotarho specifically instructed you to turn against us during the next battle."

"Oh," he breathed, "now I understand. We are to commit suicide for our chief while killing as many of you as we can?"

She lifted a shoulder. "Maybe. It would help if you told me what you expect to get out of this arrangement, Sindak. Why are you here?" To leaven the tension a little, she asked, "You're not still smitten with me, are you?"

His lips quirked. "That was a long time ago, but I have never been *smitten* with you. It was undying love. I was a silly youth."

She chuckled.

His head dropped forward until his chin rested on his chest. He had a thoughtful expression. "What do I expect to get? I haven't thought that far ahead. And I'm exhausted. Perhaps we should discuss this later in the morning, after we've both had a chance to—"

"No, now. Tell me what you hope to gain?"

He lifted his head, and his jaw went hard in annoyance. She could see his teeth grinding. "You remember that I'm a Hills warrior, correct? Maybe you should explain your perspective on the command structure here. Do you think I take orders from you?"

"You'd better."

He actually laughed, and they smiled at each other. "All right. Let me try to force my foggy souls to think." He paused for a long while, before saying, "First, I want Atotarho dead, and the People of the Hills reunited with Zateri as High Matron of all our people. Next, I want peace throughout the land, as you do. Beyond those things, I have no idea." He shoved away from the palisade. "And now, I am off to find my blanket." He strode down the catwalk.

She called, "Tell me one last thing?"

He turned. "What?"

"Where is Atotarho? Why don't we see his campfires out there? Our scouts haven't returned."

Firelight reflected in his dark eyes. "I've been wondering the same thing. My guess is that he's on the trail."

"Headed where?"

"If I knew that, Matron, my stomach would finally sink to its proper place."

"Get some sleep, Sindak."

He started to walk away, then stopped short and turned back to give her an amused look. "With regard to your earlier question about my being *smitten*. Just so you know, a part of me will always be in love with you. That's your penance for being such a great war chief. Silly young warriors become obsessed."

She laughed softly, and he gave her a sweeping bow, then continued toward the ladder.

6

Elder Brother Sun had not yet crested the eastern horizon, but already the bellies of the drifting Cloud People shimmered, and a pale lavender glow lit the forest. As the leafless maple branches swayed in the morning breeze, soft rustling filled the air.

War Chief Baji of Wild River Village rose from where she'd been rolling up her blanket and stretched her aching back muscles. The battle yesterday had been fierce. As she turned left to examine the battlefield that lay between her camp and the partly burned villages of the Standing Stone People, her gaze lingered upon the dead. Strange things happened to corpses as they froze. Yesterday afternoon most of the bodies had been lying flat. This morning, misshapen arms with clawlike hands reached high into the air, as if pleading with the sky gods—or perhaps cursing them. Necks had twisted grotesquely. Mouths gaped in silent cries. Eyes, frozen in frosty pits, seemed to strain to see a familiar face, waiting for their loved ones to find them.

She glanced expectantly at the gates of Bur Oak Village. The snow had stopped, but a dusting still frosted the shoulders of the guards who stood there.

He's coming. I know he is.

Thin streamers of smoke rose from the charred palisades. Through the gaps, she saw people gathered, engaged in a village council meeting, trying to decide what to do next. Their forces had been devastated by Chief Atotarho's attack, leaving them more vulnerable than they'd ever been. Baji and her forces could not stay to help them. She felt hollow and guilty, but she and her People had their own problems at home, not the least being that they feared Chief Atotarho would take out his vengeance on the Flint nation for supporting the Standing Stone nation against him.

Behind Baji, wooden bowls clacked against horn spoons as men and women finished their simple breakfasts of cornmeal mush, spiced with whatever variety of jerky they'd had left in their packs. Coughing and laughter carried, as well as the deep groans and fever-laced cries of the wounded. Weapons clattered as war belts were tied around waists and quivers and packs were slung over shoulders.

Baji slipped her hand beneath her buckskin cape and massaged her left arm just above the elbow where she'd sustained a blow from a war club wielded by one of the Hills People warriors. The purple lump was the size of a balled fist. Fortunately, she was right-handed. It would not impair her ability to swing her own club, though it would scream when she drew back her bow.

Her gaze returned to the gates. She tried to force her thoughts to other subjects, but, as always, Dekanawida—the man others called Sky Messenger—was there.

...beneath me, smiling, staring upward through the veil of my hair, his brown eyes filled with a dreamy warmth. Rocking, sweat-soaked, pine pollen cascading from the trees, sheathing our nakedness in pale yellow that resembles the glitter of sunlight.

Memories from last summer.

As the light strengthened, burial teams with litters began to trickle out from the villages and course through the corpses, identifying and loading relatives.

Her adopted father, Chief Cord, also dispatched two teams for the same purpose. As he led the teams onto the battlefield, Baji watched him. His black cape decorated with turtle shell carvings, symbols of his clan, waffled around his long legs.

As though he sensed her gaze, Cord turned to look at her. He had a long, pointed nose and a square jaw. The black roach of hair down the middle of his head gleamed.

To avoid his eyes, she picked up her rolled blanket, woven from twisted strips of rabbit hide, and tied it around her waist, over her cape, then knotted her weapons' belt just above it. The bone stilettos clacked against the chert knives. She was tall and muscular, with a small nose and large dark eyes. Her long black hair hung to her hips when it wasn't braided. She'd heard men call her beautiful. Were it not for the ugly knife scar that cut across her chin, she might have been.

She looked back at Bur Oak Village again. The gates were still closed.

...his deep voice singing lullabies to me in the middle of the night, holding me as though I am the only thing that stands between him and oblivion. Enough love in his eyes to sustain me for the rest of my life.

Cord frowned, broke away from the burial teams and walked toward her. When he got to within two paces, he said, "After yesterday's miracle, he must be overwhelmed with requests for audiences. Why don't you go to him?"

Baji jerked the laces of her cape tight beneath

her chin and reached down to pick up her war club. As she tucked it into her belt, she added, "Father, he is betrothed to another. Do you really think it's appropriate for me to march into his future wife's longhouse and ask for a private meeting with my former lover?"

Sympathy tightened his mouth, and she couldn't stand it. She turned away. "Camp is almost packed up," she said sternly. "How much longer will it take the burial teams? We should be going soon."

"We have some time. Time enough, I think."

Baji knew that he meant, *Time enough to wait for Dekanawida.*

"That's foolish, Father. The longer we are gone, the more likely it is that Wild River Village will be attacked. I think we should—"

The gates of Bur Oak Village swung open, and Dekanawida stepped out into the sunlight. Just the sight of him made her clamp her jaw to contain the welling emotion. She couldn't seem to get a deep breath into her lungs.

Cord didn't even turn to look. He could tell from the expression on her face. "I'll take care of making sure the war party is ready. Take as long as you need."

Father walked past her, leaving her standing alone, gazing across the expanse of frozen bodies to the only man she had ever trusted. He was very tall and broad-shouldered. He'd tucked his jet hair behind his ears. As he marched toward her, it swayed just above the shoulders of his black cape. Determination set his jaw. His slender nose flared with deep breaths. Gitchi, his old gray-faced wolf, walked at his side.

Baji strode to meet Dekanawida halfway. She suspected they both knew how things must be, though neither of them wished to admit it.

Gitchi's ears went up when he recognized her, and he loped forward to greet her with his tail wagging. Baji knelt down and put her arms around his thickly furred neck. "I miss you so much, Gitchi. How are your paws?"

She reached down to stroke his leg. His stiff joints hurt all the time, but he was still a great war dog. He'd saved her life many times. Gitchi whimpered and licked her face.

Dekanawida caught up and waited until Baji rose.

She gazed up into his eyes, and the world seemed to die around them. The voices of the war party ceased, the wind hushed. She heard only the pounding of blood in her ears.

Baji asked, "How is Tutelo? I heard her husband was killed yesterday."

As though he knew she was deliberately avoiding the only subject between them, he softly replied, "My sister is grieving, trying to be brave for her young daughters."

When they'd been slaves together as children, Tutelo had been the youngest, just eight summers, but she'd rarely cried. Love for her filled Baji. "Tutelo is the bravest person I know. I was so hoping to see her this morning, but we'll be leaving soon."

"How soon?"

"As soon as we've finished collecting our dead from the battlefield."

Their gazes held and the unbearable longing in his eyes left her feeling as empty as a shattered pot.

"I'm leaving soon, too, though I haven't told anyone yet."

Baji straightened. "Where are you going? The new alliance needs your guidance."

"Perhaps, but we need allies far more desperately. We can't be the only ones who believe that the war must end. There are others. I must find them and convince them to make peace with us."

"Father plans on doing the same thing among the People of the Mountain this winter. If everything works out, by Spring our new alliance may have tripled in size."

He swallowed hard and lowered his gaze. He seemed to be trying to decide how to tell her something. "Baji, please thank Cord for me. He—"

"He's right there." She pointed. "You can thank him yourself."

"No. I— I need to speak with you."

He lifted his gaze again. The longer they stared at each other, the more her emptiness increased.

Baji hesitated, then, in a reverent voice, asked, "Will you tell those you meet about your Dream?"

Dekanawida tenderly reached out to stroke her hair, but his hand halted before he touched her. He closed his fist on air and drew it back. In a strained voice, he said, "Baji, I know you are War Chief, and you have duties, but I want you to come with me."

She blinked in confusion. "I can't."

"Just for one moon. Surely, Cord will grant you that."

"My people are in danger, Dekanawida. It's impossible."

Dekanawida wrapped his arms around her shoulders and powerfully crushed her body against his. "I need you, Baji. Please come with me?"

A warm rush flooded her veins, frightening in its intensity. "You are betrothed to another."

His lips brushed her face, and he murmured against her hair, "My marriage is a political alliance. My future wife told me so herself." He tightened his embrace.

For a blessed timeless moment, she allowed herself to believe that she could go with him, and happiness filled her. She slipped her arms around his waist and hugged him so hard her injured arm shook. "I can't abandon my village now. Not when we may be attacked at any instant by Atotarho, or the Mountain People, or the People of the Landing. You know I can't. If you were still a deputy war chief, you would do the same."

...but he needs a body guard. There is no one better to protect his back than me.

Dekanawida slowly released her. A mixture of disappointment and despair shone in his brown eyes.

"I knew you'd say that. I had hoped not, but..." He expelled a breath. "You've always been the honorable one. I have just one last thing to say. Baji—"

"Please, don't." She knew that tone of voice. "It's useless, we can't—"

He continued as if she hadn't interrupted. "—my feelings for you have not changed. No matter what happens, I will find a way for us to be together, to marr—"

"Let it go, Dekanawida."

He frowned out at the battlefield for a long time, watching the burial teams. The Standing Stone People were piling the dead near the Bur Oak Village palisade. The mound was already three or four deep.

Finally, he softly asked, "Are you sure?"

"I have to be."

He bowed his head and seemed to be mustering his strength. At last, he said, "If you ever need me or...or want me...send word. I'll be there as soon as I can."

The Flint burial teams had lifted the litters and were carrying them toward the war party. They were almost ready to leave. She said, "If you are ever really in trouble, Dekanawida, you know I'll be there."

He balled his fists at his sides. "Yes."

Their gazes locked. Both desperate. Both at a loss for anything else to say.

She petted Gitchi's big head one last time, and smiled when he wagged his tail. "Please tell Tutelo I love her."

"I will."

The hardest thing Baji had ever done was to nod, turn her back on him, and stride away.

She did not glance back. It would have been a small selfish act that would have given him hope.

7
SKY MESSENGER

My heart slams against my ribs as I watch her walk away. Dreams die with each step.

"Come, Gitchi," I whisper.

I stride back to Bur Oak Village with Gitchi trotting slightly ahead. Hearing my Flint name, Dekanawida, and touching her, have left me feeling wounded and dazed. Everything inside me shouts to go after her, that if we have more time to talk, we will find a way to be together. But my feet resolutely do not turn from their path. They carry me down the hillside, through the dead grass, and out into the corpse-filled meadow east of Yellowtail and Bur Oak villages. As Elder Brother Sun edges higher into the sky, he casts shadows behind each frosty body. Like dark fingers, they imploringly reach for the villages, or perhaps to their relatives who walk the battlefield. To the west, beyond the burned villages, snow creates a patchwork beneath the leafless maples and sycamores that rise and fall like dove-colored waves.

My shoulder muscles contract, bulging through my shirt. Almost all the warriors of the Standing Stone nation lie dead upon the grassy plain just beyond Reed Marsh. Thousands. Their frozen bodies create a rumpled blanket of small white humps. No mourners have ventured out that far to search for loved ones, but they will, soon.

I follow Gitchi, veering around two teams carrying burial litters piled high. As the morning warms, Wind Woman blows the snow across the battlefield like a low sunlit haze. It mixes with the acrid black smoke rising from the smoldering village palisades, smoke on its way to the Sky World where it will deliver knowledge of the battle to the Blessed Ancestors.

Weeping mourners flow around me like phantoms, averting their gazes. When they do accidentally meet my eyes, they quickly bow and look away. Soft reverent murmurs carry as I pass, which makes me feel hollow. They have known me since I was a child. They watched me grow up, become a deputy war chief, and transform into what I am today. Or, rather, what I became yesterday afternoon: something alien, not quite human. A man to fear. I myself have not yet come to grips with the freak storm. How can I expect them to treat me differently?

I put my head down and walk straight for Bur Oak

Village. Though the exterior palisade has mostly been repaired, the inner palisades are little more than a collection of flimsy blackened logs, leaning against one another, ready to topple at any instant. Our People believe that the souls of lost warriors move into trees, and it is these trees that we cut for palisade logs, thereby surrounding our villages with standing warriors. I ache for these lost souls. They must feel as though they, too, failed in their duty to protect the People.

Reed Marsh is alive with birdsong. Snow coats the cattails. They are glistening white stalks in a sea of shallow blue water. I can make out the largest birds that perch upon the stems. Hawks. They sway in the cold breeze, hunting the marsh for breakfast.

Voices drift from inside Bur Oak Village. The council is still in session, awaiting my return. I pick up my pace. Wampa guards the gate. She has seen twenty-four summers and wears a slate gray cape decorated with brown spirals. A war club is tucked into her belt, but she also carries a bow and quiver slung over her left shoulder. She has already cut her black hair in mourning—as I will do later today. It hangs in irregular locks around her oval face, highlighting her wide mouth and narrow lips...which press tightly together as I approach.

I ask, "How is the council proceeding?"

A dusting of dark gray ash continues to fall, coating the snow. Gitchi trots through the gates ahead of me and into the plaza, where he stands looking back, waiting.

Unlike the mourners, Wampa stares straight at me, but there is curiosity behind her gaze, as though she's not quite sure how to respond to me. Me. A friend of more than fifteen summers. Guardedly, she says, "I haven't heard much shouting. That's a good sign."

"Generally, yes. Though this morning I think it's because no one has the strength to shout. We're all still staggering about like ducks hit in the head with rocks."

As I try to pass by, Wampa grips my sleeve to stop me, and whispers, "Sky Messenger, tell me the truth."

The warriors on the catwalk above us stop and start to gather, seeking to listen to our conversation. Four men and two women, bows and quivers slung over their shoulders, look down at us.

"I know very little, Wampa. The council hasn't decided—"

"We lost almost three thousand warriors yesterday. What are we going to do? There are barely three hundred trained warriors left in the entire Standing Stone nation. The rest are children and elders barely strong enough to draw back—"

"That is what the council is discussing, Wampa. Give them time."

With a faint tinge of panic in her voice, she says,

"I've heard that Chief Atotarho still has four thousand warriors. Four thousand of the eight thousand he started with. Do you think that's true?"

The catwalk erupts with the low hiss of conversations.

Reluctantly, I nod, and Wampa swallows hard.

"That's the best estimate we have. Two thousand of his warriors were from Coldspring, Riverbank, and Canassatego villages—the villages that made peace with us. And we think another two thousand died in the battle. That leaves four thousand. Our scouts tried to count the warriors still alive as they fled through the forest yesterday, but no one knows how accurate that number is."

She releases my sleeve and slowly lowers her hand to rest on the hilt of the war club tucked into her belt. "Even if the true number is half that..."

She doesn't have to finish. We both know what it means.

I fold my arms across my chest and stare down at her with my brows lowered. "The great warrior woman hasn't given up, has she?"

"Of course not. We're going to survive this. I just don't have the faintest idea how. The Flint People are leaving"—she flings a hand in the direction of Baji, but I dare not look—"and I've heard that Zateri's faction of the Hills People will also be heading home to their villages. It's foolish for us to remain here. Maybe we should abandon Bur Oak and Yellowtail villages and go with them?"

I shake my head. "That notion has already been entered into the council, Wampa. Chief Yellowtail suggested it, and High Matron Kittle objected. Despite our hasty battlefield alliance with Matron Zateri's faction yesterday, Kittle does not trust the Hills People. She said our newfound alliance is too uncertain, and that if we move there and they change their minds, we will be surrounded by enemies. There are so few of us left, we can't risk it."

"Then perhaps the Flint People? Chief Cord—"

"He is a good friend, yes. But our alliance with the Flint People is just as precarious. While Cord may continue to support us, we have no way of knowing what the other Flint matrons or chiefs will do once they hear that our nation was almost exterminated yesterday. They may use it as an opportunity to finish the job."

Her eyes narrow as she gazes out across the misty battlefield. She is a tough warrior. I have seen her prowess in battle. But despair touches her words: "Then we are alone."

The warriors on the catwalk are silent.

On this dreadful day, only Wind Mother's song through the marsh hallows and heals. We all seem to be listening to it.

I straighten my shoulders, and with a confident nod, say, "Others will join us. I give you my oath.

Though the gods know, befriending the Mountain People is going to take a strong stomach."

Wampa laughs. Before Atotarho came to power and changed the Hills People, the Mountain People were the most unfathomable, contrary, and brutal People in the land. It's inconceivable that the Standing Stone nation and the Mountain People could ever be friends. Nervous chuckles eddy across the catwalk. On the war trail, when things looked hopeless, I was always able to make my warriors laugh. I laugh, too, joining them.

"That's the old Sky Messenger talking," Wampa says softly, for my ears alone. "He was one of the finest warriors in the Standing Stone nation. But I think he is gone. I heard Matron Jigonsaseh talking this morning. She says you have given up your weapons for good. So while many of us will be fighting to the death for our people...you will not."

Her words are not an accusation, but a subtle question. "My duty rests elsewhere, old friend. I must gather more allies for our cause—the cause of peace. If I march into the villages of the People of the Landing or the Mountain People with a war party at my back, or a war club in my hand, my message will ring hollow. They will not listen to me. I must go alone...and unarmed."

She glances up at the warriors gazing down upon us, judging their expressions. "You'll be killed on sight, Sky Messenger. We have, after all, been slaughtering their people, burning their villages, and stealing their families for slaves for generations."

"They may kill me. But if they don't and I have a chance to speak honestly with their councils, I believe I can win them to our side."

Wampa utters a disbelieving grunt. "You are either deluded or a very great Dreamer."

"I'm hoping for the latter."

The catwalk erupts in laughter again.

Wampa smiles and points through the gate to the council house. "Go on. I've delayed you long enough. The council needs you."

Before I pass by, I grip her shoulder hard and stare into her dark eyes. "My Dream is true, Wampa. We must make peace with our enemies or we are all doomed. I..."

My voice fades as the vision blossoms behind my eyes and consumes my world.

...An amorphous darkness rises from the watery depths and slithers along the horizon like the legendary Horned Serpent who almost destroyed the world at the dawn of creation. Strange black curls, like gigantic antlers, spin from the darkness and rake through the cloud-sea—

"Sky Messenger?" Wampa shakes me.

I snap from the vision and return with a gasp. The sunlight is so bright it hurts. "S-sorry. I-I'm sorry."

I close my eyes for a moment, trying to see nothing, not this world, not the world of the vision. Just nothing. Still, somewhere inside me there is brilliance...*and I'm falling...tumbling through nothingness with the flowers of the World Tree, made of pure light, fluttering down around me—*

"Are you all right?" Wampa asks. "You were there, weren't you? When the sky splits and Elder Brother Sun flees into the dark hole in the sky, leaving the world to die?"

I rub my eyes and nod.

Wampa edges closer and hisses to me, "I believe you. So do our warriors. We all believe. Just tell us how to help you make peace, and we'll do it. Even if we have to eat at the same fire as those accursed Mountain People."

I suck in a breath, and the smoke from the smoldering palisades stings the back of my throat. "You're a good friend, Wampa. When I know what to ask, I will. Thank you."

From the catwalk, a man says, "We believe you, Sky Messenger." A woman adds, "We won't let you down, Sky Messenger." More voices rise.

I look up into their blazing eyes, eyes alight with faith in me, and their hope is suddenly like a cape of iron around my shoulders. It is I who cannot let them down.

I give them a confident nod, lift a hand, and walk through each of the three gates in the palisades. When I step into the village, Gitchi falls into step beside me.

Refugees from destroyed Standing Stone villages crowd the plaza. In the entire Standing Stone nation, there are only two villages left now, Bur Oak and Yellowtail, and they almost ceased to exist yesterday. Lean-to shelters line the entire eastern wall. Children race in front of them with dogs trotting at their heels. Every child is half-starved. Their bellies are distended. Bars of ribs press against thin leather shirts and dresses. High Matron Kittle had to send food to every Standing Stone village last autumn, and even to one Hills village that requested help: Sedge Marsh Village.

In an unfathomable twist of fate, the deaths of three thousand warriors yesterday suddenly means we have plenty of food. Ordinarily, we would survive by raiding other nations, taking food, slaves, and other necessities. After yesterday's battle, we no longer have to do that. To keep it safe, we have hundreds of caches of food buried in wooden barrels in the forest nearby. It will be enough to last until next summer. Soon, these starved faces will fill out and the children will smile and play again...unless we are raided and our caches discovered and stolen.

Because High Matron Kittle fears this, she'll ration food for moons.

I gaze around the plaza at the adults clustered in groups, talking. Desperation lines their faces.

I pass by without a word, heading for the council house where it squats to the left of the central plaza bonfire. The bonfire burns in the very center of the village. As I walk, I glance to my right at the Deer Clan longhouse, Kittle's longhouse, then the Hawk Clan longhouse. The houses are constructed of pole frames covered with elm bark. Their arched roofs soar forty hands high. Straight ahead, to the south, the longhouses of the Wolf and Snipe clans stand. Every roof has been burned through in several places. Many of the bark walls are blackened. Once the palisades have been fully repaired, the clans will begin rebuilding the longhouses. That is, unless the council decides we should abandon these villages and throw ourselves on the mercy of our neighbors. If we beg to be adopted into another nation, the Standing Stone People will cease to exist.

None of us can bear the thought.

I stride for the council house door. Just before I enter, I say, "Gitchi, I want you to stay here. Guard the door to the council house."

He obediently drops to his haunches, and vigilantly begins studying each person who passes by.

The leather curtain over the entry billows in the breeze, and a rush of warm air envelops me. I shiver and duck past the curtain into the house. As I do, a hush descends. After the brilliant sunlight, my eyes need time to adjust to the firelit darkness. I see only the faint curve of the house walls, hundreds of black shapes, and orange flames.

Jigonsaseh, the village matron of Yellowtail

Village, and my mother, calls, "Please join us, Sky Messenger."

I blink, trying to hurry my eyes, and see the rings of benches that encircle the fire in the middle of the house. Each person and clan has a place. The Ruling Council of the nation, composed of six clan matrons and the High Matron, Kittle, sit on the innermost ring, nearest the fire. The next ring is reserved for village chiefs, war chiefs, and visiting matrons. The outermost ring is crowded with Speakers. Each of the villages in the Standing Stone nation has four Speakers, elected representatives who convey group decisions and ask questions on the group's behalf. The Speakers for the Warriors cluster on the north side of the outer bench. The Speakers for the Women are on the east bench. The Speakers for the Men sit to the west. The Speakers for the Shamans fill the south bench. The rest of the house is open. Anyone from any village who wishes to listen to the council's deliberations may attend these meetings. Today, people line the walls, packed shoulder-to-shoulder. As my eyes grow accustomed to the firelight, I see that every head is turned in my direction.

Mother and High Matron Kittle stand together before the Ruling Council. Both watch me as I weave through the benches to reach them.

The sacred False Face masks, representing the Faces of the Forest who control sickness, perch high upon the walls. Their empty eye sockets capture the firelight and seem to glow. Carved by expert hands, they are made of wood, feathers, human hair, cedar bark, shell, and fur. They have bent noses and crooked mouths. Each is alive—watching and listening to the puny affairs of men. Their Powers come from the Spirit creatures who live in the forests, the air, and under water.

My gaze clings to the Doorkeeper Mask. It represents the Spirits who dwell at the rim of Great Grandmother Earth. Long black hair drapes over the red forehead and black chin, making the bent nose protrude from between the silken strands. The whistling mouth sucks sickness from wounded bodies and blows it into the Sky World where Elder Brother Sun burns it to ashes that are then used to purify the sick or scare away evil Spirits.

"Are the Flint People headed home?" Mother asks. She has seen thirty-nine summers and is very tall, as tall as I am, twelve hands. Short black hair, streaked with silver, frames her oval face. She has a narrow nose and full lips. Through the fine doe hide leather of her white cape—painted with black bear paws—muscles bulge. She was once a great war chief. She still practices with her bow and club every day. Despite the fact that she is now a village matron, yesterday she led the Yellowtail warriors into the fight.

"They are," I answer, and move to stand at her side before the flickering fire.

"I pray their journey is safe and they arrive home

to find all is well." Mother turns to the matrons on the second ring of benches. "When will the Hills People be leaving?"

Matron Zateri rises, and I spot Hiyawento, who sits on the bench next to her, his arm around his eight-summers-old daughter, Kahn-Tineta. Just seeing Hiyawento and Zateri, knowing they are here, soothes me. Because of the horrors we endured together as children, we are inextricably linked. They live inside me as much as my own souls do.

Zateri smoothes her hands on her buckskin cape. She is just twenty-two summers old, short and girlish. From the back, she is often mistaken for a child. Her two front teeth stick out slightly. To those who do not know her, she appears frail and weak. Slowly, with precision, she says, "I have discussed the issue with Matron Kwahseti of Riverbank Village and Matron Gwinodje of Canassatego Village. We will be leaving as soon as we have identified and collected the bodies of our warriors from the battlefield. Hopefully, we'll be gone by midday."

Matron Kwahseti stands up beside Zateri. She is thirty-five with gray hair. "Please understand, we do not wish to leave you. We know how many warriors you lost yesterday before we entered the fight on your side, but we fear our own home villages will be Atotarho's next targets. We must make certain our relatives are safe."

High Matron Kittle turns and firelight sheaths her

beautiful face, reflecting from her large dark eyes and perfect nose. Even at forty-four summers, she is renowned as the most beautiful woman in the Standing Stone nation. She does not wear a cape, just a smoked elk hide dress, painted around the collar with yellow hawk wings, that molds to every curve. "We understand, but could you possibly leave a few hundred of your warriors with us, as a symbol of the new alliance between our two nations?"

"As you know, Sindak and his forty warriors asked to remain to help you," Zateri answers. "We approved their request."

"Yes, but we need more, High Matron."

Kwahseti, Gwinodje, and Zateri whisper together.

I search the gathering. Where is my betrothed, Taya? She must be here. Because she is only fourteen, a woman of no position, she cannot sit on the reserved benches. But somewhere out in the crowd, she must be watching me. While I do not see Taya, I do see my sister, Tutelo. She stands with her arms crossed over her chest, her gaze fixed upon me. Mourning hair drapes irregularly around her pretty face. Where are her young daughters? Perhaps they remained in the Bear Clan longhouse, speaking to their dead father, saying goodbye.

Zateri turns away from the other Hills matrons to gaze at me. "Sky Messenger, have you Dreamed anything about the next few days?"

I spread my arms. "You know my Dream, Zateri.

Whether it will come true tomorrow or next summer, I cannot say."

"But you haven't Dreamed anything specific about any of our villages?"

"No."

"Then we must assume the worst." Kwahseti exhales hard.

Murmuring passes along the walls as speculations fill the council house.

Kittle holds up a hand, and the voices die down. "Please, continue, High Matron Zateri."

Zateri hesitates before she says, "We have a great deal to do when we get home. We have decided that we must combine our villages so that we may protect each other. Coldspring Village and Riverbank Village will be moving to join Canassatego Village, since it is the farthest away from Atotarho Village. We dispatched messengers last night, instructing our villages to pack up and move as soon as possible. But our children and elders will make it slow-going. Once they arrive, they will still be very vulnerable. And they must pack and transport every kernel of corn they have."

Kwahseti adds, "You know how many warriors Chief Atotarho still has. After yesterday's battle between our three villages, we possess only around two thousand warriors. One thousand five hundred are here. In addition, we left a total of around five hundred at home to protect our three villages. They will have to hold off any attacks upon Canassatego Village until we arrive. Atotarho will destroy our families if he can."

Zateri says, "We're sorry, High Matron Kittle. We've already discussed this possibility. We would leave a contingent here if we could, but we honestly can't spare a single person at this point in time. However, when we have secured our new village, we give you our oaths that we will send you warriors. We don't guarantee that there will be many, but we will send as many as we can."

Kittle clamps her jaw. "How long will that be?"

"Perhaps ten days. Fifteen at most."

Kittle boldly looks around the council house, meeting each person's gaze, as though silently assuring them that they can survive until then. She projects a confidence that, at terrible times such as these, seems to calm the world. When her gaze returns to Zateri, she says, "We are deeply grateful for what you did yesterday. Without your help, the entire Standing Stone nation would have been wiped from the face of Great Grandmother Earth. We are in your debt. As you journey, we pray Sodowegowah does not see your faces."

Sodowegowah was the harbinger of death. Once he saw your face, you could not escape.

"Thank you, High Matron," Zateri responds with a nod and asks, "May we ask, High Matron, what you plan to do? Will you move or stay to fight? You know, of course, that my father is already planning to attack you again."

Kittle turns to gaze into Matron Jigonsaseh's eyes. Mother gives her a stony look. I know that look. They must have argued about this issue. Mother did not agree with the decision, but she will back Kittle no matter what.

Kittle runs a hand through her black hair, and replies, "We will stay and fight."

Dire whispers move through the people standing along the walls. They shift like a herd of deer, shying at a strange sound, preparing to flee.

I say, "High Matron, may I address the council?"

Kittle's head dips. "Of course."

My gaze locks with Hiyawento's. He is War Chief of Coldspring Village in the Hills nation, and my oldest and dearest friend. The first time he saved my life, I'd only seen eleven summers. He has chopped his black hair short in mourning for his two murdered daughters. His eagle-like face, with its beaked nose, shines in the firelight. When the end comes, he will be there. I have seen it. He is with me when the Great Face shakes the World Tree and Elder Brother Sun flies away into a black hole in the sky. I lift my chin and in a loud voice announce, "I will be leaving, as well. I—"

"*What?*" Matron Kittle shouts. "Are you insane? I forbid it! We need every warrior now!"

Mother's gaze is upon me, stern, unblinking. "Please, let him finish, Kittle."

Kittle glares at Mother, then flicks a hand at me. "Finish."

The crowd rustles as people shove to get closer, to hear me better. My gaze remains locked with Hiyawento's. Despite his grief, Power lives in his eyes. He is the strongest man I've ever known. He nods to me, as though encouraging me to continue. He knows the Dream, and knows the end is swiftly rushing toward us.

As I draw breath, something catches my attention in the rear of the house. Gitchi noses aside the door curtain. As the wolf's lean body slides into the council house, a dark form follows him. The figure's black cape flares around his legs. The old, tarnished copper beads that ring his collar flash azure in the firelight. He has his hood pulled up, but when he turns to look at me, the blood drains from my body, leaving me lightheaded. Inside, where his face should be, it is empty. Just a black oval, darker than his black hood. It is as though I'm staring straight into a bottomless obsidian abyss. Gitchi remains by the entry, but Black Cape slips through the crowd. As he moves, he doesn't seem to be tethered to the ground, but floating above it.

I force myself to look away, knowing he will find me soon enough.

I say, "Chief Atotarho has refused to make peace, but there are other potential allies out there. I wish to go to the People of the Landing to ask them to join our peace alliance. I will not leave until they agree. Then I will proceed to the People of the Mountain, and perhaps even venture into the Islander's Confederacy north of Skanodario Lake."

The silence is so powerful it has an ominous presence. Only the crackling fire disturbs the council house.

Kittle breaks the spell. "Are you so anxious to throw away your life? We need you here! If nothing else, you can wander among the People repeating your vision to give them hope. As High Matron of this nation, I refuse to—"

Mother reaches out and touches Kittle's hand, urging her not to continue this tirade. "As part of the Ruling Council, I will cast my voice to allow Sky Messenger to walk among the other nations, seeking peace. If he fails, we are no worse off than we are today. But if he succeeds—"

"He won't succeed!" Old Matron Daga, from the destroyed White Dog Village, blurts as she rises on spindly legs. Toothless, with snowy hair, she has a fierce expression. "The Landing People despise us as much as we do them. If Sky Messenger goes to them begging for peace, they will see it as a sign of weakness and attack us faster than lightning! I agree with High Matron Kittle. I will not approve this peace mission." The way she says "peace" makes it sound like a curse. She sits back down and glowers at me.

On the third ring of benches, to the west, a man

stands up. I can't see his face, but I know the way he moves. My father, Gonda, says, "May I be recognized, High Matron?"

Kittle nods.

Gonda hesitates for a moment, before he says, "I have spoken long and hard with my son. I may not agree with his method, but I understand his goal. Sky Messenger is no longer a deputy war chief. Instead, he has become a peace chief. One man, more or less, will make no difference to our survival here. I beseech the council to approve his mission."

Conversations erupt across the house, forcing High Matron Kittle to lift her hands and shout, "Silence! This council is in session. Is there anyone else who wishes to address this matter?"

"I do." Hiyawento rises. His gray cape, still blood-soaked from yesterday's battle, sways around his tall body. His lean face is haggard. He turns all the way around, letting the crowd see him and know him. He was born in Yellowtail Village. When he left to marry the Hills woman, Zateri, he was declared Outcast and a traitor. Yesterday, when Hiyawento and Zateri turned their forces against Atotarho's army, they became the stuff of legend, heroes whose names will forever be spoken with reverence throughout the Standing Stone nation.

Hiyawento calls, "I have already discussed what I am about to tell you with Matrons Zateri, Kwahseti, and Gwinodje, and they have approved my request.

As War Chief, I must lead my People home and make sure they are safe, but if this council approves Sky Messenger's mission, I will finish my duties at Coldspring Village and meet him on the trail to the east of Shookas Village. I—"

A mixture of clapping and cheers rumbles through the house.

High Matron Kittle lifts both hands and holds them in the warm firelit air until the disturbance dies down. Her beautiful face has gone somber. Firelight makes the yellow hawk wings around her collar appear to flutter. She says, "I assume that the assembled Hills matrons believe in Sky Messenger's mission?"

Zateri answers, "We do, High Matron."

Gonda calls, "If you please, High Matron, may I say that I think it will make an impression on the Landing People when representatives from both the Standing Stone nation and the Hills nation approach them about peace."

Nods go through the chiefs and matrons, and spread to the crowd.

I dip my head to Hiyawento, thanking him. He gives me a small smile. We both know the Dream. We must face it together. I only wish Baji was going with us. If we had a Flint War Chief along, our peace delegation would be even more impressive.

Just the thought of her leaves my heart beating a dull staccato in my chest.

Blessed Ancestors, I need her. She is my strength.

Father continues, "I would ask one other thing, if I may?"

"What is it?" Kittle says coldly. She appears anxious, eager to end this council meeting so that village repairs can continue. She must be terrified every instant that we're already being surrounded.

"I would ask that when Sky Messenger and Hiyawento decide to head for the country of the Mountain People—"

"If they make it that far," Kittle says ominously.

"Yes, if they do, I wish to be allowed to go and meet them there. Other than Atotarho, I believe the Mountain People will be the greatest obstacle to our alliance, and I may be able to help win them to the side of peace."

Mother's face tenses. She takes a step toward Father before she catches herself. They have been divorced for twelve summers, and Father's new wife, Pawen, is standing in the crowd behind him. Mother says, "Gonda, you know as well as I do that Yenda has been made Chief of Wenisa Village. Surely you do not expect to—"

"I do, in fact." Father smiles broadly. "I'm looking forward to sitting across the fire from my old enemy— the man who destroyed Yellowtail Village twelve summers ago—and discussing peace."

"He will laugh in your face," Mother warns.

"Perhaps. Nonetheless, I understand him. I've

fought against him often enough that I believe I know how he thinks, and therefore, I may be of use."

Kittle massages her forehead. This must seem bizarre to her. She is desperately worried that the Standing Stone nation is on the brink of destruction, and she has three fools who, instead of planning to defend their decimated villages, wish to trot out, preaching peace to neighboring nations.

Kittle says, "There are two requests before the council. How do you cast your voices?"

Matron Daga immediately says, "No."

Mother votes, "Yes."

One by one, every other matron votes yes, including High Matron Kittle.

Kittle returns to Matron Daga. While the vote was being taken, Chief Yellowtail has been speaking with her in a low calm voice, perhaps explaining the benefits. Her elderly face has gone from fierce to resigned. She lifts her hand and calls, "High Matron, if you please."

"Yes, Matron Daga?"

"As Chief Yellowtail has pointed out to me, we should all be united on this issue. If Sky Messenger, Hiyawento, and Gonda can go to the other nations and say that we all agree peace is the way, it will, perhaps, lend more weight to their message. I would, therefore, like to change my vote to yes."

Every person standing along the walls quiets. "Is there any further discussion of this issue?"

No one speaks.

"Very well. We have achieved One Mind of Consensus. Your requests have been approved by the High Council of the Standing Stone nation. Sky Messenger, you may leave any time you wish. Gonda, you will wait until Sky Messenger sends word for you to meet him at Wenisa Village, then you may leave."

Gonda nods his thanks.

"As for the rest of us..." Kittle pauses. "We must begin preparing for war."

Kittle gazes out at the crowd. "You all know your assignments. We do not have enough warriors to effectively defend two villages. So, temporarily, the people from Yellowtail Village will be moving into Bur Oak Village. The Snipe Clan and Wolf Clan will get the Bur Oak Village palisades rebuilt as soon as possible, while the Deer Clan fills Bur Oak with water and food. The Hawk Clan will be responsible for making good arrows that fly true, and stockpiling them beneath the catwalks of the three rings of palisades. While the repairs are coming along, the Bear and Turtle clans will be responsible for protecting the villages. Any questions?"

There were none.

"Very well, I fear we haven't much time. This council is dismissed. Let us get to work."

A soft din rises as people begin filing out of the council house.

Kittle stalks past me with barely a glance.

People rise from the benches and filter around me. Over Mother's shoulder, I see Father making his way through the crowd, heading for the exit. Atotarho's former war chief, Sindak, walks at his side. They glance at each other uneasily. It is a strange sight. Less than one-half moon ago, Sindak led the war party that destroyed Father's village, White Dog Village.

Black Cape, whom I call The Voice, since frequently that is all I know of him, is slowly circling the walls of the house, waiting for me. The hair at the nape of my neck prickles. *What does he want? It must be urgent for him to brave the crowds of the council house.*

Tutelo stands alone on the southern wall, beside Gitchi. But she seems to be watching The Voice. A long time ago she named him Shagoniyoh. None of us know his true name.

Mother says, "Are you still committed to this foolishness of going alone into the heart of enemy territory?"

"I am."

"You know, of course, that as soon as Atotarho hears of your mission, he will dispatch warriors to murder you."

"Oh, I'm sure of it," I casually reply.

Mother scowls at me. "And you still refuse to carry weapons?"

"When Hiyawento arrives, he will guard me."

"That may be many days."

"I'll be all right."

She shakes her head. "This is a bad decision, my son. I pray the Forest Spirits take pity upon you."

As Mother walks away, following the crowd outside, the black form closes in, and I smell his distinctive scent, as though the odor of ancient destruction clings to his cape.

When only Tutelo, Gitchi, and I stand alone in the council house, The Voice walks straight to me, leans close, and whispers, *"Sodowegowah has seen her face."*

"Who? Whose face?"

As if blown by a wind I cannot feel, his cape billows. He backs away and gracefully walks out the door.

When he is gone, it takes me a moment before I can manage to get a deep breath into my lungs.

My sister walks forward with Gitchi at her side. Her eyes are tired, tortured. She loved her husband very much. "What did he say?"

"That Sodowegowah has seen her face."

"Did you understand?"

"No." I reach down to stroke Gitchi's gray muzzle. He affectionately licks my hand.

As we walk outside into the morning sunshine, I slip my arm around her shoulders. "How are my nieces?"

"Still sleeping, I hope. It was a hard night for us."

"Baji said to tell you she loves you. She says you're the bravest person she's ever known."

Tutelo looks up. "I wanted so to see her this morning. Is she gone?"

"Yes."

"And when are you leaving, brother?"

"As soon as I've filled my pack, and said goodbye to Taya."

"I didn't see her at the council meeting."

"She wasn't feeling well this morning."

Tutelo slips her arm around my waist and holds me close as we cross the crowded plaza to the Deer Clan longhouse.

8

Though afternoon sunlight painted the rolling hills with swaths and streaks of gold, indigo shadows encircled the patches of snow that lingered in the most thickly wooded areas, mostly on the north slopes. War Chief Baji kept searching them, identifying the slightest movement, or shift of colors. Fortunately, the only things she'd seen all day were animals and birds. The rich scents of damp earth and old autumn leaves filled the air.

When the trail curved through a rocky defile, Baji's pace slowed to a walk. Breathing hard, she looked around. Massive gray boulders the size of longhouses piled atop one another here, and extended for perhaps four hundred paces. She turned, saw her deputy, and called, "Dzadi, take four men and scout the top of the rocks."

Deputy Dzadi, a big man who'd seen forty-six summers, lifted a hand, selected his scouts, and trotted away. She watched two men climb up and scamper across the rocks that lined the northern side of the trail. Dzadi and two other warriors took the southern side. Dzadi was out front, searching the boulders for hidden warriors. He was known far and wide for the puckered burn scars that discolored his face and muscular arms. He'd been captured by the enemy three times during his life, and escaped each time. He was one of the bravest men she knew, though age was beginning to slow him down. The village warriors had at first voted Dzadi as War Chief, but he had refused the honor, saying he was too old. Instead, he'd thrown his support behind Baji. Afterward, the warriors had overwhelmingly cast their voices to make Baji the new War Chief of Wild River Village.

Baji took the time to untie her belt pouch and pull out a strip of venison jerky. She ripped off a chunk and chewed it slowly. Five hundred warriors slowed behind her, and conversations broke out. She heaved a sigh. As she did, Cord came up beside her and scanned the way ahead. In the distance, the trail ascended a steep hill, rising up out of the valley like a dark serpent.

"What do you think?" she asked her adopted father.

Cord's eyes narrowed. "We're probably safe.

The footing on top of the rocks is treacherous, too many gaps and cracks to negotiate, but I'm glad you are vigilant." The black roach of hair that thrust up from the middle of his shaved head had just a touch of silver, and lines etched the flesh across his tanned forehead. Otherwise, he did not look his forty-one summers. The snake tattoos on his cheeks still appeared crisp and detailed, not shriveled with wrinkles. The thick knife scar that slashed his square jaw shone whitely in the winter glare.

Cord said, "How are the wounded faring?"

"Better than I would have thought. Those who can run are managing to keep up. Those who can't have crawled upon the litters, joining the dead, and are being carried. Tomorrow we'll be able to move a little faster. The litters will be lighter."

As her lean body cooled down, her sweat-soaked war shirt clung to her body, chilling her. She shivered and bit off another chunk of jerky. The meat had been smoked over a hickory fire. The rich tang tasted wonderful. She finished it slowly, then retied her belt pouch.

At the far end of the rocks, she saw Dzadi wave to her, indicting the defile was safe. She nodded to Cord, and they broke into a trot again, running side-by-side through the deep shadows. Behind them, the low drone of hundreds of feet beat the air.

As they plunged down the trail between the

boulders, Cord said, "Did you come to an agreement?"

"With whom?"

He gave her a disgruntled look—his silent way of asking if she thought him stupid.

Baji sighed. At least he'd waited to ask until afternoon when it didn't hurt so much. "He asked me to go away with him."

"He's leaving?"

"Yes."

"Where is he going?"

"In search of allies. He says we are not alone. There are others out there who agree that the war must end. Others who may wish to join us."

Cord frowned, and the snakes tattooed on his cheeks seemed to coil tighter. "He's right. The alliance needs more warriors. As it stands, we have barely half the forces of our enemy."

"And the war has been long and difficult. Every nation south of Skanodario Lake is ripe for harvest. Atotarho knows it. He will not wait for us to move. His own faction of the People of the Hills is starving."

"Every nation is starving, except ours."

Baji looked at him askance. "That's the problem. We have food. You can be certain they'll be coming for it."

They trotted out of the rocks and over the crest of the hill where she gazed down upon the thickly forested valley below. It was all second-growth, dense stands of stubby trees that had invaded after a lightning-caused fire. Blackened stumps and trees still dotted the landscape. Stripped from their branches by the fierce winter winds, leaves had piled knee-deep in the middle of the trail. Her war party would be forced to slog through them.

A finger of breeze tugged hair loose from Baji's long braid and left it hanging in black curls around her sweating face. She brushed it aside. "I don't like the looks of that trail."

"I don't either. Even after we clear the leaves, we'll have to pass through that section where the trees grow so densely they resemble black walls on either side of the path."

Even worse than the trees along the trail, the small valley was rocky and steep-sided. If they were attacked here, there was no place to run. Carefully, she searched the high points for evidence of treachery, but saw only windblown leafless trees.

Baji gestured with her bow. "I'm going to dispatch a party to clear the leaves. That will make it easier going and give us a warning if someone is hiding in the shadows."

"Good idea. Our warriors will appreciate having time to catch their breaths," Cord said. "You've been pushing them hard."

"I want to get home."

"And, I suspect," he said in a knowing voice, "as far from Dekanawida as you can. But I will miss him. He is a great warrior and a—"

"*Was*," she corrected. "He *was* a great warrior. He's abandoned his weapons for good."

"Well, that is the way of many Dreamers, though I've never thought it wise."

Baji picked up her pace, pounding down the incline toward the leaf-choked trail where they would temporarily stop. Cord trotted beside her. "I'm worried about him, Father. If he is attacked—and you and I both know he's made himself a target—he has no way to defend himself. He needs a guard, someone to protect him."

Cord laughed softly. "Perhaps you've forgotten the storm yesterday?"

"I haven't." The images had been seared into her souls. "Father, do you really believe he called the storm? Or was it coincidence?" She felt like a traitorous dog asking the question. If she, who loved him more than life, didn't fully believe, did anyone?

"He called the storm, my daughter. I saw it."

She shook her head, not in denial, just uncertainty. "Faith is a hard thing. How do you do it?"

He smiled at her. "Simple. Believing is the doorway to believing."

As they neared the leaves, he slowed to a walk, and the warriors behind them sighed in relief.

Laughter broke out, followed by happy voices. Cord said, "Not only that, I believe Dekanawida has Powerful allies in the Spirit World. I met one of them once."

Baji gripped his arm and dragged him to a stop in the middle of the trail, forcing warriors to flood around her. *"When?"*

Cord tilted his head to a small clearing off the trail, a place where they would not be overheard. She followed him to the sun-splashed meadow, surrounded by maples. Snow glistened at the base of the trunks and frosted the leafless limbs.

She called, "Dzadi, please select a group to clear the leaves from the path and scout the area, then start moving the war party through."

"Yes, War Chief."

Dzadi walked through the warriors, tapping men on the shoulders. In less than twenty heartbeats, thirty men had trotted out and begun using their war clubs to beat a path through the deep leaves and scout the forest.

Baji turned to study Cord with sharp black eyes, waiting for him to answer her question. His eyes took on a glazed look, as though remembering.

"Twelve summers ago, that last night when the old woman attacked us on the river. I had followed Odion's path, seen where he'd been captured by her warriors. I was tracking him. I still don't know what to make of what had happened next."

Baji waited. "What did you see?"

"At first? Just a strange ripple, as though the darkness itself was blowing in the wind, then a shine of tarnished copper beads. Finally, a black cape appeared, and a man seemed to coalesce inside it. He glided weightlessly through the trees, apparently also following Odion's steps."

Baji stopped breathing. Her eyes felt like burning coals. "Did you speak with him?"

"Oh, yes," Cord answered with a laugh. "For a long time. I spoke with him twice that night. The first thing he told me was that if I was going to help my friends, I had to hurry, because you were surrounded and outnumbered three to one—"

"Meaning us?"

"Yes, your party was down on the riverbank. When I arrived, I saw War Chief Koracoo...sorry. I mean Jigonsaseh...I saw her standing facing the evil old woman. You were all surrounded, just as Black Cape had said." He paused to study Dzadi's team. They had managed to knock about half the leaves out of the trail. She couldn't see the scouts. They were probably examining the depths of the forest. "That's when the Spirit came to me again."

"Again? Why?"

He exhaled the words, "It's a long story. I had my bow aimed at the old woman's chest, and he told me that I could not kill her. He said there were many who had claims upon her life, but I was not one of them. He said I didn't have the right. I think he meant that only you, Wrass, Odion, and Tutelo had the right to kill her for what she'd done to you."

Baji had never told anyone the grim details of what had happened to her that long ago winter. She didn't want to see it in their eyes when they gazed at her. "Was he handsome? With long black hair and nose bent slightly to the right?"

Cord's eyes narrowed. "How do you know that?"

"Tutelo named him Shagoniyoh. We all saw him."

Cord held her gaze. It was powerful, like wings lifting her. He asked, "What is he? Do you know? Is he one of the Faces of the Forest, or a—"

"I think he's lost, Father. A warrior condemned to wander the earth forever. He helped us escape."

"Why have you never told me this?"

She gave him a lopsided smile. "Why have you never told me of your encounter with him?"

Cord hesitated, as though trying to decide. "I don't know. I wasn't sure anyone would believe me, and I guess I thought it was...personal."

Baji untied her water bag from her belt and lifted it to her lips, taking a long drink. The cool water soothed her throat as it went down. She took another greedy swallow, then she handed the bag to Cord, and looked out at the valley again. This area was known as Rocky Meadows for the gray slabs of cap rock that jutted up at odd angles across the flats and along the crests of the surrounding hills. She said, "Shagoniyoh is more than a lost soul. He's Dekanawida's personal Spirit Helper."

"Blessed gods, I knew it. Even that night, I had the feeling the creature was watching over Odion."

When the trail had been mostly cleared, Dzadi waved to the war party, and led the warriors down into the dense tree-lined portion of the trail, kicking up leaves as they went. Almost impenetrable walls of forest lined the trail ahead of them. Their colorful capes and headbands contrasted sharply with the cold shadows. A few men laughed nervously when the trail narrowed, and they had to fall into single file.

As he watched their progress, Cord said, "Have you ever seen him again?"

"No." Her gaze remained on her warriors. "Have you?"

"No."

Their war party had gotten too far ahead for her comfort. "Come on. Let's catch up."

Cord's steps pounded behind her.

The leaves on the trail were still ankle-deep and slick beneath her moccasins. They caught up with the party just as it started up the far side of the valley. Hundreds of warriors were stretched out ahead of them, moving like ants up the steep incline in the distance. At the top, dark green pines stood like sentinels.

Baji's gaze lingered on the trees. Wind Woman touched the branches, causing sunlight to flash through the needles.

But there was something...odd.

Glitters. In the sunlit air in front of the pines.

"Oh, dear gods!" she shouted. She broke into a dead run, crying, *"Go back! Take cover. Form defensive positions! Run!"*

The shining arrows toppled the first twenty men in line, cutting them down like dry blades of grass beneath a chert scythe. The battlefield roared, its distinctive voice striking terror into her heart—a mixture of shrieks, grunts, and wails. The wounded were crawling, trying to make it to the safety of the—

"Baji!" Cord's heavy body struck her and knocked her to the ground just as arrows cut the air over her head—coming from behind her!

Laughter erupted as enemy warriors flooded from the trees with triumphant grins on their faces. Hills People warriors. She'd seen many of these faces during yesterday's battle. Atotarho's men. They let out whoops and dashed for Baji and Cord.

She glanced at Cord. Blood streamed around the arrow that had pierced his right side. "Stay down, Father!"

In one smooth movement, Baji rolled to her

feet, drew an arrow from her quiver, nocked it in her bow, and let fly. Her first arrow lanced through the closest man's heart. She killed two more. The warriors behind them didn't even slow down. They leaped over the dead bodies and charged Baji.

One arrogant fool cried, "My brothers are hunting down your filthy lover right now. I wanted you to know before I crush your skull!"

As her own men tried to rush to her side, the feathered shafts of Hills People arrows streaked past. Her friends went down, some shot as many as four times.

How did my scouts miss this?

Baji tossed her bow aside and jerked her war club from her belt. Spinning low, she slammed the fool's feet out from under him, rose and crushed the second man's chest, and lunged for the third. As she swung for his head, she saw Cord stumble to his feet with his war club in his hand and wade into the onslaught. His distinctive Turtle Clan war cry rang out. Grunts and cries rent the blood-scented air.

As if he were here, fighting at her side, as he had so many times, she heard Dekanawida shout, *Baji, get down!*

And at the far corner of her vision...to her left... she saw a flash. Just a small glint, but like a rock thrown into a pond, it seemed to leave a wake in the cold air. Baji just had time to leap...

9

Blighted as though by perpetual wind, the moonlit slope bristled with tormented shapes: pines with branches on only one side, the twisted trunks of leafless sycamores, rocks scoured as smooth as polished agate. Some of the boulders stood half-again as tall as War Chief Negano, and he was a tall man, lean and muscular, with long black hair. His plain undecorated buckskin cape flapped around his legs as he hiked up the trail through the icy wind.

Across the narrow valley, hundreds of campfires glistened. He could hear the laughter of his warriors and the hum of conversations. They made a strange contrast to the deep bass notes of the battlefield, where low groans and sobs lilted like perverse music. They had used their clubs to silence the Flint wounded. These cries came from his own people.

Negano had just visited the field where his wounded had been carried. The grasping hands, the pleading voices of men and women who just wanted to be carried home to die so that their families could Requicken their souls in new bodies and they could live again—all of it had made him ill.

When dry leaves crunched behind Negano, he spun around with his war club lifted...but all he saw were the glowing white faces in the valley below. Moonlit visages of the Flint warriors they'd slaughtered that afternoon. The valley bottom had been the heart of the ambush, the killing pen. Hundreds sprawled there, a feast for the wolves whose shining eyes winked up and down the valley. Negano sucked in a breath and let it out slowly. He should have been ecstatic. His ambush had been perfect! Brilliantly planned and executed.

But on nights like this, he swore he was being tracked by enemy ghosts. He lowered his club, silently berated himself, and turned back to the trail, heading up to where Chief Atotarho camped just below the crest of the hill. Five men, the Chief's personal guards, stood behind the old man.

As he walked, Negano continued to hear footsteps, soft, carefully placed. It took an act of will not to whirl around again.

The Flint People were fighters. It did not surprise him that death would not stop them. Negano's cape was spattered with their gore. In the distance, to the west, he could see the bodies of those who'd made it out of the killing pen and desperately tried to flee. They'd scrambled up the wind-combed hills like terrified rabbits. Few had escaped. Negano had commanded two thousand warriors to Baji's five hundred. The enemy hadn't had a chance.

A twig snapped behind him. Negano instinctively spun on his toes to face his attacker...only to see nothing.

Laughter erupted from the Chief's personal guards, and Negano clamped his jaw. Were they laughing at him, or at some joke that had been told?

"You're being a fool," he growled at himself. "Stop it." At the age of thirty-two summers, Negano had lived with death, and the dead, for so long they rarely left him, waking or sleeping. Somehow, though, tonight was worse than usual. He could feel vast solitudes pressing down upon his lungs, squeezing the air out, and he felt certain Sodowegowah was standing right there, backed by an army of ghosts, all staring him in the face.

Negano cursed himself and marched straight toward where his chief sat on a rock, clutching a long stick in his hand. Atotarho's hunched back looked like a misshapen pack hidden beneath his clothing. When the old man heard him coming, he looked up. The black pits of his eyes, staring out of a cadaverous face, made Negano's belly muscles go tight. They were alive with malice.

Negano called, "It is I, my Chief. Do not be alarmed."

The circlets of human skull that decorated Atotarho's black cape flashed as he prodded his fire with the stick, sending tornadoes of sparks swirling into the cold night air.

He didn't appear to be in good humor. Negano inhaled to prepare himself. He knew perhaps better than anyone, for Negano had been the head of the old man's personal guards until last night. Negano had never had designs on the position of War Chief...too much responsibility, too little reward...but here he was. No choice now but to try and make the best of things.

Out on the far side of the narrow valley, a group of warriors began singing the Victory Song. Deep and triumphant, their voices swelled over the winter-bare trees. Other warriors joined in, then more, until the valley of the dead echoed with exultation.

Chief Atotarho stopped tormenting his fire to listen. His wrinkled face twitched. He had seen sixty-four summers pass and had suffered from the joint-stiffening disease for the past twenty. His bent, crooked body pained him constantly. His enemies said it was the Spirits' revenge for his witchery. Negano knew better. The old chief wasn't a witch, but he hired witches, like the frightening Ohsinoh, to do his bidding. In this way, entire villages vanished, poisoned or decimated by strange plagues. No man in the world was feared more than Chief Atotarho...except perhaps Sky Messenger. That must be galling the old man.

As Negano approached, he saw the freshly chewed human ribs that lay around the fire pit, cast there by the chief after his teeth had stripped the cooked flesh away. Who had the person been? A chief, probably, or maybe a war chief. Possibly the great Cord himself? Atotarho refused to consume lowly warriors.

Atotarho snapped, "What took you so long? I summoned you over one-half hand of time ago."

Negano bowed. "Forgive me, my Chief, I had to check on the wounded. They—"

"In the future, you will come immediately when I call for you."

Negano straightened, confused. "But, my Chief, I am now War Chief. It is my duty to make certain the wounded are being well cared for. When we return to Atotarho Village, their families will wish to know that I did everything possible to—"

"We'll be leaving the wounded here tomorrow. We have other priorities."

Negano stiffened. The words were a slap in the face. It was inconceivable that they would not carry the wounded home to their families as quickly as possible. "I don't understand?"

"That doesn't surprise me. When I divided our forces yesterday, sending two thousand warriors back into Hills country, did you think I did it for no reason?" Atotarho glared at him. As a symbol of his dedication to war, he'd braided rattlesnake skins into his gray hair. They lay in plaits along his sunken cheeks.

"I'm sorry, my Chief," Negano apologized again, "I understood that you wished to punish the rogue Hills villages that had sided with the enemy and fought against us, but I thought that as soon as our group of two thousand had taken care of the Flint war party, we would, naturally, return home."

"In the future, you will not assume. Have you determined how many total warriors deserted after the Standing Stone battle and today's fight with the Flint People?"

"Out of the four thousand that lived and remained loyal to you, only a few hundred. Some went home, but some will certainly return. They're just out in the forest, hunting, getting their bellies full and trying to make sense of what happened. They'll be back. Yesterday, when Zateri, Gwinodje, and Kwahseti betrayed us and joined the enemy, I think many of our warriors could not bear the thought of killing their own relatives. Then, when Sky Messenger called that monstrous storm... a few fled to join the enemy, including War Chief Sindak. Gods, while I do not agree with Sindak's actions, I understand his reasons. It was like watching one of the great heroes at the dawn of creation."

The awe in Negano's voice seemed to anger the old man. Atotarho's teeth ground beneath the thin veneer of wrinkled skin that covered his jaw. In a thin, reedy voice, he asked, "Fortunately, he'll soon be dead. Providing you followed my orders and dispatched warriors to hunt him down?"

"I did so last night. If they managed to slip by Jigonsaseh's scouts, they should have arrived at Bur Oak this morning and have been watching for him."

Atotarho used one of his clawlike hands to massage his aching knee. "I want every deserter hunted down and killed, starting with Sindak."

"Of course. I thought that once we'd carried the wounded home, we would—"

"We're not going home."

Negano blinked, as though clearing his eyes would make it easier to grasp this latest lunacy. His gaze sought out the chief's personal guards, standing in a group five paces away. They'd been listening to his conversation with the chief, and now stared at Negano as though expecting him to do something about this madness. After all, he was War Chief. The wounded must be carried home. It was his duty to explain these facts to the Chief.

The new leader of the Chief's personal guards, Nesi, sharply dipped his head toward Atotarho, urging Negano to say something. Nesi was a big, square-jawed giant with a heavily scarred face. He had seen forty summers pass. A decade ago, Nesi had been the War Chief of Atotarho Village. He understood Negano's new duties better than Negano did.

Negano braced his feet. "My Chief, as you well know, our warriors have fought two hard battles in as many days. They're exhausted. Many of their friends and family members are injured. Some are dying. Our warriors expect to take them home where they can be properly cared for."

Atotarho calmly rested his stick across his lap, and sternly repeated, "I told you, we are not returning home."

"Do you plan to remain here until the wounded can travel?" It was the only reason he could think of.

"At dawn, we're going back to Bur Oak and Yellowtail villages."

When Negano cast a glance at Nesi, the giant frowned and shook his head; he was just as confused as Negano.

Negano said, "Do you plan to attack those villages again?"

Wolves got into a fight over one of the bodies in the killing pen, and a snarling, growling cacophony arose. Negano could see eyes coalescing around the pair that fought, creating a jewel-like silver ring. The battle lasted barely ten heartbeats before one of the wolves yelped and whimpered away.

Atotarho waited for the commotion to die down. "I wish you to dispatch a messenger tonight to the new High Matron of our nation. Inform Kelek that we will remain in Standing Stone country for another half moon, perhaps even a moon. That should be long enough. Also, after our war parties have destroyed the traitorous villages, she should immediately dispatch two thousand warriors back to Bur Oak Village to aid us."

"Very well."

"I also wish you to dispatch messengers under white arrows to carry the news of our great victory to other nations. Have them say that the Standing Stone nation is on the verge of extinction, and we are about to assure it." He aimed a crooked finger at Negano's heart. "I especially wish messengers to be sent to the Mountain People. Tell them that if they wish to ally with us for a few days, we will be able to exterminate the Standing Stone nation even faster."

"I doubt they'll accept, my Chief. They hate

us. Even if they do accept, it will take them seven or eight days to arrive."

Atotarho just stared at him.

"I'll dispatch the messengers immediately. Now, Chief, if we may, I'd like to return to our former discussion. What will we be doing in Standing Stone country for another moon? How will we feed our warriors while camping in a winter forest?"

Negano waited for an explanation of how he planned to use their current force of one thousand seven hundred warriors, and then another two thousand.

Atotarho did not answer. He'd occupied himself tossing more branches on the fire. Sparks whirled through the air.

"Chief, three thousand seven hundred warriors is a huge force. I ask again, how will we feed them?"

"Now that you know we are not going home, you should start by stripping the Flint bodies of every shred of food they have in their packs, then ration it to our warriors. It will take days for our reinforcements to arrive. By then, I'm sure you will have thought of something to keep the army fed. After all, you are War Chief. It's your responsibility."

When Atotarho offered no further information, Nesi, who stood where the chief couldn't see him, stabbed his war club at the Chief, insisting that Negano ask the necessary questions to finish the discussion.

Negano sighed and asked, "What is it you wish to accomplish in Standing Stone country, my Chief?"

Atotarho prodded the fire again. The burning logs crackled and spat. Orange light fluttered like huge wings through the nearby pines, and sparks gushed into the darkness. Atotarho lifted his wrinkled face to watch them climb into the Sky World. He appeared to be offering a silent prayer.

When he looked back at Negano, the old Chief murmured, "I plan to teach a lesson none of our enemies will ever forget."

Negano's eyes narrowed. "What lesson? Do you plan to take the Standing Stone villagers hostage? To make them slaves? I'm sure our villages would appreciate being able to increase their numbers, but there are thousands of survivors from the Bur Oak and Yellowtail battle. How will we feed so many on the way home?"

In a low deadly voice, the Chief replied, "We're not going to feed them."

Negano let that sink in. "Very well, but it is my duty to inform you that I believe capturing them will be harder than you perhaps realize. Despite the fact that we have one thousand seven hundred warriors left after this afternoon's battle, the

Standing Stone clans will have spent all day repairing their damaged palisades—*and three rows of palisades surround each village,*" he added forcefully, and saw Nesi nod in approval. "They are not fools. We nearly destroyed their entire army yesterday. They must be expecting us to return to finish the job. By the time we arrive, they will be prepared for us. We—"

"Get to your question."

"My Chief, we have less than one-quarter the warriors we did when we attacked yesterday. If we assault their palisades, it will be a long, drawn-out struggle. We will lose at least half our current forces, leaving us with perhaps eight hundred. Truly, my Chief, I do not believe it's worth the blood. Our warriors are tired and they wish to go home. Next Spring, we can undertake such a campaign with the full force of our army and—"

"Are your ears filled with pine sap?"

Negano shifted. "How have I offended you?"

"We are not going to assault their palisades."

"But how will we get hostages if we do not attack?"

"Oh," he replied in a gloating voice, "they'll walk right out of their gates and into our arms. You see, we're going to starve them to death."

Negano stood perfectly still. The old chief was clenching and unclenching his grotesquely deformed hands, as though ready to twist Negano's head off.

He glanced at Nesi, and the former War Chief's stern expression gave him no leeway. Negano said, "My Chief, I feel I must make you understand what's going on in our warriors' hearts. It's not just the wounded and dead that concern them. Yesterday was like a blunt beam swung to their bellies. They are stunned. It appeared to them"—*and to me*—"that Elder Brother Sun obeyed Sky Messenger's commands. He has become a walking, breathing legend. They're terrified of him. Not only that, your own War Chief defected to Sky Messenger's side yesterday." He spread his arms. "Chief, *your own daughter* fought on Sky Messenger's side. Your daughter!" More softly, he continued, "Your warriors are reeling. They need to think about all this. If you insist that they immediately engage in another battle, they may—"

"Insolent fool!" Atotarho roared in rage. "Pray you don't find yourself staring as your guts come tumbling out of your belly in the middle of the night!"

Negano had no doubt but that his life was in danger. There was more he needed to say, and should say. Instead, he opted to protect his own hide, and bowed deeply. "Forgive me, my Chief. I realize you have not yet finished your plan. When you do, I would appreciate it if you could explain it to me in detail."

Behind the chief, he saw Nesi roll his eyes and throw up his hands. He thought Negano a coward —which is exactly how he felt.

Atotarho ordered, "Leave me. Find and dispatch the messengers as I instructed. If you're still alive, I'll call for you again in the morning."

"Yes, my Chief."

Negano turned, and with as much dignity as he could, walked down the hillside, but he could feel Nesi's stare lancing through the back of his head.

10

The high-pitched scream punctured the night, waking Hiyawento from a sound sleep. Instinctively, he leaped to his feet with his war club in his hand. Breathing hard, he frantically tried to identify the threat. An uproar rose as other sleeping warriors threw off their blankets and grabbed for weapons. In less than ten heartbeats, dozens of people had gathered around Hiyawento's fire, murmuring, asking questions. Conversations carried on the frigid night breeze.

It took Hiyawento a few instants to hear Zateri say, "Hush, you're all right. We're safe."

He swung around to see his wife holding Kahn-Tineta against her chest. Their daughter clutched Zateri's sleeves in sheer terror, and her huge eyes darted over the darkness.

"But Mother, I saw him! He was right there!" She thrust an arm toward the dense sumacs to the north. Their leafless branches had a spiky appearance.

Their camp stretched over the hilltop like a glimmering blanket, dotted with hundreds of campfires. Though camped close together, each village had separated. Coldspring Village occupied the southern portion of the hilltop. Riverbank was to the north, and Canassatego Village stood on the highest point to the west. In the distance, to the east, the Forks River twisted through the bottom country like a silver serpent.

Hiyawento held up a hand and called, "Forgive us, please return to your bedding hides. Everything is well."

Warriors muttered and eventually drifted back to their own camps, leaving Hiyawento and Zateri alone with their wildly sobbing daughter. All three of them had cut their hair in mourning over the deaths of little Jimer and Catta, his murdered daughters. As well, they were mourning the passing of the High Matron of the People of the Hills, Zateri's grandmother, Tila.

Virtually no one these days has hair longer than his or her shoulders.

Zateri asked, "Are you better?"

"No!" Kahn-Tineta choked out and buried her

face against her mother's cape. "He's still out there."

As the panic drained from Hiyawento's muscles, his heartbeat began to slow, and the feeling of impending doom that had become his constant companion returned. He couldn't seem to shake it. It was as though he could feel Sodowegowah's icy breath upon his cheek.

As he walked toward Zateri, Kahn-Tineta shrieked, "Father! Father!"

She wriggled out of Zateri's arms and ran to him, her arms up, her fingers working in a "take me, take me" gesture.

Hiyawento lifted her, and her legs went around his waist. He kissed her hair and said, "Let's sit down beside your mother."

Kahn-Tineta had her chin propped on his shoulder, and every muscle in the girl's body trembled. He stroked her hair softly. "You're all right," he whispered. "Look around you. The camps are quiet and still."

"The witch is out there, Father! I saw him!"

Hiyawento lowered himself to a cross-legged position on the hides beside Zateri and shifted Kahn-Tineta to his lap where he could look into her wild eyes. "Where did you see him? Show me."

"Right there!" she pointed again. "He sneaked from the trees and was watching me. He's going to get me!"

Zateri gave him a wrenching look. Firelight flickered over her flat face with its wide nose. Her two front teeth, which stuck out slightly, made her lips appear to protrude. She mouthed the word, "Again."

This was the second night in a row that the "witch" had come to Kahn-Tineta in her dreams.

Hiyawento stroked his daughter's back and gazed directly into her dark eyes. "I told you, my daughter, the witch is dead. I killed him. What did I do after that? Do you remember?"

"You dismembered his corpse and scattered the pieces far and wide so that no one could ever find him and Sing him to the afterlife."

"That's right. Dismemberment also immobilizes the angry Spirit of the Dead, so it can't run off seeking revenge."

She sobbed. "But he came back to life, Father! Just like the stories said he would. He can't die! He's still after me."

Zateri folded her arms over her chest, hugging herself, and lifted her face to study the moon-silvered night sky. A few Cloud People drifted across the charcoal background, their edges gleaming. It had only been seven days since they'd left Kahn-Tineta with her grandmother Tila and trotted off to war with the Standing Stone nation. How could they have known that Zateri's father, Atotarho, would hire Ohsinoh to kidnap their last daughter so that he could use the little girl as leverage against them? He was unnaturally canny. Even then, Atotarho must have suspected that Coldspring, Riverbank, and Canassatego villages were secretly aligning against him.

"Well, don't worry," Hiyawento said, pandering to her fear. "If he returns, I'll shoot him through the heart and crush his skull again. He'll never get you. I'll—"

"He got me once! He stole me right out of Atotarho Village!"

He adjusted her cape, straightening it around her small body. "Well, I wasn't there to protect you, but I am—"

"Father, I—I wish Sky Messenger was here to protect me."

Hiyawento smiled sadly. "I wish he were here, too. I miss him. But if he were here, do you know what he would tell you about the witch?"

She blinked wide eyes. "What?"

"Sky Messenger would tell you that condemned souls change after death. When souls discover they can never reach the Land of the Dead, they are so overwhelmed with grief that they seek out the comfort of loved ones. Usually, they return to their home villages to move unseen among their relatives. They eat the dregs from the cooking pots—that's why we often hear them rattling for no reason at night. Lost souls take comfort from familiar surroundings. They are too distraught to even think of kidnapping little girls they barely know."

Kahn-Tineta tucked a finger in her mouth and began sucking on it...a thing she had not done in five summers since she was three.

In a firm voice, Hiyawento said, "You're safe, Kahn-Tineta. I give you my oath."

His daughter slowly began to relax in his arms. Her cries became less choked but still punctuated with occasional sobs.

"Not only that..." He reached down to pull the small medicine bag from her cape. It hung around her neck, suspended on a braided leather cord. "Your mother is one of the greatest Healers in the land. She makes powerful Spirit medicines." He held the bag up to his daughter's nose. "What do you smell?"

She sniffed. "Wood nettle and white oak."

"That's right. They can counteract even the most powerful witchcraft. That's why your mother told you never to take this off."

Kahn-Tineta angrily wept. "Why didn't Mother give it to me before you both left to go to war? Maybe the witch wouldn't have gotten me!"

As her fear receded, it was replaced with anger, which was a good sign, but the words seemed to tear Zateri's heart. Tears filled her eyes. She rose. When she ambled over to the fire to place two more branches on the flames, sparks swirled up around her. An orange gleam coated the tears on her cheeks.

"We were just overwhelmed and not thinking right," Hiyawento explained. "It won't happen again."

Kahn-Tineta stared hard into his eyes, as though judging the truth of his words, then her arms went around his neck in a stranglehold, and she pressed her cheek against his. "Give me your oath as a warrior of the Hills nation."

In a deep, solemn voice, Hiyawento replied, "On my life, as the War Chief of Coldspring Village, I give you my oath that you will never be alone again. One of us will always be with you to protect you."

She pushed away to stare at him, judging his sincerity. "I believe you."

"I appreciate that." Hiyawento kissed her forehead. "Now, if you'll try to sleep, I'll stand guard."

"Will you? Really?"

"I'll be standing right there." He pointed to the place where Zateri stood by the fire.

Kahn-Tineta rested her head on his shoulder and sighed deeply. "Thank you, Father."

Hiyawento rocked her in his arms until she fell asleep, then he carried her back to her bed and drew the hides up around her throat. When he started to rise, her tiny hand shot out and grabbed his, clutching it. Her eyes were still closed, half-asleep, but she wouldn't let go.

Hiyawento knelt at her bedside, holding her hand until sleep loosened her grip. Only then did he tiptoe away and walk to the fire to stand beside Zateri.

"She's asleep?"

"Yes. Finally." Unconsciously, he lifted his hand to massage his injured left arm, just below the shoulder, where Deputy War Chief Negano's war club had connected. The bruise ran deep, probably all the way to the bone. The pain was intense.

"Hiyawento, you must sleep tonight. You're hurt and exhausted. I'll find someone else—"

"If she wakes in the night, I want her to see me standing here."

When Zateri gazed up at him with tormented eyes, his own unbearable grief returned. He wrapped an arm around her narrow shoulders and hugged her. "I'll be all right."

Neither of them spoke for a time. Between them lay the indestructible bond of two people who have seen their worlds destroyed, of childhood captivity and torture, of horrific battles, and friends lost...and two people who have held beloved children in their arms while they convulsed and died. They had been through so much together, but never before had Hiyawento felt this gut-deep mixture of rage and despair. The emotion was unnatural, even inhuman. It covered everything like an impenetrable black cloak, blotting out the light, draining joy from the very air he breathed.

Out in the forest, branches smashed into each other as Wind Mother's violent son, *Hadui,* beat his way through the trees and dashed across the hilltop, battering anything in his path. He appeared to be headed north, chasing after the flocks of moonlit Cloud People. Whirlwinds of old leaves and twigs careened in his wake. As he rushed through the camps, people cursed in surprise and sparks exploded from fire pits. They trailed through the night sky like swirling ribbons.

Zateri asked, "What do you think we're going to find when we make it to Canassatego Village?"

He wasn't sure how to answer that, though he'd been thinking of little else. "The night I killed the witch, he told me we wouldn't make it home in time."

"Gods, I pray that was just bluster." Her eyes reflected the firelight. "Do you think he meant our villages would be destroyed before they could move? If Atotarho did that, our warriors' indignation and rage will be uncontrollable." She sucked in a breath and exhaled hard. "It will mean civil war."

He tossed another branch onto the fire, expecting the night to be long and cold. "We started the civil war, my wife, the instant we ordered our warriors to fight against their own nation. Nothing can stop it now."

Zateri's delicate eyebrows drew together. Thoughtfully, she whispered, "There must be a way."

11

Wind blew Matron Jigonsaseh's hair into her eyes and rattled the wooden beads around her throat. She shoved the strands away and continued striding across the sunny Bur Oak plaza. She could tell from the sudden gusts and the change in temperature that another storm was coming. They had even less time to complete repairs than she'd thought.

Near the center of the plaza, High Matron Kittle stood observing six warriors who used ropes to pull the new logs into place in the exterior palisade. The men grunted with the effort, and their faces streamed sweat. Autumn had been very rainy, followed by several deep snows. The sodden logs were heavy and unwieldy. The workers struggled to keep them from falling back to the earth and crushing the men beneath.

Jigonsaseh stopped at Kittle's side. Four longhouses arched in a semi-circle around them. Lines of men, women, and children filed in and out of each one, carrying pots of water and baskets of seeds, corn, and beans. One woman had dried squash vines around her neck. The squashes, still attached, knocked together as she walked, producing a hollow thumping sound. The villagers wore no capes, just knee-length shirts, dresses, and brightly painted leggings. A light shower of brown autumn leaves pirouetted around them as they worked.

Jigonsaseh counted the number of women carrying water pots. Not enough. She would have to tend to that. They could live far longer without food than they could without water.

Without turning, Kittle asked, "How is our defense?"

"Almost nonexistent. Deploying our warriors outside the palisade is a waste, Kittle. I know that's what the council approved, but—"

"And Wampa?"

Jigonsaseh gauged the hard lines in Kittle's face. There would be no convincing her to shift their forces now. Jigonsaseh sighed and said, "Though she is the new War Chief of Bur Oak Village, she has no objections to subordinating herself to War Chief Deru for as long as necessary. She knows he has more experience."

"What of our scouts and lines? Is everyone in place?"

Jigonsaseh quietly took a breath and let it out. "Yes, we have scouts in the tallest trees. As for our lines, we have barely enough warriors to encircle the village. Even then, they are so widely spread out that they are almost no protection at all. They will, perhaps, be able to let one arrow fly before they'll have to turn tail and run for safety. It's a waste of effort. We should pull them all in to defend the village so that when the scouts signal a warning, we'll be ready."

Kittle watched the groaning laborers slowly haul the log, hand-over-hand, into place. Muscles bulged and sweat ran down their faces. When the logs were in place, warriors on the catwalk lashed them to the standing logs, securing them into the palisade. Finally, she said, "That's the last section of the exterior palisade to need repairing, isn't it?"

"Yes."

"Good. They're working fast."

"They'd better. At this rate, we won't even be able to start repairing the longhouses until tomorrow afternoon."

"I know that," Kittle said in a clipped voice.

"We must repair the inner palisades first, then we—"

"*I know.*" Kittle glared up at her, for Jigonsaseh was two heads taller, and an exhausted expression slackened her features. "There's another subject I'd like to discuss with you, and I want you to tell me the bald facts."

"Have I ever done otherwise?"

"No, but we've never been in a position like this before."

Wind tormented her cape until it whipped around her legs in snapping folds. Kittle paused until the gust passed. "If you were Atotarho would you still be in camp, tending your wounded? On your way home? Or on your way here?" A swallow went down her throat. "How much time do we have?"

Jigonsaseh spread her legs and her war club, CorpseEye, swayed where it was tied to her belt. She reached down to wrap her fingers around the smooth polished shaft. It took less than five heartbeats for a tingle of warmth to spread through her palm and up her arm. "Not long, Kittle. He knows how vulnerable we are. However, if he's decided to attack us again, his warriors will be upset, grousing about not being able to carry their injured friends and loved ones home. I think he's so crazy now that he doesn't care about tradition or the souls of his dead relatives. I think he'll push this thing to the end."

Kittle's oval face with its perfect nose and large dark eyes, sagged. She tucked her shoulder-length black hair behind her ears and said simply, "I'd give anything for two hands of sleep."

No one in either village had slept well last night. The wails and groans of the wounded had wrung shudders from the very wood of the longhouses. Fortunately, the worst off had died during the night. This morning, the bodies had been carried outside to await the burial ceremony, and the last of the wounded had been moved into the Council House. Constant whimpering and cries filled the air.

Out in the forest a flock of jays burst into flight and soared away amid a riot of squawks and chirps. One of their lines had probably shifted and startled the birds.

Jigonsaseh gazed out through the open gates to her own village thirty paces distant. "How much of Yellowtail Village has been cleaned out?"

When they'd decided to repair Bur Oak Village and abandon Yellowtail Village, there had been an outcry among Yellowtail villagers. Every chamber in Yellowtail Village was filled with the injured or dying. Everyone knew that moving them might kill them. It had required great patience for Jigonsaseh to go to each family and convince them that if they were attacked again, it might be the only way to save their children.

"About half, last I heard."

Jigonsaseh's eyes narrowed. "If you do not

object, I think I'll take over supervising the evacuation. Perhaps I can speed up the process. As you know, many of my villagers are not happy about this move."

"I would appreciate your help. And"—she exhaled the word—"when that's done, I want you to take over our entire defense."

Jigonsaseh shifted uneasily. "I will if you wish, but I'm not sure that's a good decision. War Chief Deru is perfectly competent to—"

"I know that. I want you up there leading our warriors. They trust you."

She nodded. "Very well."

Kittle's gaze lifted to the sky where Cloud People gathered over the northern hills. The trees visible through the gates had already taken on the curious sheen of stormlight. "We'll have snow by nightfall."

The refugee lean-tos propped against the innermost palisade were falling down. Currently empty, they resembled little more than piles of sticks and bark. Yesterday's miraculous storm had ripped apart every lean-to, and shredded the longhouse roofs, before rolling out into the forest where it tore whole trees from the earth and cast them about like kindling.

Kittle said, "We'll have to find a way to roof those lean-tos before snowfall. What of your villagers? We have no more room in any of our longhouses. Where will your people sleep? Do you plan to have them stay one more night in Yellowtail Village, tending the wounded, until we can—"

"I don't think that's wise. If we're attacked, it will split our meager forces in two. No, we will move the wounded here, as well as the rest of my villagers."

"Where will you move them to?"

"I've ordered the children of the Turtle Clan to collect every sleeping hide in Yellowtail Village. After that, they will gather the branches torn from the trees by yesterday's storm, and bring them here. We'll throw up branch frames and cover them with hides. It will do."

Memories of the black whirling winds yesterday made her think of Sky Messenger. If he'd been running at a good steady trot, by now he should be close to the territorial boundary of the Standing Stone nation. She prayed he was still safe.

"Worried about Sky Messenger?" Kittle said.

"How did you know?"

"Because I'm worried about Taya. After they said goodbye, Taya spent a good two hands of time lying in her hides weeping."

Jigonsaseh frowned. "They barely know each other, Kittle. I hardly think she is pining away—"

"I suspect her emotional mood may mean she carries your son's child."

Jigonsaseh straightened. Sky Messenger and

Taya could not marry until she had proven her worthiness by conceiving. If it were true, they could wed as soon as he returned. Jigonsaseh did not know if that fact would please her son or not. Sky Messenger wanted Baji. Clan politics precluded any such marriage. Perhaps, if Taya was with child, he would finally accept his fate, marry her, and fulfill his duty to his clan.

She said, "At most, your granddaughter is one moon pregnant. Her emotional mood could be nothing more than the aftermath of the battle. Let us wait before we rejoice."

"Agreed."

The wind shifted, and the odors of sweating bodies and wood smoke wafted over them. Jigonsaseh evaluated the holes in the inner palisades. At least five or six gaping charred ovals remained. If they didn't replace that burned wood before the next attack came, the enemy would only have to breach the exterior palisade in one place, and they could flood through the entire village.

"Let's talk about the inner palisades. I think we need to reorganize the work so that—"

"That's because you think like a war chief. If you'd been a village matron for summers, you'd realize that food and water will be just as essential when we are attacked. I can't afford to shift anyone now."

Three boys, five or six summers old, dashed by

with dogs loping at their heels, laughing as they weaved through the lines of workers. Their faces were sheathed in afternoon gleam. One of the dogs, overeager to play, took a flying leap and knocked the lead boy down. The other two boys saw their chance and piled on top of him, squealing as they wrestled.

Jigonsaseh said, "If you don't wish to shift workers, perhaps we could organize the youngest children to fill water jars."

Kittle didn't answer. Her thoughts seemed far away.

"Did you hear me?"

Kittle blinked. "Don't you think it's odd that none of the surrounding villages have sent runners to inquire about our welfare? They must have seen the smoke from our burning villages yesterday morning. At least a few runners should have arrived by dawn today."

"Perhaps they fear Atotarho's army is still here."

"Nonsense. Any responsible matron would have sent at least one man to sneak in, take a look, and hightail it home with the news. Don't they care if we're alive or dead?"

"Perhaps they are more afraid of being attacked themselves and are keeping every warrior inside their palisade walls."

Kittle fumbled with her shell bracelets, rearranging them. They clicked. "But we also haven't seen that odious little Trader, Tagosah. He's always here showing off his latest trinkets around the first day of the moon. He's never late."

"Rarely late. Not never. Don't exaggerate."

Jigonsaseh studied the warriors on the catwalk. Their gazes were fixed on the scouts who stood in the tallest trees, searching for threats. No alarm had been given. They hadn't even signaled that a lone passerby approached.

"There's another thing I wish for you to consider, Kittle. Once everyone has cleared out of Yellowtail Village, we should dismantle it. We need stronger logs for the interior palisades, and we must build more housing in Bur Oak Village. More important, we don't want our enemies to capture it."

Kittle heaved a breath. "You're right. The last thing we need is to have Hills warriors lining the palisade of Yellowtail Village and shooting into Bur Oak Village. Very well, I will leave it to you to tear down your own village."

A strange silence caught her attention. Her right hand unconsciously tightened around CorpseEye while she searched the longhouse roofs and leafless branches of the surrounding trees. "There are no birds."

"Hmm? What?" Kittle stared at Jigonsaseh as though her soul were loose.

Jigonsaseh's senses abruptly sharpened, focused on sound, and sound alone. She sifted out the village noise, and let her attention drift beyond the walls of the palisade. No dove calls. No finch chirps. There was no flutter of panicked wings in the air.

Because they'd already burst into flight or taken cover.

Any decent warrior knew to stop and listen when animals started warning one another. The fact that she'd barely noticed the flock of panicked jays spoke to the gravity of her morning.

The warriors on the catwalk stirred. Two men ran to the side overlooking Reed Marsh, and a clipped conversation broke out.

The scouts in the trees.

Panicked cries rose from the marsh.

Kittle looked up. "What's happening?"

As Jigonsaseh started to back away, to run for the catwalk, she said. "Get everyone inside the palisade."

"What? Why?"

"Just do it!"

Jigonsaseh ran hard for the nearest ladder. Hundreds of arrows leaned against the palisade wall behind the ladder, along with pots of water, wooden drinking cups, and bags of jerky to be used only by warriors protecting the village.

In the plaza below, Kittle shouted at two young

men, "Tell everyone in Yellowtail Village to grab what they can, and get inside our palisades immediately!"

"Yes, High Matron." They dashed away.

Just as Jigonsaseh set foot upon the catwalk, cries came from the warriors in the field to the north...then more came from the south. A corresponding roar went up from the warriors on the catwalk, and they started charging around, scrambling for a better position.

"Matron?" War Chief Wampa called. "Our lines are falling back! War Chief Deru must have ordered them to flee!"

Jigonsaseh leaned on the palisade to survey the situation. To the north, over the top of Yellowtail Village, she caught glimpses of warriors fleeing through the trees. The northern line had broken and warriors sprinted for Bur Oak Village like terrified mice with a mountain lion bounding behind them.

Jigonsaseh strode for the knot of warriors who stood gaping, their gazes leveled on the grassy plain to the west, beyond Reed Marsh. Several gestured wildly with their arms.

"Where is the enemy? Show me."

Wampa used her bow to point. "Look at the tree line, Matron, just out of bow range. They just appeared."

Jigonsaseh scanned the weave of trunks and

brush with a practiced eye. Barely visible, enemy warriors casually lined out, as though they had all the time in the world to get into position. She swung around. "War Chief Wampa, dispatch teams to gather arrows and stack them on the catwalk. After that, not a single warrior leaves his or her position without my permission. Do you understand? Keep the gates open until the Yellowtail Villagers are inside, then open it only as necessary for our retreating warriors to enter."

"Yes, Matron!"

Wampa ran. First, she assigned warriors to bring up the arrows, then she trotted to the portion of the catwalk overlooking the gates, where she leaned over and shouted to the men below, "Open the gates! But I want them closed the instant our last warrior is inside. After that, open them only on my order or the order of Matron Jigonsaseh!"

"Yes, War Chief!"

Along the eastern palisade wall of Yellowtail Village, people flooded, carrying armloads of belongings. More supported litters. The wounded and dying moaned each time one of the rushing litter bearers stumbled.

Tutelo and her young daughters trotted beside the litter carrying her dead husband, Idos. He'd been washed and dressed in his finest war shirt, the one with blue beads down the sleeves. His eyes had sunken, his lips pulled back from his gums.

"Wampa?" she shouted. "Leave the dead outside along the walls. There's no space for them inside!"

Wampa nodded and leaned over the palisade to relay the latest order.

Tutelo drew her daughters against her sides and watched as her beloved husband's body was gently lowered onto the pile of dead stacked along the eastern wall.

Blessed Ancestors, there would be no time now to perform the proper rituals to send the dead on their journey to the Land of the Dead. Thousands of afterlife souls would be wandering around the village, crying out to their relatives.

Frightened voices erupted from the plaza. Jigonsaseh turned. A group of elders surrounded High Matron Kittle and the flurry of conversation was growing louder. Matron Daga shook a fist in Kittle's face. Chief Yellowtail kept speaking to her in a tranquil voice, trying to calm her down.

Jigonsaseh's thoughts began working out the permutations, trying to decipher her enemy's strategy. Who was Atotarho's new War Chief? Did she know him? What were his weaknesses? Not that such knowledge would give her much time. If the Hills army encircled Bur Oak Village and laid siege, eventually they would walk right through the front gates, kill all of the elders, and take the women and children hostage to serve as slaves.

After that, they'd burn the villages so that anyone who escaped had nothing to return to.

Her duty was clear. She had to keep her people alive for as long as she could, and make certain that Atotarho knew the valor of the Standing Stone nation. If it took the last breath in her body, she would make sure his losses were staggering.

Jigonsaseh unslung her bow, pulled an arrow from her quiver, and nocked it. As she monitored her retreating lines, she prepared herself for the worst she could imagine.

12

As twilight engulfed the valley, the falling snow resembled wavering sheets of gray silk blowing in the faint wind.

Jigonsaseh stood beside Sindak with her legs braced, staring out at the field of dead to the west. For more than two hands of time, Atotarho's warriors had been stripping corpses, and mutilating the bodies.

"What's he doing? Why hasn't he attacked?"

Sindak wiped snow from the bridge of his hooked nose. "He knows feeding the army comes first. Men with empty bellies desert and flee. As to the mutilation, he's feeding his warriors' souls. Condemning your relatives to wander the earth forever will make Atotarho's army feel better."

Clan war cries erupted, and she saw several

men start dancing, holding severed heads in their fists."

Sindak said, "I've tried to get a rough count, but people have been shifting around so much, I haven't been able to. How many men, women, and children are in this village?"

"Too many," she answered, seeing no reason to lie to him. "Around two thousand four hundred. Most are elderly or children."

His gaze bored into hers. Snow had accumulated on his black hair. As though he'd just realized it, he brushed it off, and flipped up his hood. The edges of the tan leather caught the firelight and framed his narrow face with a flickering oval. "You're in serious trouble, Matron."

She laughed grimly and turned away.

Sindak asked, "Do you know why Atotarho allowed all of your warriors to return unharmed today? They were fleeing like rabbits. He could have dispatched a few hundred men to chase after them, and they would have killed many. But he didn't. He let them return to the safety of the village."

His features had set into hard unyielding lines. The lines of a War Chief's face, a man struggling to understand every possible nuance of his enemy's actions.

While she stared into his eyes, blood surged so loudly in her ears that it dimmed the noise in the plaza. "Blessed gods, I've been so occupied with the council and the village's defense—"

"That you haven't had time to think like Atotarho? Of course not. Besides, I know him better than you do, and I have had the time."

Jigonsaseh massaged her brow as she cursed herself for being a fool. "Atotarho knows that no matter how much food and water we managed to pack into the village before he arrived, it will run out eventually."

"Yes, and the more mouths that need water and food, the faster it will run out. How long can we last?"

The fact that he'd said "we" interested her. Had he truly thrown his lot in with theirs? Wind flapped his hood around his face. He reached up to clasp it beneath his chin, holding it in place until the gust passed.

She answered. "If it was just food, we could last seven days with what we have stockpiled inside Bur Oak Village, and if we can get to our buried caches outside, we could last all winter. But—"

"How much water is there?" The crow's-feet at the corners of his eyes deepened. He looked at the longhouses.

"Three or four day's worth, but the marsh is ten paces away. If we're lucky, we'll be able to send out teams in the night—"

"You won't," he cut her off. As he shook his

head, firelight gilded the hook of his nose with an edge of flame. "Accept that fact now. The marsh provides excellent cover. He'll have it surrounded by noon tomorrow. Maybe even tonight. Anyone who steps out of this village will be dead. The cover of darkness won't matter."

"Maybe, but the cover of darkness works both ways. The hunters can easily become the hunted."

Jigonsaseh's fingers tightened around CorpseEye until her hand ached. Of course, Atotarho had men to waste. If his warriors were killed, he had plenty more. She did not. She would have to institute drastic measures to conserve their water. Suddenly, every flake of snow drew her attention.

She lurched forward and called, "War Chief Deru?"

Deru, who stood ten paces away down the catwalk, tramped toward her with his red cape swaying around him. He was a big, muscular man with a squashed nose. His left cheek had been crushed by a war club many summers ago. As he walked passed Sindak, he gave his former enemy a slit-eyed glare. Clearly, Deru didn't trust Sindak.

Sindak just stared back, expressionless.

Deru bowed. "Yes, Matron?"

"I want you to organize teams. Find every pot in the village not already full of water and empty it. We need to dispatch people to the marsh to fill them. After that, as they are emptied, I want the pots placed along the drip lines of the longhouses to catch the snow runoff."

"I'll see to both immediately."

He started to turn away, but she gripped his arm, forcing him to look back at her. They'd fought side-by-side for many summers. He'd once been her deputy war chief, yet she had no idea how he would respond to her next order. Quietly, she added, "I must discuss this with the Ruling Council before we can implement it, but I want you to begin making preparations. Mark every dying victim in the village. Consult with the Healers, Bahna and Genonsgwa. If they agree that there is no hope of the victim's recovery, we need to stop wasting food and water on them."

Deru's jaw clamped. A swallow went down his throat. He briefly looked over her shoulder, out at the campfires. "You and I must talk soon. I need to know what you know." He gave Sindak an unpleasant glance, as though blaming him for the order.

"Give me one-half hand of time, Deru, then meet me here."

"Yes, Matron." Deru strode away.

Jigonsaseh's gaze must have been like a lance. As though in defense, Sindak folded his arms beneath his cape, shielding his vulnerable chest.

"The time for pleasantries is over, *old friend*. I

need to know every detail of Atotarho's army, every possible vulnerability, Atotarho's quirks, his habits, every weakness of the new War Chief, every—"

"Matron, I'm not sure who the new War Chief—"

"Speculate."

Sindak rubbed his jaw. He probably hoped that once Atotarho was dead, the Hills nation would reunite and he and his warriors could return home to take up their old lives. But if that did not happen, Sindak would become the most hated traitor in the history of his people, his name cursed forever. His actions would also cause all of his warriors to be declared Outcasts by Atotarho's faction of the People of the Hills. None of them would be able to return home again.

He seemed to be thinking about that. After what seemed a long time, he replied, "Maybe Negano. He was in charge of Atotarho's personal guards for five summers. The chief trusts him, but it could just as easily be—"

"Tell me about Negano."

Sindak tightened his folded arms. Muscles bulged through the leather of his cape.

Through a tense exhalation, he said, "His weaknesses...all right. First, he's inexperienced. While he carried the title of deputy war chief, he's never actually served as one. He was the leader of Atotarho's personal guards, composed of five or six warriors. He doesn't understand how an army works. As well, if he's been promoted over other, more worthy people, there will be a lot of resentment. As the leader of the chief's personal guards, he's used to respect. It will be a shock for him. He's going to stumble for a while as he finds his way and earns the trust of the men and women who were passed over."

"What do you think of him personally?"

Sindak shrugged. "He's not innovative, but he's competent. Once he gets settled into the position, I think he's capable of being a good War Chief. However, you should be aware that it won't really matter who Atotarho's war chief is... because Atotarho gives most of the commands himself."

She listened, processing the information, trying to determine how she might be able to use it. Below, High Matron Kittle and Gonda exited the council house, carrying teacups, and wearily tramped across the plaza toward the Deer Clan Longhouse, undoubtedly praying they could finally get some sleep. Every few paces, someone stopped and demanded to speak with them. The Ruling Council had ordered Jigonsaseh to lead the fight for as long as necessary, which excused her from council meetings—at least until she was sent for. She wondered what decisions had been arrived at, and how it would affect the fight.

"Who do you think was promoted as the leader of Atotarho's personal guards?"

Sindak shrugged. "That's more difficult. I don't think the chief really liked any of his other guards, though they were all good men. Honestly, I can't even guess."

"Try."

Suspiciously, he cocked his head. "Why?"

"I need to know if he can be bribed or convinced that his chief is insane and leading his people to destruction."

"What you're really saying is you want to know if we can convince him to kill the evil old man. Correct?"

"Yes."

Sindak unfolded his arms and, as he turned toward her, his dark, deeply sunken eyes reflected the wavering firelight. "Well, he might have opted for a young, strong warrior like Lonkol, or a seasoned veteran like Nesi, his War Chief of many summers ago." Sindak's brows plunged down over his hooked nose. "If it's Nesi, there is no chance whatsoever of swaying him in our direction. He is a man of great integrity. Loyal to a fault."

"And if it's Lonkol?"

His head waffled. "Maybe."

In the plaza, Kittle finally made it to her longhouse, said a few final words to Gonda, and ducked beneath the curtain, disappearing into the warmth.

A line of people followed her inside, calling questions.

Gonda took a drink from his teacup and surveyed the village. No one had remained to question him. He was merely a refugee, the Speaker for the Warriors from White Dog Village, a village destroyed by the man standing next to her, War Chief Sindak of the People of the Hills. When Gonda saw Jigonsaseh and Sindak standing together on the catwalk, he tiredly walked toward them.

"If you were still in charge of Atotarho's army, how would your warriors be lined out?"

Sindak's gaze roamed the surrounding hills, then he knelt on the catwalk and started drawing lines in the snow. "Keep in mind, after he left here, Atotarho probably split his army down the middle. He wanted to punish the rogue villages, so I suspect he dispatched three war parties to each village—Coldspring, Riverbank, and Canassatego—with orders to burn them to the ground. He—"

"Explain why you think he would split his army. It would be sheer foolishness."

Sindak looked up at her. Snowflakes melted on his cheeks. "He's insane. The fact that his daughter Zateri led the betrayal will be eating him alive."

"If you're right, that means there are only two thousand out there."

Sindak didn't even blink. "Yes, so we're only

outnumbered eight to one. Are you telling me you feel better?"

Gonda's steps crunched the snow as he came up behind Sindak and, teacup in hand, peered inquiringly over Sindak's shoulder at the sketch. His long red cape had an orange tint in the firelight.

Sindak continued, "He has two thousand trained warriors—not children carrying their childhood bows, as fill your ranks. Atotarho's forces will be bedded down on every high point around this village. They'll be concentrated here"—he sketched the position—"here and here. In addition, substantial forces will have been deployed to cut off the trails, to isolate you. Lastly, a thin line will fill in the most vulnerable gaps. Over here in this drainage, and up here where the trail cuts through the cap rock." He stared for a time at the lines he'd made in the snow, nodded, and stood up again. "At least, that's what I'd do."

As Gonda handed the warm teacup to Jigonsaseh, he said, "I thought you might be cold."

"I am. Thank you."

Gonda glanced back at the lines Sindak had sketched in the snow, and pointedly asked, "Why do we care what Atotarho's *former* War Chief would do? He's not out there. He's in here with us."

"Because he trained those warriors, you fool," Sindak defended. "Even you should grasp that. You once trained warriors when you were War Chief Koracoo's deputy—before she removed you in favor of War Chief Cord."

The lines of Gonda's round face drooped. "Not very subtle, Sindak, pointing out that we both qualify as *former*."

"I thought you'd appreciate that."

A small amount of her distrust had seeped away as Sindak talked. He didn't appear to be holding anything back, or trying to deceive her. "I heard that Gonda offered to adopt you and your warriors into his clan."

Gonda nodded. "I did. He refused."

Sindak knocked off the snow that had accumulated on the shoulders of his cape. "My warriors are considering it. But you know as well as I do that they believe themselves patriots. They desperately want to go home to their families."

Bluntly, Jigonsaseh said, "Atotarho is going to kill their families, Sindak. They may already be dead. If not, their relatives need to get out now and make their way here. Perhaps you should dispatch one of your warriors with that message? I give you my oath that the Standing Stone nation will adopt any member of their families who—"

"I'll tell them."

Jigonsaseh turned to watch the enraged sobbing people in the plaza.

The circle broke up and men and women sauntered away in different directions.

"Now, Matron, I want you to tell me something," Sindak said.

Gonda scowled. "That sounded like a command, not a request. You are addressing a member of the Ruling Council, you pusillanimous insect. You will keep a civil tongue—"

She cut Gonda off, "What is it, Sindak?"

Sindak gave Gonda a disgruntled look, then propped his hands on his hips. The motion caused his tan cape to flare out around his body. The white geometric designs on the bottom flashed in the firelight. "We've heard a thousand versions of Sky Messenger's vision. I want to hear it from you. I assume you memorized it to make sure you could repeat it exactly. You wouldn't want to make an error before an enemy council that Sky Messenger would later have to correct." He pointed a stern finger at her, a warning gesture. "Word for word, Matron."

She chuckled at his audacity. This was the man she remembered from twelve summers ago. Too brash for his own good.

Gonda's mouth opened to say something vituperative, but she replied, "I did memorize it."

"Good. I'm listening."

Images from the vision flared behind her eyes.

Brilliant and dark, and reverence filtered through her exhaustion.

13

"Keep in mind, I don't tell it as well as he does."

"I suspect no one does," Sindak answered.

Jigonsaseh shook the snow from her hood. Clumps of white fell onto the catwalk. "It will probably help if you imagine his deep voice, not mine."

Sindak sank back against the palisade again, his intent gaze upon her, totally ignoring Gonda. Snow lilted through the air around him, the big flakes falling slowly. "I'll try."

She took a drink from the cup of spruce needle tea, and steam curled up around her face. The sweet tangy flavor didn't soothe her taut nerves, but it warmed her belly.

"When the dream begins he can't feel his body,

just the air cooling as color leaches from the forest, leaving the land strangely gray and shimmering. As he watches, the blue sky goes leaden, and the rounded patches of light falling through the trees curve into bladelike crescents. That's when he first senses his skin...but it's a faint, not really there, sensation. He has the overwhelming urge to run, but he can't feel his legs at all. His fingers work, clenching into hard fists, unclenching. A great cloud-sea swims beneath him. He says it's a dark restless ocean, punctured by a great tree with flowers of pure light."

"The sacred World Tree? Whose roots sink through Great Grandmother Earth and plant themselves upon the back of the Great Tortoise floating in the primeval ocean below?"

As images from the Creation Story filled her, she clutched Gonda's teacup more tightly. "Yes."

Her gaze briefly fixed on Gonda's, then focused on the palisade at the opposite end of the village, behind the Snipe Clan longhouse. Through the veil of snow she saw a group of four warriors talking, their bows slung over muscular shoulders.

"As though the birds know the unthinkable is about to happen, they tuck their beaks beneath their wings and close their eyes, roosting in the middle of the day. Noisy clouds of insects that, only moments ago, twisted through the forest like tiny tornadoes, vanish. Butterflies settle to the ground at Sky Messenger's feet and secret themselves amid the clouds. An eerie silence descends."

Sindak didn't seem to be breathing. He watched her with slightly narrowed, unblinking eyes.

"Morning Star flares in the darkening sky and, as though she's caused it, fantastic shadow-bands, rapidly moving strips of light and dark, flicker across the meadow. He—"

"So..." Sindak interrupted, "now he's standing in a meadow. The cloud-sea is gone?"

"Let her finish," Gonda said.

"It's complicated," she added. "Spirit Dreams have a logic of their own."

"But where is the meadow? Has he ever seen it before?"

"At this point in the Dream," she replied, "it nestles in the heart of the cloud-sea."

"Ah, I understand." He sank back against the palisade. As Jigonsaseh told the story, she could hear Sky Messenger's voice, filled with awe and foreboding. "Dimly, he becomes aware that he is not alone. Gray shades drift through the air around him, their hushed voices like the distant cries of lost souls. He knows that they are the last congregation. The dead who still walk and breathe. Then he hears Hiyawento call, 'Odion?' and he turns to see Hiyawento standing in the meadow beside him. Hiyawento points out beyond the cloud-sea. At the western edge of the world, an amorphous darkness rises from the watery depths and slithers along the horizon—"

"Horned Serpent? The Spirit beast who almost destroyed the world at the dawn of creation?"

Annoyed, she said, "Will you let me finish?"

Sindak's mouth pursed then he said, "But it's hard not to ask questions."

"Endeavor," Gonda said.

"I apologize."

Jigonsaseh sighed. "When strange black curls, like gigantic antlers, spin from the darkness and rake through the cloud-sea, Elder Brother Sun trembles in the sky. Right beside him, a black hole opens in the universe, and Elder Brother Sun slowly turns his back on the world to flee. There is a final brilliant flash, and blindingly white feathers sprout from his edges. Sky Messenger is certain that he's flying. Flying away. And he knows that if Elder Brother Sun leaves us, the world will die... unless he does something."

She swiveled her head to peer at Sindak. He stared at her fixedly. His narrow beaked face was beaded with melted snow.

"Just as Sky Messenger realizes that it is up to him to stop the death of the world, a crack—like the sky splitting—blasts him. He looks down and sees a great pine tree pushing up through a hole in the earth, its four white roots slashing like lightning to the four directions. A snowy blanket of thistledown blows toward it like a great wave, spreading out all over the world."

Sindak stood so still, he resembled a stuffed man-skin.

"Sky Messenger staggers as his body comes alive in a raging flood. When he turns to speak to the Shades, a child cries out. The sound is muffled and wavering, seeping through the ocean of other voices. It sounds like the little boy is suffocating, his mouth covered with a hand or hide. Fear freezes the air in his lungs. As though the man has his lips pressed to Sky Messenger's ear, he orders, 'Lie down, boy. Stop crying or I'll cut your heart out.'"

Sindak moved, shifting his back to a new position against the palisade. Clearly, he longed to ask a question, but he held his tongue.

"Then the Dream bursts. For a time, there is only brilliance. Then Sky Messenger sees the flowers of the World Tree, made of pure light, fluttering down. They're all around him, fluttering down into utter darkness...and he's falling, tumbling through nothingness with tufts of cloud trailing behind him."

When she'd finished, she lifted the teacup, and took another drink. Each telling was like a journey to another world, a place where time ran more slowly, as though the Creator himself were dragging his feet, afraid of what was to come.

"Who is the man?" Sindak's dark eyes had gone wide and wet.

"The man we cut apart outside Bog Willow Village."

Sindak's forehead furrowed, then his awed expression dissolved like mist in sunshine, becoming hard and filled with hatred. "What does that piece of filth have to do with the vision?"

Jigonsaseh said, "I don't really understand it, Sindak, though I was there when Old Bahna, our village holy man, explained it to Sky Messenger. He told Sky Messenger that 'A man who hates has no eyes. He is a prisoner of darkness.' Bahna said the point was forgiveness."

Sindak made a deep-throated sound of disgust. "Forgiveness? He wants Sky Messenger to forgive that piece of filth? That's a bad idea."

"I thought so, too," Gonda remarked.

Jigonsaseh said, "Bahna told Sky Messenger that all of his life he's been hiding from a memory, and that he's been afraid for so long, he doesn't know how to stop. He told Sky Messenger that he lived in a prison that he repaired every day. He added new chinking, new logs, and sealed himself in, over and over. Bahna told Sky Messenger that he had to stop it, to escape, or he'd never be able to truly see the ghosts of grief and desperation that haunt this land. That's why that foul War Chief—"

"That foul War Chief is dead, Matron," Sindak

noted. "How can forgiving him accomplish anything?"

"Bahna says he's not dead. He says that just as a warrior breathes soul into every arrow he creates, a man can breathe soul into a memory. He said Sky Messenger's hatred has kept the War Chief alive."

"How is Sky Messenger supposed to accomplish this foolish task of forgiveness?"

Logs cracked in the plaza bonfire, belching gouts of black smoke and blue-green flames. People yipped and ran a short distance away, then returned, one at a time, to the stew pots. Sparks whirled upward into the falling snow.

"He already has. Sky Messenger and his betrothed, Taya, returned to Bog Willow Village and collected as many of his bones as they could find, then Sky Messenger prayed the *piece of filth's* soul to the afterlife. He says he forgave the man."

Jigonsaseh turned and leaned her back against the palisade beside Sindak, staring out at the fire-warmed roofs of the longhouses, still mostly free of snow. Smoke escaped from the smokeholes and curled through the air in blue streamers. The workers had used rolls of bark stripped from the Yellowtail Village to repair the roofs. They were a different color, lighter brown, and created a patchwork.

"All right, let's return to my original question. In the vision"—Sindak crossed his arms—"when

Elder Brother Sun flees into the black hole, where are Sky Messenger and Hiyawento standing? Where is the meadow? Does Sky Messenger think it's a real place?"

"He does. But he doesn't know where it is. Why?"

Sindak turned sideways and propped his right elbow on the palisade, facing her. "I want to be there, that's why. They're going to need loyal friends."

After all the summers of war between their peoples, she found it a curious statement. Refugees from the White Dog Village battle filled the plaza below: Gonda's village. "And are you a loyal friend, War Chief Sindak?"

He stared at her, apparently unoffended. "During the battle yesterday, both Sky Messenger and Hiyawento were right beside me. I could have killed them a hundred times. I have never, except in self-defense, lifted a weapon against either man." He paused for two heartbeats. "Everything goes back to those children, Matron. They were chosen by Power. And you and I both know it."

When she didn't respond, he gruffly shoved away from the palisade, glared at Gonda, and walked to the closest ladder, where he climbed down to the crowded plaza.

Jigonsaseh watched him until he rejoined his warriors, then she turned her attention back to the campfires on the distant hills, wavering through the veils of snow.

She propped her elbows on the palisade and finished the dregs of spruce needle tea in her cup. It had gone stone cold. "How did the Council Meeting go?"

"They're all terrified beyond the capacity for thought. No decisions were made."

She handed his cup back. When he took it, their fingers briefly overlapped, which she found comforting. Over the long summers since their marriage ended, their enmity had faded and transformed into a deep friendship that she cherished.

"Sindak says Atotarho may have sent half his warriors away to punish the three Hills villages that opposed him."

Gonda paused as though thinking it over. "Do you believe it?"

"I'm not sure it matters. He's speculating just like we are. We won't know anything until daylight tomorrow."

14

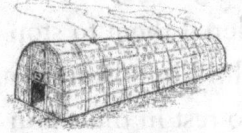

The sloping hillside in front of Zateri descended to the west, flattening out into a broad gently rolling plain. For the most part, winter-gray oaks and maples covered the plain, but here and there, red veins of willows stood out, tracing the paths of creeks and rivers that flowed into Skanodario Lake. In the low places, mist created shimmering white spots.

She glanced back at Kwahseti and Gwinodje. They stood with their war chiefs, surrounded by a few warriors, asking questions. They had donned their white ritual capes, and the folds of the painted leather shone in the bright light. The color of the wolf paws painted on their capes defined their lineages. Kwahseti's white cape had red paws for Yi's lineage. Gwinodje's had black paws for Inawa's lineage. Zateri's white cape had blue wolf paws. All of her life they had symbolized Tila's lineage. With the death of her grandmother, however, they now symbolized Zateri's lineage. While the other matrons endeavored to extricate themselves, Zateri gazed out across the vista.

She had ordered them to stop for one hand of time to allow the litter bearers and the walking wounded time to rest in the warm meadow, and to give her the time to speak with matrons Gwinodje and Kwahseti. They would reach Riverbank Village tomorrow and had no idea what they would find. If they were lucky, Kwahseti's messenger had reached the village first, and her people had packed up and moved to Canassatego Village. In that case, they would find just an empty village, a place to rest for a time before they themselves continued on to Canassatego Village. But if Kwahseti's messenger had not arrived in time...if Atotarho's warriors had reached Riverbank Village first, they would find it burned to the ground and the slaughtered bodies of their relatives strewn across the forest.

Zateri shivered in the cold breath of wind that swept the hilltop and rustled through the bare-branched maples. Old autumn leaves whirled around her. If Riverbank was gone, it meant her own Coldspring Village was also probably gone. And she had no doubt but that her father had told his warriors to be especially destructive. Since

Atotarho knew that cannibalism horrified Zateri, she'd already begun preparing herself for a burned-out husk of a village filled with gigantic piles of half-eaten human bones.

We live in an age of madness.

She looked at Hiyawento. Two paces away, he sat cross-legged in a patch of sunlight, gently rocking their sleeping daughter in his arms. They'd cut Kahn-Tineta's long hair in mourning for her dead sisters. As Hiyawento gazed down at her pretty face, her mouth opened slightly, revealing her missing front teeth. She could tell from Hiyawento's expression that he longed to touch her, to stroke her chopped-off hair, but didn't wish to wake her.

Hiyawento's gaze shifted to the beaded belt he'd been stringing just before Kahn-Tineta had crawled into his lap. After the deaths of Catta and Jimer, he'd started gathering fresh water shells, white and purple, grinding them into long cylinder-shaped beads, and stringing them on thread made from twisted elm bark. Almost finished, the belt was completely white except for two tiny human figures near the front ties. They were deep dark purple. As he studied them, silent rage twisted Hiyawento's features.

A chill went through Zateri. No matter what role Ohsinoh had played, ultimately his baby daughters had been taken from him by Atotarho.

The need for vengeance was consuming his soul. So far, he had managed to contain it, accepting that they had to get their warriors to Canassatego Village. But when they'd accomplished that, when he knew Zateri and Kahn-Tineta were safe, his inner dam would burst, and he would leave his enemy's world in flames.

Kwahseti and Gwinodje separated from the group of warriors and walked toward Zateri's fire with their heads down in quiet conversation. Their war chiefs, Thona and Waswanosh, trailed a few paces behind them. The war chiefs made a strange duo. While Waswanosh was of medium height and slender, Thona was the tallest and most heavily scarred man in the Hills nation. The scars on his face and burly arms resembled tangles of white cords. He was known for his skill with the war ax. Waswanosh's skill was battle strategy. Together, along with Hiyawento's brilliance at tactics, they made formidable leaders.

As Gwinodje and Kwahseti neared her position, they both gave her worried looks.

Kwahseti apologized, "Forgive us for taking so long. Our warriors are concerned about what we will do tomorrow."

Zateri didn't have to ask what she meant. The word *if* hung in the air like a granite boulder suspended over their heads. "As am I. That's one of the things I wish to discuss with you."

As the matrons seated themselves on woven willow mats spread around the fire, Zateri added another branch to the flames. She waited until Kwahseti had dipped two cups of tea from the pot nestled at the edge of the flames and handed one to Gwinodje. "Zateri, shall I dip one for you also?"

"No, I've had my fill, but thank you."

Zateri waited a few moments longer, giving them time to get settled, then she lifted her voice: "Come. Let us bring order to the world."

Gwinodje and Kwahseti respectfully bowed their heads, waiting for Zateri to finish the opening, as her Grandmother Tila had done for more than thirty summers. Midday sunlight streamed through the windblown branches. Kwahseti, Gwinodje, and Zateri sat in a perfect triangle. Their white ritual capes signified their *ohwachiras,* or maternal lineages. Since the deaths of Zateri's two aunts, she was the only female left in Tila's direct line. It was a daunting position. Their ohwachira, kinship group, could trace its descent for thousands of summers back to a common ancestor. In the case of the Wolf Clan, that descent traced back to the Creation of the World, and a great woman leader named Dancing Fox who had bravely led their clan through a dark underworld and into this world of light.

All of Zateri's life, Grandmother had trained her to understand the role of the Wolf Clan ohwachiras. They had power because of them. Ohwachiras possessed and bestowed chieftainship titles, and held the other great names of their lineages. They bestowed those names by raising up the souls of the dead and Requickening them in the bodies of newly elected chiefs, adoptees, matrons, or others. The ohwachira also had the right to remove a soul, and take back the name from anyone who disgraced it. The nation's sisterhood of ohwachiras also decided when to go to war, and when to make peace.

Zateri finished the opening, "I pray that Great Grandmother Earth hears our voices and guides us in our decisions for the good of all things, great and small. I would speak first, if there are no objections."

The matrons shook their heads and glanced at their war chiefs.

Three paces behind Kwahseti, her War Chief, Thona, crouched, waiting to be called upon should the council find it necessary. Three paces behind Gwinodje, her War Chief, Waswanosh, stood with his arms folded tightly across his broad chest. Hiyawento had not moved, but he'd lifted his head to listen.

Zateri smoothed her hands over her white cape and squared her narrow shoulders. "Let me speak straightly, I need to know how you think your lineages view Matron Kelek's ascension to the position of High Matron of our nation."

Usually, upon a High Matron's death, the oldest female in her direct line underwent the Requickening ceremony, received the dead High Matron's name, and—if the former High Matron had so specified—was installed not only as the new matron of the entire clan, but also as the High Matron of the Hills nation. However, during the last meeting of the Wolf Clan ohwachiras, where Tila had presented the possibility of Zateri following her, there had been objections. Unfortunately, Tila had died without making her final successor known. Regardless of who was selected as High Matron, there should have been no question but that the High Matron would come from one of the Wolf Clan ohwachiras, which meant that Zateri, Inawa, or Yi should have ascended to the position. No one understood yet what Chief Atotarho had done to assure that the Wolf Clan would be replaced by the Bear Clan in Atotarho Village, but he'd obviously made some kind of "arrangement."

Kwahseti shoved short gray hair away from her eyes. "The leader of my lineage, Yi, must be livid. The Wolf Clan has led the nation well for more than thirty summers. To have the Bear Clan suddenly assume leadership is an outrage."

Zateri waited for her to continue. When she didn't, Zateri said, "Gwinodje?"

Gwinodje had been staring at her fingers, lacing and unlacing them in her lap. She and Zateri were both small-boned and childlike. "I think Inawa, the leader of my lineage, must be deeply troubled. She will suspect foul play on Atotarho's part. I imagine she is wondering what kind of deal was struck between Kelek and Atotarho to accomplish the task. Everyone knows the Wolf Clan is the largest and most powerful clan in the nation. By all rights, a woman from one of our lineages should have ascended to the High Matronship."

Zateri's short black hair hung at chin level, shining at the corners of her vision. "Since Yi and Inawa both live in Atotarho Village, what sort of repercussions have there been?"

Kwahseti snorted. "Repercussions? I imagine Yi is on a rampage, organizing our lineage for a political campaign to overturn Kelek's ascension. Things must be getting ugly between the clans."

Zateri looked across the fire.

Gwinodje's heart-shaped face tensed. She thought about it before quietly answering, "Zateri, you know that Inawa objected heartily to having you follow your grandmother. She knew that if your grandmother did not appoint you, her own lineage would assume the leadership of the Wolf Clan. Inawa would have become High

Matron of the nation. She must be stalking about like a stiff-legged dog. In fact, I imagine her indignation enlivens every conversation in Atotarho Village."

Zateri took a moment to glance at Thona and Waswanosh, judging the war chiefs' expressions. Both appeared to be analyzing the information.

Zateri said, "As we are all aware, my appointment as High Matron of our faction of the Hills People is temporary. Once we have melded our villages with Canassatego Village, every ohwachira will have a chance to speak with its members about who they wish for High Matron. Until then, I plan to—"

"But, Mother," Kahn-Tineta said with a sleepy yawn and opened her eyes. She rolled over in Hiyawento's arms to stare at the matrons' council.

Zateri turned to look at her daughter. Black tangles framed her pretty young face. "My daughter, we are in council. Perhaps your question could wait—"

"But, Mother, Great Grandmother wanted you to be High Matron." Kahn-Tineta sat up and rubbed her eyes. "She told me."

Zateri started to dismiss the suggestion, but Kwahseti held up a hand. "Wait. I wish to hear this story. When did your great-grandmother tell you this?"

Zateri sighed, and turned around to face her

daughter. Hiyawento's gaze focused on Kahn-Tineta with eagle-sharpness.

Kahn-Tineta must have felt the weight of the council's attention. She tucked a finger into the corner of her mouth, and slurred, "The day she died. I was lying beside her on her shleeping bench while she stroked my hair, and said she was going to tell me a secret that I couldn't tell anyone."

Gwinodje and Kwahseti glanced at each other.

Gwinodje calmly asked, "We need to know her exact words, Kahn-Tineta. Do you understand what that means? Her *exact* words."

Kahn-Tineta nodded. She removed her finger from her mouth to say, "Grandmother hugged me very tightly and said, 'Can I tell you a secret?' I said, 'What is it?' and she said, 'I'm going to name your mother as Matron of the Wolf Clan when she returns, but you mustn't tell anyone.'"

Kwahseti said, "And you've been a very good girl, because you haven't, have you?"

Zateri understood Kwahseti's meaning. If the event truly had occurred, why hadn't Kahn-Tineta told them such important news?

"No, Matron Kwahseti," Kahn-Tineta answered. "Great-grandmother asked me if I could keep her words locked in my heart until it was announced." Kahn-Tineta looked around, meeting each person's eyes. "That's why I haven't said anything. I'm good at keeping secrets...and it hasn't been announced...has it?"

Kwahseti replied, "No, dear girl, because your great-grandmother left for the Land of the Dead before she could tell anyone. What else did she say?"

Kahn-Tineta's eyes narrowed slightly, as though something had occurred to her but she wasn't certain she should say it. She glanced up hesitantly at Hiyawento.

He gently said, "It's all right, Kahn-Tineta. You can tell us."

Kahn-Tineta licked her lips and swallowed. "I told great-grandmother that I wasn't sure Mother wished to be High Matron."

Zateri bowed her head. "What did she say to that?"

"Oh, she said, 'That's not a surprise. No one does.' Then she poked me in the chest with her finger"—Kahn-Tineta rubbed the spot—"and said, 'You remember I said that. Someday, you will have to make the choice of whether or not to lead your people. It is an overwhelming responsibility. But I suspect in the end you will choose to place the welfare of the Hills nation above your own. You will shoulder the burden for the nation's sake. Just as your mother will.'"

Zateri's throat suddenly ached with emotion. "Was that all she said?"

Kahn-Tineta crossed her legs in Hiyawento's lap and shook one moccasin while she frowned at the swirls of blue smoke gliding above her.

"No. I told her I wasn't so sure you would because Father didn't wish to move to Atotarho Village, because he hated Grandfather Atotarho."

At the mention of Atotarho's name, Hiyawento's arm muscles tightened as though fit to burst through his shirt. He frowned down at his daughter. "Kahn-Tineta, look at me."

The girl looked up but cringed at his stern expression.

"Are you telling the truth?"

"Yes, Father!" she cried indignantly. "I wouldn't lie about this!"

He glared at her for a few moments until he'd satisfied himself. "All right. Go on. What else did your great-grandmother say?"

"She told me a story," Kahn-Tineta replied weakly, as though her father's expression made her wish she hadn't said anything at all.

"What story?"

Kahn-Tineta tucked her finger in her mouth again, sucking it for a time to soothe her fears, before saying, "She told me that my great-great-great grandmother used to have a saying. She said that for every one person hacking at the roots of hatred, there were thousands swinging in its branches, and I'd better not do that or I'd fall and break my neck. Great Grandmother told me the only way to survive in this world was to make sure I was the one with the hatchet." Around her finger, Kahn-Tineta slurred, "I liked that shtory."

Gwinodje blinked thoughtfully and turned to Zateri. "That sounds very much like something your grandmother would have said, Zateri."

"Yes," she smiled sadly. "Grandmother told me that same story when I was a child. I loved it, too."

Below them, stretched across the hillside, warriors began rising, dusting off their clothing, and preparing to leave. Sounds of weapons clattering replaced the low drone of conversation.

Thona rose to his feet to stand like a scarred giant behind Kwahseti, waiting to be recognized.

Zateri looked up at him. "Please ask your question, War Chief Thona."

Thona's eyes narrowed. He turned first to Hiyawento, then to Waswanosh, as though silently asking what they thought, before he gazed at Zateri with hard eyes. "High Matron, no child could make up such words. We all agree upon that, yes?"

Hiyawento said, "Yes."

Nods went round the fire.

Thona continued, "If your daughter speaks the truth, as we all suspect, you have been robbed of your rightful position in this nation."

Waswanosh hesitated, rubbing his chin while he considered. "I agree, High Matron."

"You must do something about this crime," Thona said.

Waswanosh nodded. "You can't just stand by and allow this to happen. Despite the fact that we have the largest and most powerful clan in the nation, it will make us look like feeble fools."

Zateri turned around to look at Hiyawento. He seemed to be glaring at the ground, but he was seeing something at a great distance, perhaps in the future, or the past. Kahn-Tineta had leaned her head against his broad chest and continued to suck her finger while she glanced around at the adults.

"Hiyawento?"

He looked up with fiery eyes, then they slowly cleared as he returned to the here and now. In a powerful voice, he said, "This only makes a difference if you've decided that our nation should be reunited. If we plan to remain as a separate nation, it should be of no concern to us whom the Old Hills People choose as their High Matron. We must define what our *nation* is. Are we the New People of the Hills or not?"

Hisses passed around the fire, Gwinodje shaking her head at something Kwahseti whispered. Thona and Waswanosh stared at Hiyawento with pensive eyes, deep in thought. Finally, Thona nodded in agreement.

Hiyawento said, "Every action we take in the next few days depends upon that decision. If we wish to reunite we cannot, must not, attack our relatives in any of the Hills villages."

"But what if they attack us?" Waswanosh asked.

"We defend ourselves, but we do not send out warriors to attack them."

Thona shifted. As his teeth ground, the crisscrossing scars on his face moved like a tangle of white worms. "I do not wish to sit by and allow our villagers to be relentlessly attacked while we bide our time in the hopes that the new High Matron, Kelek, will see the wisdom of reuniting our peoples."

Zateri noted that he'd said "peoples," not "people." Thona had already been thinking along the same lines as Hiyawento, assuming that the separation into two nations was inevitable. A similar thing had happened generations ago among the People of the Dawnland. One faction had split off and called themselves the People Who Separated.

Zateri said, "Kwahseti, your thoughts on this?"

Kwahseti ran a hand through her gray hair, and shook her head. "I would hear Gwinodje's thoughts first."

Zateri turned to Gwinodje. As all eyes fixed on her, Gwinodje blinked and frowned at the flickering fire.

She said, "I confess that, after Atotarho is dead, I would like to see our peoples become one nation again. We all have relatives scattered throughout the other Hills villages. Frankly, I don't wish to consider them my enemy forever."

Zateri nodded and turned back to Kwahseti. "And you?"

Kwahseti toyed with the cup in her hands. "There is another possibility. If we remain as two nations, and Sky Messenger can create a Peace Alliance between all our peoples, we will still be able to see our relatives—"

"Forgive me for interrupting, Matron," Thona said. "But that is a very big *if*. I do not believe we should base our decisions upon that possibility. A Peace Alliance is, in my thoughts, the least likely outcome of this war."

"Yes, probably," Kwahseti exhaled the words. "But in my heart, it is what I most hope for, and what I am willing to risk almost everything for. What of you, Zateri?"

Zateri's brow lined. Her gaze went around the fire, studying the tense expressions. At last, she looked at Hiyawento. "My husband?"

Hiyawento seemed to think about it for a time, then he set Kahn-Tineta on the ground, and rose to his feet. As he straightened to his full height, his beaked face went hard. His soft words were powerful, striking at the heart like knives: "Sky Messenger's vision *will* come to pass. Elder Brother Sun will cover his face with the soot of the dying world and everything we love will die...unless we do something to stop it. Peace is not an option. It's a necessity for survival."

Like the pause after an indrawn breath, a curious silence held them. Wind gusted through their camp, scattered the embers in the fire, and whipped the flames into crackling fury.

When it died down, Thona said, "Peace is a comforting notion. I understand. However, at this very instant, Atotarho is planning to wipe our faction of the Hills People from the face of Great Grandmother Earth. If we do not strike him first, that is exactly what's going to happen. Perhaps, peace can wait a little longer."

"No," Zateri said firmly. "I, like my husband and Sky Messenger, believe peace is our only hope."

Gwinodje and Kwahseti spoke softly again, then Gwinodje turned. "Yes, Zateri, but how do we accomplish it before our villages are annihilated?"

She sat for some time on the mat before the fire that overlooked the long slope to the west, her shell bracelets flashing in the sunlight that fell through the swaying branches. A queer rhythm pulsed her blood, not like her heartbeat, more like music trickling up from a covered pit that fell forever into a black abyss.

"We must use the clan mothers, not warriors."

Kwahseti's brows drew together as she frowned. "How?"

Gwinodje sat forward. "I think I understand! First, we must dispatch messengers to Yi and Inawa, telling them that Tila's last words were to appoint Zateri as her successor—and Zateri claims that right." Words spilled from her lips. "Then we must ask them to dispatch messengers to the other ohwachiras! We—"

"Every ohwachira except those of the Bear Clan. We should leave that decision to Yi and Inawa," Zateri said with a lifted finger. "The Bear Clan must be overjoyed at Kelek's ascension, probably celebrating their new power. Our words will be of no consequence. We are traitors in their minds."

"But if you think the Wolf Clan should take a stand against Kelek, we should tell Yi and Inawa," Kwahseti said.

Zateri carefully considered her next words. She had the sense that they were all suspended upon a zephyr above oblivion. The slightest wrong move now...

"I think Yi and Inawa will know what to do without any suggestions from us, Kwahseti. We are at a great disadvantage. We must be careful. While we have declared independence, if we ever wish to reunite the nation, we must work with the established clan authorities. Yi and Inawa face Kelek every day. Kelek must be swelled with triumph right now, and lauding her victory. However, the Wolf Clan must give her a chance to defend herself before it—"

"Zateri," Kwahseti said with a touch of malice, "she ascended to her position as High Matron through underhanded negotiations with Atotarho. You know it's true. Atotarho must have assured Kelek that she would become High Matron in exchange for something. What?"

Hiyawento said, "In exchange for retaining his position as chief. He knew that as soon as Zateri became High Matron she would remove him."

Zateri nodded. "I would have."

Thona spread his feet and squared his broad shoulders. "How do we survive long enough for the clans to take action? And I think we must fight back if Kelek does not step down as High Matron."

Zateri quietly said, "I don't think so, War Chief. I agree with my husband. We must take no action against Kelek or the rest of the nation. It's not up to us. No matter what Kelek has done, punishing her must remain the prerogative of the Bear Clan. If a Wolf Clan matron had ascended to the position of High Matron through treachery, we would claim the right to deal with it ourselves, wouldn't we?"

Kwahseti nodded. "Absolutely, and if any other clan tried to depose her, regardless of her crimes, we would declare a blood oath and hunt them down."

Gwinodje turned to look at her war chief. "Waswanosh? You have not spoken in a while. Should we fight, as Thona suggests, or merely defend ourselves while we rally the support of the other ohwachiras?"

"Forgive me, Matron. I am...off-balance. However, I find myself more in agreement with High Matron Zateri. If we *can* use the ohwachiras to accomplish our task, we should. Thona is right, too, though. There must be a time limit. If we wait too long, we will be two nations forever."

Zateri waited for more comments.

They all stared at her.

"I fear our patience will be determined by what we find at Riverbank Village tomorrow."

"And at Canassatego Village the day after," Gwinodje said with trepidation in her voice. "If all of our villages are gone..." She sucked in a breath at the thought. "I will cast my voice with War Chief Thona and commit my warriors to destroying Atotarho, and anyone who sides with him, no matter the cost."

Kwahseti nodded, then Waswanosh. When Zateri turned to Hiyawento, she found him staring directly at her with slitted eyes. "My husband?"

His teeth ground for several moments, while he

met each person's eyes. "That will be for the rest of you to decide. I won't be there."

Thona half-shouted, "*What?* You would leave at a moment like—"

"I would," Hiyawento interrupted in a commanding voice. He and Thona glared at each other. "I must be at Sky Messenger's side when the end comes. I *will be* at his side."

Thona leaned toward him threateningly, his hand on his belted war club. "Without you here to lead your warriors, it may come faster than you anticipate." He turned to Kwahseti. "Matron, with your permission, I will return to my duties before I cause a disturbance."

"You may go, Thona. Thank you for your counsel."

Thona bowed to the matrons, glared at Hiyawento again, then stalked away with his cape jerking around him.

Kwahseti vented a sigh. "Please excuse him. He's desperate."

"As we all are," Hiyawento countered.

Gwinodje stared at her hands, twisting them in her lap. Waswanosh stood silently behind her.

Quietly, Zateri said, "If there are no more issues to be presented, I will dismiss this council."

15

Snow fell from the night sky like weightless white feathers, drifting down around Sonon, frosting the hood and shoulders of his black cape, and softly alighting on the bowed head of the woman kneeling in the trail five paces in front of him. Leafless maples swayed gently behind her, their branches already shining with a thin white crust.

The woman was exhausted, gasping hoarse lungfuls of air. She'd un-braided her long hair, and it draped in perfect glistening waves around her beautiful face. Tiny arcs of snow-crested her high cheekbones and iced the lashes that fringed her large black eyes. She'd been running all day without a break, desperately trying to reach Sky Messenger.

Unbeknownst to her, Sonon had been at her

side the entire time. Sooner or later, he knew she would see him.

She collapsed in the middle of the path and curled into a fetal position. She made no sound, but when she succumbed to shivering, the dark curve of trail seemed to tighten around her, holding her tall body in a lover's grasp.

Sonon tilted his head.

There were always souls whose burden of suffering seemed so great that it became an obscenity, a thing that could not be borne by any sane person. At the age of twelve summers, her village had been burned, her parents killed, and she and her two sisters had been sold into slavery. All three of them had been brutalized. Then her sisters were sold to bad men and hauled away. Within hours, they'd both been murdered— leaving her alone. Or rather, in the company of a small group of children from many nations. Among them, Wrass, who was now called Hiyawento, Tutelo, Zateri, and the man she knew as Dekanawida.

She had lost so much.

He hurt for her.

For a time, he watched the snow fall. The forest had gone silent. He could hear each flake that settled upon the branches and rocks.

The woman on the trail shoved up on one elbow. Snow-covered jet waves cascaded around her slender, muscular body. Her shoulders heaved.

Was she weeping? He couldn't see her face. She'd rolled onto her hands and knees, and fought to shove to her feet, but her legs shook too violently.

Flakes whirled and spun around the woman, tousling her hair over her eyes. The woman angrily brushed it aside, sat up, and propped her elbows atop her knees as she massaged her temples. Forlorn, she murmured, "Dear gods, I can't believe I'm lost. I know this country."

Slowly, so as not to startle her, Sonon moved out of the trees and onto the path directly ahead of her. His black cape must be almost invisible in the darkness and falling snow.

But Baji was a warrior. She saw him.

Fast as lightning, she lunged to her feet and pulled the war club from her belt, ready to swing it with deadly accuracy. Her legs wobbled so badly, they barely held her. "Show yourself now, you worthless worm!"

He opened his arms, revealing that he carried no weapons, and called, "I mean you no harm."

Her eyes widened, and the war club in her fists trembled. Barely above a whisper, she called, "*Shagoniyoh?* Dear gods, please tell me Dekanawida is all right?"

It didn't surprise him that her first question was not for herself, but for the only man she'd ever loved. "He is well enough."

Her shoulders sagged. The white chert nodule

lashed to the club's head dipped toward the snow and blended with it. She spread her feet to brace her weak knees. "There are warriors after him, trying to kill him. Do you know that?"

"Yes, I know."

Angry, she said, "Then why are you here? You should be with him!"

He walked toward her and she stiffened. When he stood less than three paces away, he said, "I thought, perhaps, you might have questions for me."

Using the sleeve of her war shirt, she wiped the tears from her cheeks. "Get away from me. Dekanawida is the one who needs you."

Sonon cautiously took another step toward her. She did not back away, but her fingers clutched her war club so tightly that her nails went white. The scent of her fear pervaded the night air.

Softly, he asked, "How are you feeling?" and gestured to her head wound. Blood caked the area behind her right ear.

Baji ignored him while she tied the club back to her belt. A bold move, given how close he stood. "It's healing. I'll be all right."

"And what of your father, Chief Cord? Did he escape?"

Her gaze searched the white-sheathed branches of the maples and darted over the brush. Out in the forest, a few large boulders hunched like white-caped monsters. She stared at them. "I saw him carried from the field of battle, but I...I can't..." She shook her head and dread twisted her features. "I can't remember. Gods, what's wrong with me?"

Gently, he said, "Head wounds. They knock the souls loose for a time."

Her black eyes riveted on Sonon's face, at once pleading and demanding. "Is Father all right? Do you know?"

"No, I'm sorry. I followed you when you left the battlefield. I don't know what happened after that."

Apprehensive, she asked, "Why did you follow me?"

He replied gently, "Most people have questions. About themselves. About where they are. I know these trails very well."

She sucked in a breath and turned around, bewildered, studying the forest. The white veil was growing heavier by the instant. "The only thing I want to know is how to find Dekanawida. Is he on this trail?"

He heaved a sad sigh. "Yes."

"How far ahead of me?"

"Are you sure you wish to find him? You don't have to, Baji. There are other—"

"I *must* find him!" The slightest hint of panic entered her eyes, then it turned into a glare. "I told you, he's being hunted by murderers. The last thing Atotarho's warrior—"

"And you believed him." She must have or she wouldn't be here.

She gave Sonon a withering look. She'd always had a fierce way about her. "You mean he lied to me?"

"No. There are two warriors on Sky Messenger's backtrail. It's just that your belief is what—"

"Blessed Spirits, he has no weapons!" she cried. "Don't you understand? Stop wasting my time and tell me how far ahead he is. He needs me."

She clamped her jaw, and her beautiful face went as hard as granite. Her patience was wearing thin. He could tell from the killing glitter in her eyes.

"Baji, he does need you. He always has, but just this once, you must think of yourself. You—"

"Can I help him?"

The straightforward simplicity of the question touched him.

Blessed gods, she knows...and she doesn't care. I underestimated her.

He stood still for a long time, holding her gaze, before he nodded. "Yes, but there is a great risk. You could be a distraction, and many people get so turned around here that they never—"

She stalked by him, just brushing his shoulder

with hers, and broke into a shambling dog-tired trot.

"Baji, please don't do this."

She didn't slow down, but called, "You did, didn't you?"

She disappeared into the darkness and storm.

Sonon hung his head and studied the place where she'd lain in the trail. Her body had sculpted the snow. When she'd seen twelve summers, he'd often charted her course by such impressions. Her course and those of the other captive children. What had he expected her to do? He was, after all, the ghost that inhabited the murdering place. She had always chosen life, especially life for those she loved.

Nothing could stop her from trying to save them, not even the threat of losing her own soul and being condemned to wander the earth forever.

The snowfall dwindled and through breaks in the clouds, he glimpsed the brilliant Path of Souls that led to the afterlife. The campfires of the dead sparkled and winked, as though the ancestors passed back and forth in front of them.

Such longing swelled his heart that he had to look away.

An old hermit, a Trader from the far West, had once told Sonon that those who suffered long enough for the sake of others would always be found. He said that while all lost souls would be shown the way to the Land of the Dead after the human False Face wiped the world clean of evil, even before that, there was hope—because faithful friends never gave up.

He wanted to believe. For her sake.

Unbidden, a face flashed and vanished behind his eyes.

Hopocan.

He tried to block the images, but like all true horrors, they paid no attention to individual wants and needs.

She, too, had been a great warrior woman. In his sixteenth summer, Sonon and Hopocan had been trotting down the war trail, side-by-side, smiling at each other, when the attack came. An arrow pierced Hopocan's back. He'd carried her home and covered her with soft elk hides from which she never again rose. At first, she'd grown ashen and corpse-like. Then her real suffering began. The evil Spirits of gangrene edged from her wound and slithered into her body. Puss leaked from her mouth, and enormous worms lived in her flesh. Her muscles decayed, hanging together only by transparent sinews. Had her affliction come from a natural source, she would blessedly have died one moon earlier. But the malignant living creature had been sent by the Ancestors. Sonon had rocked her in his arms until it was over.

He lifted his eyes to the Cloud People. Grandmother Moon's light slivered their edges as they traveled south, trailing the veil of snow beneath them. Hopocan was up there somewhere, sitting before the campfires of the dead, laughing and telling stories. He prayed she had forgotten him. The possibility that she might be waiting for him was too great a burden to bear.

After her death he had spent many torturous moons trying to make sense of it and had come to believe that her staggering sufferings were, in reality, a glimpse granted by the Ancestors of a greater truth: The "Law of Retribution" extended far beyond the world of the living. It coiled in the heart of existence itself—and existence demanded that someone pay the price of war. Hopocan had not been called, he had.

He turned to look back at the trail.

The white slash weaved through the forest, glistening as it filled up with snow, obliterating Baji's tracks. He couldn't let her get too far ahead.

When he fell into a steady, distance-eating trot, he whispered, "Yes, Baji, I did."

16

War Chief Hiyawento stood tall and straight, his nocked bow gripped in his hands, watching his warriors appear and disappear, moving through the stark trees, searching the forest for either intruders or survivors of the Riverbank Village battle. The stench of carrion was everywhere. Drawn by it, wolves had come in the night, prowling for the food inevitably left in the wake of war parties. Occasionally, a man shouted at the animals, and warning growls and barks erupted in response.

Wind Woman flapped his short hair around his eagle face as he turned to examine the smoldering palisades that sent black smoke trailing across the blue midmorning sky. The village sat on the highest terrace of the Sundrop River, a small rushing stream that babbled over rocks as it cut its way across the tree-covered hills. Inside the village, Zateri, Kwahseti, and Gwinodje wandered through the destroyed longhouses. Their ominous voices carried.

The story was clear. The villagers had received Kwahseti's message to leave as soon as possible, but a small contingent of warriors had remained behind. If he'd been at Coldspring Village when such a message came, he would have done the same thing. Get most of the people out, but leave warriors—all volunteers—to guard the walls for as long as possible, delaying the enemy and giving their fleeing relatives more time to reach the safety of Canassatego Village. As best he could tell, thirty warriors had remained. Men and women who knew it was a death sentence, but stayed anyway.

War Chief Thona wandered the ruins with his jaw clamped, a handful of trusted deputies at his side. When Thona pointed, deputies bent to collect the bones of the fallen. Most were blackened. Those warriors had died in the fires, still at their posts on the walls. Others, the survivors, had been chopped apart. Their bones bore the unmistakable evidence of cannibalism. The long bones of the legs and arms had been split open with war clubs to get to the roasted marrow inside. Several showed "pot polish," the sheen associated with having been stirred in a ceramic pot for a long time.

Hiyawento's pulse beat a dull rhythm in his

ears. Did Coldspring Village look like this? Or worse? Had any of the villagers managed to escape? Or had they been attacked before they could leave? His souls spun hideous images.

Curses rang out in the forest. A man shouted. A woman tried to calm him down. Dread tingled the winter-scented air. Every person feared this place and the lost souls who roamed the shadows. They were all anxious to be away, to get to Canassatego Village to find out which of their relatives had survived.

Hiyawento looked inside the destroyed village again. Sky Messenger had told Hiyawento once, just a few days ago, that he could see them...the lost souls. They appeared as small yellowish lights bobbing across battlefields or through the husks of destroyed villages. Sometimes, he heard them weeping, confused because their relatives wouldn't talk to them, not understanding they were dead.

Hiyawento bowed his head and glared at the brown oak leaves tumbling across the ground in the cold gusts of wind. He felt dead inside. *Too much violence.* It gutted the world. His body echoed with emptiness, as though the deaths of his daughters, and the constant warfare, had chased his souls away, leaving behind a hollow cocoon filled with rage. Is that how these lost souls felt?

He searched for any glint of bobbing soul

lights, but saw only wind-tormented branches and ash and smoke whirling through the air.

Thona stalked across the decimated village, exited the gates, and came to stand beside Hiyawento. His heavily scarred face was grim and determined. "We should be on our way."

"Matron Kwahseti has decided not to bury the remains of your relatives?"

Thona shook his head. "We'll return when we can and care for them.

Right now, we must care for the living. Canassatego Village may be under attack as we speak. If so, our living relatives need our help more."

Zateri, Kwahseti, and Gwinodje walked through the smoking gates, talking softly, their faces pale and cold, as though what they'd seen had drained them of warm blood from their bodies.

Zateri's desperate gaze clung to Hiyawento's. She must be seeing the same hideous images he was: Their home burned to the ground, cannibalized dead bodies strewn across the forest...

Kwahseti's gray hair flipped around her squinted eyes. She stared at Hiyawento, then Thona. "Call in our warriors. We're leaving now."

"Yes, Matron," Thona answered. He cupped a hand to his mouth and yipped his distinctive lone wolf cry.

Warriors instantly began to emerge from the forest and trot toward the village, coalescing into a whispering, eddying army of exhausted men and women.

Just before Hiyawento turned toward the trail, voices went up at the outer margins of the army, but they were not warning voices. A path opened as warriors backed away, allowing a single man to trot forward.

"Who is it?" Zateri asked as she moved to stand at Hiyawento's side. "Can you tell?"

"No."

The man came forward at a sluggish trot, as though his legs felt like granite weights. He was tall, with a Trader's burly shoulders. Long black hair draped the front of his undecorated, soot-coated cape. Faint recognition began to dawn on Hiyawento. The man had a straight nose. His mouth clamped into a white line. He kept squinting, as though he couldn't see very well at a distance.

"*Towa!*" Hiyawento broke into a run, rushing to meet him.

When Towa recognized him, a tired smile came to his lips. They embraced, pounding each other's back hard enough to leave them breathless.

"Blessed gods," Towa said. "We feared you were all dead."

"No, my friend, we—"

"Tell me quickly," Towa said as he shoved away. "Are the stories true? Did Sky Messenger lift his hands and call a gigantic storm that swept the warriors from the battlefield?"

"Yes, yes, he did. Now tell me, did everyone make it safely to Canassatego Village?"

Zateri, Kwahseti, and Gwinodje crowded around them, listening. Chief Canassatego came up behind Gwinodje, his wrinkled face somber, framed with gray braids. Thona stood behind Kwahseti like an angry giant.

Towa swallowed hard and nodded. "Yes. I led the Riverbank Villagers there. A few hands of time later, villagers from Coldspring Village rushed the palisades, crying that Atotarho's forces were right behind them." He took a deep breath and took a few moments to look at the assembled matrons. "Matron Gwinodje, Chief Canassatego, your village was so well prepared it was astonishing. They flung open the gates for the Coldspring refugees, then lowered bracing logs across them and ran to man the catwalks. Our warriors were already up there, standing shoulder-to-shoulder with yours. When Atotarho's forces hit the walls, it...it was a grisly sight. Within the first quarter-hour, we killed so many that the dead piled against the palisades three deep." He bowed his head as though unable to continue. A dread silence possessed the army. Every ear strained to hear his story. "After three hands of time, it was over. The remnant of Atotarho's army that survived fled."

Thona looked shocked. "What fool led the attack? Why didn't he back away when he saw he couldn't breach the walls?"

"A deputy war chief from Turtleback Village appeared to be in charge, but you can't blame him. He died very early in the attack. After his death, his forces seemed to have no head. They just threw themselves at the walls as though senseless rage motivated them."

"How many died?" Zateri asked in an emotionless voice as though she'd already braced herself for the worst.

Towa stared at her with an agonized expression. "Inside Canassatego Village, we lost one-hundred-eleven. Another one hundred fifty-two were wounded. But outside...I'd say Atotarho attacked with maybe seven hundred warriors, and when it was done, maybe two hundred fled back through the forest."

Whispers began to eddy through the army, men and women relaying the story to those farther back who hadn't been able to hear. A low moan, composed of many voices, drifted on the wind. They had been forced to kill their relatives. There would be blood feuds and weeping for generations.

Zateri said, "We can hear the rest of the story after we've arrived at Canassatego Village. Let's move out."

As Thona tramped onto the trail and fell into a

steady trot, warriors swarmed onto the trail behind him. The sound of thousands of feet striking the frozen earth resembled a deep-throated growl. The forest went still, the animals afraid to move.

Hiyawento said, "Give me a moment, matrons?"

Zateri, Kwahseti, and Gwinodje turned to him. Chief Canassatego waited, as well.

"Now that we know our villagers have made it safely to Canassatego Village, I request permission to join Sky Messenger. He should soon be in the Landing People villages. That's a single day's run for me."

Towa gripped his shoulder, and a smile came to his exhausted face. "Will you let me join you? I know the Landing elders. I can make introductions."

"Towa, you're exhausted. I'll be moving as fast as I can."

"Even if I hold you back so that it takes two days to get there, I was in Shookas Village only one moon ago. They hate the Hills People so much that I assure you, without me, they will kill you on sight."

Hiyawento studied the man's fatigued eyes and trembling legs, but said, "Then I would welcome having you along, Towa."

Kwahseti tucked short gray hair behind one ear. "I have no objections to this."

Gwinodje turned to Canassatego. "What is your opinion, Chief?"

The man's deeply wrinkled face twisted. "One man will make no difference at our village."

Gwinodje nodded. "I agree."

Zateri's eyes tightened with worry. For a long time, she looked at him, as if memorizing his face should she never see it again. "I pray the Forest Spirits guide you. Be careful."

Hiyawento hugged her tightly, kissed her, and said, "Thank you. We'll return to Canassatego Village as quickly as we can."

17

Pewter moonlight penetrated the gaps between the Cloud People and shone upon the narrow trail that wound through the towering chestnuts and sycamores. Baji took another step, maintaining the tension on her bowstring.

The scent of snow and wet bark suffused the wind. As Grandmother Moon traveled across the night sky, the branch shadows that created a lattice on the forest floor shifted, striping the snow and the white bark of birches. Then it flashed upon faces. Sometimes, owl eyes reflected, other times, wolf eyes. Neither held her attention for more than an instant. Instead, she focused on the two men and the dog in the forest ahead of her.

Dekanawida's knee-length cape, worn and soiled from the soot of many campfires, swayed around his tall body. Since she'd last seen him, he'd cut his black hair short in mourning for friends lost in the battle. It draped over his round face in irregular chopped-off locks. His brown eyes seemed focused on a small copse of pawpaws to his right, which meant he was paying no attention at all to his backtrail. Did he see another threat on the trail ahead? It was the only reason she could determine that he would be this careless. The unknown man sneaking through the forest twenty paces to Dekanawida's left had already nocked his bow. He was smiling, his rotted front teeth exposed in the moonlit gleam.

Gitchi had his white muzzle up, dutifully scenting the air for danger, but the breeze was blowing in his face, shoving the man's stink back over Baji. Gitchi's eyes, too, clung to the pawpaws.

With ghostly skill, Baji used the massive sycamore trunks—four times as wide as her body—as cover, slipping from one to another, slowly moving around behind the unknown man. He seemed oblivious to her presence.

She flared her nostrils. The odor of the man's sweat carried a particular pungency that she recognized. Despite his smile, he was afraid. Dekanawida was a formidable warrior. Even without weapons, if he got close enough, he would snap his assailant's spine in less than three heartbeats. Not only that, if this man had been involved in the battle at Bur Oak and Yellowtail villages, he'd seen the freak storm rise over the eastern hills, and crash down upon him like a ferocious monster. He was probably terrified that Dekanawida's Spirit Helpers were, even now, secreted in the forest shadows, waiting to attack anyone who attempted to harm the Dreamer.

Baji silently lifted her foot, tested the ground for snow-covered twigs that might snap beneath her weight, then eased her moccasin down. The hired killer paused suddenly, as though he'd heard something, and turned to look in her direction.

Baji shifted enough that she could just barely see him from the corner of her vision. Eyes drew eyes. Even in the darkness. It was an almost unnatural thing. A warrior may not see weapons, or capes, or distinctive human shapes, but his gaze would rivet upon other human eyes as though he sensed more than saw them. Once eyes caught his attention, everything else fell into place: arms, legs, weapons.

The man fidgeted, uneasy, as though he knew he was being tracked but saw nothing behind him. He looked back at Dekanawida and Gitchi, who'd continued up the trail, and were now too far ahead of him for a sure bowshot. The unknown man's lips moved in what appeared to be a curse, and he foolishly hurried to catch up.

As he dodged behind trees and carelessly

crunched twigs beneath his moccasins, Baji patiently stalked him.

The forest always knew what was about to happen long before humans did, and the land exuded an exotic fragrance. To Baji's right, thirty paces distant, a single lynx eye shone, half-hidden behind a boulder, focused on a snowshoe hare's glistening ears, almost invisible in the white blanket that littered the ground. There was an air of expectancy, as though the animals waited for the final moment so that they could thaw their muscles and continue on their nightly search for food.

When the killer was again in range of Dekanawida, he halted, leaned his shoulder against a tree to brace his shot, and drew back his bow.

An unearthly calm descended, as though the silence of eternity had smothered the pitiful sounds of the world's struggle. Peaceful eons seemed to pass as Baji spread her feet and aimed at his broad back. The white spirals on the fool's black cape provided excellent targets. She took a breath, held it, and let fly. The arrow glistened in the moonlight as it sailed between the tree trunks, hissing slightly as it lanced the darkness. *Shish-thump*. It was a soft sound, but the man stumbled and loosed his arrow. The shot went high and clattered in the branches over Dekanawida's head.

Gitchi barked, whirled, and lunged for the man.

Dekanawida breathlessly spun around.

Gitchi leaped upon the warrior, knocked him to the ground, and transformed from warm companion to a snarling whirlwind of muscled fur. When the dying man's scream erupted, it seemed to come from nowhere, directionless and terrifying.

As the lynx and snowshoe hare thrashed away into the forest, flurries of startled wings erupted from the branches. The night sky suddenly filled with birds.

Baji nocked another arrow and charged forward, leaping fallen branches, trying to get to the man before he could pick up his bow again.

Dekanawida must have seen her. He dashed for the dying man, too.

Just before she and Dekanawida converged, Gitchi ripped the murderer's throat out and danced back, barking and growling, leaving Baji and Dekanawida to finish the job. The man, who'd managed to get on his knees, toppled face-first into the snow.

Baji kept her bow aimed at him, but her first arrow had done the job. Taking him through the left side, it had pierced his lung. A dark stain spread across his back. The man briefly struggled and groaned. His fingers clenched nothing but snow.

When the killer sagged and his limbs stopped twitching, Baji looked up.

Dekanawida stood frozen, staring at her. His mouth was open, his brown eyes wide, as though stunned. "Baji. What...what are you doing here?"

She slung her bow over her shoulder and stalked forward to glare at him. "What's the matter with you? How could you let anyone get this close? If I hadn't been here, you'd be dead."

Sputtering with surprise, he said, "I—I thought I saw someone...ahead of me on the trail. I never even heard this warrior."

"Obviously," she chided. "Has your Dream killed your warrior's instincts?"

Gitchi, who'd waited as he'd been taught and now understood the danger was over, loped forward and leaped up to put his big paws in the middle of Baji's chest. She staggered beneath his weight, and ruffled the thick fur of his neck. "Gitchi, the warrior dog, good work!"

The love in his eyes was palpable. His tail swiped the air.

When Gitchi jumped down, Dekanawida embraced her hard enough to drive the air from her lungs. Tears filled Baji's eyes.

"I can't believe you're here. Blessed gods, how did you find me? I didn't myself know the trail I'd take, let alone—"

"Shh," she cautioned.

The feel of his muscular arms around her somewhat eased her panic, but her eyes continued to scan the forest over his shoulder, searching for the second killer she knew was out there somewhere.

"Where did you think you saw the other man?"

Dekanawida reluctantly released her and turned. He dipped his head, indicating a dense copse of pawpaw saplings to the right of the trail. "Over there."

They stood side-by-side staring at it, their gazes sweeping the shadows, moving across the moonlit snow.

Gitchi noted their gazes and sniffed the wind, then trotted to stand at Dekanawida's side.

"I don't see anything now," Dekanawida whispered.

"Let's look for tracks, just to make certain."

"I'll go left. You go right."

"Not a good idea," she said bluntly. "I have weapons, you don't. I can't protect you if we're widely separated. Come with me."

Baji led the way, taking a few careful steps at a time, stopping to survey every moonlit shape, then taking a few more steps toward the saplings. As they neared the copse, she noticed the single gigantic pignut hickory that stood behind the pawpaws. Twenty times her height, its leafless branches created a dark tracery against the moonlit Cloud People. The egg-shaped nuts had fallen all over the ground. They resembled a bumpy blanket beneath the snow. Dangerous to walk upon, they rolled beneath a warrior's feet.

"You're sure this is where you saw him?" she asked. "No warrior with sensibilities would walk here."

"I know," he whispered behind her shoulder. "But this is where I saw movement. It might have just been a deer...but it looked human-shaped."

Baji's eyes narrowed. She veered right around the copse, glanced down at the ground, then up to scan the forest for the man. As she tip-toed around behind the pawpaws, she saw the fresh tracks.

"Well, there they are," she murmured.

Gitchi bounded forward to sniff them.

"Just one man," Dekanawida said.

He slid around her and went to kneel beside Gitchi, examining the tracks, while Baji kept her eyes on the forest. Snow had collected in the crook of the hickory and resembled a white sparkling nest. Against the cobalt background of moon-silvered forest, it seemed unnaturally bright. Deeper in the shadows, white cedars dotted the landscape. Half the height of the hickory, slender, bell-shaped cones hung from their evergreen branches. If she concentrated, she could just smell their sweet scent. Nothing moved out there. Even Wind Woman had fled this part of the forest.

"Baji, come take a look."

When Dekanawida stood up and heaved a

sigh, Gitchi trotted away, suddenly unconcerned, to sniff out a rabbit trail.

Baji worked her way over to Dekanawida, her bow still half-drawn, and glanced down at the clear tracks in the fresh snow. A big man, his feet had sunken deep, but there was something more interesting. As her gaze roved the area, she saw no tracks coming in or going out. It was as though he'd just appeared here, took a few steps, and disappeared into the moonlight.

Baji released the tension on her bow. "Sandal tracks. Herringbone pattern. Hills People."

Dekanawida's handsome face relaxed. "But if Shagoniyoh came to see me, why didn't he stay to speak—"

"He may have come to see me."

Dekanawida paused. "To see you?"

Baji listened to the night. The distant howling of wolves drifted through the moonlight. "Shagoniyoh visited me on the trail yesterday. Right after the battle."

Dekanawida didn't seem to be breathing. "What battle?"

"The day we left Bur Oak Village, we were ambushed by Atotarho's forces." A mixture of fear and hatred warmed her breast when she remembered the enemy flooding from the trees. *My fault. I am War Chief. I should have seen them long before we entered the valley. How many dead? How many friends...* "We lost hundreds in the first few moments. Father was wounded."

Dekanawida gripped her arm hard. "Is he all right?"

"I—I don't know." She rubbed behind her right ear. She'd combed out the caked blood, but the hair remained stiff. The swollen lump had given her an almost unbearable headache that dimmed her wits.

Dekanawida stepped around, pulled the long waves of her black hair aside, and sucked in a breath when he saw the club wound. "Blessed Ancestors, Baji! Why aren't you in bed somewhere? You should have stopped at the first village to see a Healer. You know better than to ignore a head wound—"

"There's another killer after you," she explained.

He backed away slightly. "How do you know?"

"Just before I received this club wound, the man yelled at me: 'Before I crush your skull, you should know that my brothers are hunting down your filthy lover right now.'"

"Sent by Atotarho?"

"Who else?"

Dekanawida eased her hair back into place over her wound, and reached down to tightly clasp her hand. "I was going to walk for most of the night, but I've changed my mind. We're making camp so I can tend that head wound."

Baji let him lead her out of the pawpaw copse and to a place beneath the arching branches of the pignut hickory, where an old log lay. After he'd brushed the snow from the wood, he ordered, "Sit down and rest while I get a fire going."

"Just for a moment." She sat on the log.

As Dekanawida went about cracking dead limbs from the tree trunk, Baji forced herself to concentrate. Her legs were shaking. When had that happened? She pulled bow and quiver from her shoulder and propped them against the log beside her. Suddenly, she felt utterly exhausted. Her head now hurt so badly she knew it would explode at any instant. She leaned forward, braced her elbows on her knees, and massaged her temples. Fiery pokers stabbed behind her eyes.

Gitchi came around the log, apparently satisfied that the rabbit was nowhere to be found, and curled up at Baji's feet. She lowered one hand to pat his side, and went back to massaging her temple.

Dekanawida returned, dropped one armload of branches on the ground, smiled at her, and went back to gathering wood, cracking twigs from one of the nearby chestnuts.

Baji granted herself the luxury of closing her eyes. After all, Shagoniyoh was close. Surely, he and Gitchi would protect Dekanawida while she rested.

A short while later, Baji sneaked through the forest, coming up behind the camp of the Hills warrior who'd shot Cord. The man sat with five friends before a campfire, tearing off big chunks of venison jerky with his rotted teeth, laughing too loudly. He liked to wave his hands as he talked. It made him appear a blustering fool. How strange. She thought she'd killed him. But here he was, surrounded by relatives, chortling like an imbecile, and obviously enjoying himself. One of the men had left a war ax lying at the edge of the trees. He'd probably been using it to hack off branches for the fire and forgotten it.

It lay half-covered with snow five paces in front of her.

She might have let the man go if Dzadi hadn't appeared in the trees on the opposite side of the clearing and nodded his head to her, encouraging her to continue. Then her friend Ogwed appeared just to her right and whispered, "We have them surrounded, War Chief."

"Good."

Ogwed led her forward, picked up the ax, brushed the snow off on his pants, then put it in her hand. "We all wish to kill him, but it is your right."

Baji's fingers went tight around the handle. Glimmering through the trees, she saw the firelit faces of many friends—men and women she had fought with. They would guard her back while she completed her task.

Baji stalked into the clearing, and the men around the fire leaped to their feet. From the trees, arrows hissed and each fell silently to the ground, leaving only her quarry standing.

"Hello, fool."

Like the coward he was, the man rushed to put the fire between them. As he thrust out his empty hands, he said, "War Chief Baji! What are you doing here?"

Baji cautiously flanked him. She felt neither pity nor hatred, just the calculation of a warrior fulfilling her duty.

"Wait. Let's talk this over!" the man shouted and tried to run.

Baji raced forward to cut off his escape. They circled each other.

The man said, "You bitch in heat! I'll club you like a fish." He kept glancing at a red-painted war club a few paces away, lying canted against a rolled blanket.

As Baji closed in, the man lunged for the club, grabbed it, and rolled away.

Baji dove for him. Her ax chopped into the spine at the base of his neck, and he went limp. Lying broken on the ground, his eyes were still upon hers, blinking feverishly. His fingers twitched and jerked. His lungs desperately sucked and expelled air. She tossed the ax aside and got her hands around his throat, grunting as she fought to strangle him.

Dzadi, Ogwed, and the others edged out of the trees to watch.

When she felt the enemy warrior's heart stop, when his frantic lungs no longer pulled at his throat, she staggered to her feet and stared down into his dead eyes. The fire had gone out. How quickly the night cooled! Darkness seeped close around her. She looked past Dzadi's blank face to a narrow starlit trail that weaved through the trees. In the distance, at the end of the trail, a bridge spanned a dark, glistening river. Flint country lay on the other side. She knew it, could feel home in her bones, calling to her.

How would Cord take it when he heard that she had avenged him?

Baji walked out of the clearing, her friends following behind, and passed on into Wild River Village in search of a warm longhouse. The familiar crowd filled the plaza. Women used mallets to pound corn in hollowed-out logs. Old men slept in the sunshine beneath the porches, with dogs curled at their sides. Children played stick-and-ball games along the palisade wall. None seemed to notice that Baji and a remnant of her war party had returned home. Not that it mattered.

The day was warm and fragrant with the scent of dogwood blossoms. They would gather around the plaza bonfire with the other warriors who stood eating heaping bowls of freshly roasted grouse and talking of the latest news. And what was that in their hands? Cornmeal biscuits dripping with bumblebee honey! As she led her party closer, Baji saw twenty or more grouse, skewered on poles, being cooked over the flames, sizzling with fat.

"Baji?" Dzadi called happily. "How will we ever eat so much?" She turned, smiling, but... "*Baji?*"

Not Dzadi.

She suffered a moment of disorientation. Couldn't figure out...

"*Baji, I need you to wake up.*"

Dekanawida's deep voice. A hand rested lightly on her shoulder.

She opened her eyes. "Gods, I'm sorry. I must have fallen asleep."

She sat up and braced her hands on the log on either side of her hips. Her long black hair fell forward over her cape.

"I didn't want to wake you, but I need you to lie on your left side so I can get to your head wound. I must care for it tonight before the Evil Spirits smell the blood and fly to nest in your flesh."

A wooden bowl clacked as he set it on the log, and she noticed in surprise that a small fire burned not two paces away. The bowl, filled with warm water and a piece of soaked hide, steamed.

She nodded tiredly. "Thank you. I'm just so tired."

Dekanawida's thick brows drew down over his slender nose. His jagged locks of short hair sleeked down around his wide mouth and blunt chin. In a tender voice, he instructed, "If you'll stretch out on your left side on the log, I'll try to work. I don't want any of the water to drip down and soak your cape. You need to stay dry and warm tonight. When I'm done, I'll wrap you in my blanket."

Baji's wounded arm shook as she braced it to ease down onto her left side, so that Dekanawida could clean the swollen lump behind her right ear.

In a stern voice, he said, "I'm heating willow bark tea for you. When I've finished cleaning, I want you to drink it. It will help with the headache."

"If I'm awake."

She thought he nodded. She wasn't sure.

Dekanawida squeezed out the soaked hide and started washing the lump. The warm water hurt. But his touch was a balm upon her soul. He had large hands, strong, and they worked with practiced skill. As a deputy war chief, he'd tended many wounds in his time. Tonight, though, his face was aspen-bark white, his eyes blazing like polished brown chert.

"Close your eyes and try to rest," he ordered.

Hundreds of summers from now, while she slumbered in an old tree, the sound of his deep voice would fill her lonely dreams.

The firelight threw faint multiple shadows across his concerned face.

Gitchi's ears suddenly pricked, and he turned to stare out at the white cedars. Baji glimpsed something. The hem of a windblown black cape, flapping wildly, like a trick of moonlight in the saplings, for the forest around her was absolutely still.

A faint smile came to her lips.

He's standing guard. I don't have to.

18

For the moment, Yi ignored the dusty messenger who stood, breathing hard, on the opposite side of the fire. A shaft of afternoon sunlight streamed down through the smoke hole, landing like a golden scarf across his dirty, trail-weary face. Yi continued pacing the floor of the longhouse, thinking.

Yi's chamber in the Wolf Clan longhouse in Atotarho Village sat at the far end, eight hundred hands away from the former High Matron's chamber. Tila was gone, her chamber empty, but Yi still felt the weight of her presence, as if Tila's Spirit had refused to travel to the afterlife, and remained in the longhouse. Her afterlife soul had not been Requickened yet, and it was a terrible spiritual loss for the clan. It weakened all of them. Almost everyone had assumed that when Zateri returned from the battle, she would receive her grandmother's soul.

Yi looked down the length of the house, her gaze passing over the many chambers and people sitting around their fires. Women nearby weaved baskets from willow staves. Children played with cornhusk toys. Yi missed Tila desperately. Especially now when the clan needed her guidance so desperately.

So much had happened in the past half moon that she was having trouble making sense of things.

First, High Matron Tila had died, then had come the shocking news, delivered by one of Atotarho's messengers, that Tila had named Kelek, Matron of the Bear Clan, to replace her. One did not question the Chief without good cause, but they'd all known Tila for more than forty summers. It was simply impossible. Then, yesterday morning, news had come that Coldspring Village, their sister village, had been completely abandoned. The villagers had fled in a hurry, carrying only food and blankets with them. The rest of their possessions remained in place, as if awaiting their owners' return. Scouts had seen the Coldspring villagers running up the Canassatego Village trail. Later, Atotarho Village had been flooded with returning warriors, charging through the gates, proclaiming that they'd lost the battle against the Standing Stone nation after the prophet, Sky Messenger, had called a gigantic storm that swept their forces from the field of battle. There had also been wild rumors of betrayal and civil war. Finally, *finally,* this morning, more warriors had flooded in, fresh from burning Coldspring Village to the ground. Along with them, a messenger arrived from Atotarho, verifying the rumor that Zateri, Kwahseti, and Gwinodje had betrayed the Hills nation and fought on the side of the Standing Stone People. Despite their treachery, Atotarho reported that he had won the battle, and devastated the Standing Stone nation. He'd said they were but a pitiful remnant of what they had once been, and informed the Ruling Council that he would remain in Standing Stone country for perhaps one more moon, by the end of which, he said, he would have completely destroyed the Standing Stone nation.

Atotarho's report had humiliated the Wolf Clan. Matrons from all three of its ohwachiras had betrayed the nation! Where just a few days ago, the Wolf Clan had been the most numerous and powerful clan among the People of the Hills, the news had thrown them down to the lowest level of society. People had actually spat upon Yi and Inawa when they'd gone to grovel before High Matron Kelek, begging forgiveness, and promising to do anything necessary to prove their clan's loyalty to the Hills nation.

And now this...

Yi stopped pacing and looked at the messenger. He'd run hard to get to her. His elk hide cape bore a thick coating of grime and dust, as did his black hair and round face. He looked to have seen perhaps seventeen summers.

"What is your name, warrior?"

"Skanawati, great Matron."

"Of Riverbank Village, I assume?"

"I am. Matron Kwahseti sent me to you."

Two little boys raced by, laughing, and ducked through the door curtain out into the cold afternoon air.

The messenger shifted, clearly wishing to be on his way. His gaze appeared fixed on the beautiful False Face masks that decorated the rear wall of Yi's chamber. They did not have bent noses, as other masks did, rather, they had extremely long noses and fanged mouths. Her masks had been handed down from grandmother to grandmother for more than three centuries. The legends of her ohwachira said they came from the great cities of the ancient mound builders, from a distant ancestor named Lichen. Sometimes, late at night, she heard them whispering to one another.

"Well, Skanawati, your message has left me with many questions. Please, sit. Let us talk for a time."

The man nodded respectfully and knelt on the

mat on the opposite side of the fire. As he did so, a slave girl rushed to dunk a teacup, made from the skull of a Flint warrior, into the boiling bag that hung on the tripod near the fire, and brought it to him.

"You must be hungry and thirsty. I'll have food brought." Yi waved to the girl, who ran to fetch a basket of bread. She set it beside the warrior and dutifully backed away.

"Thank you for your kindness." Skanawati finished the tea in four gulps, looking like he cherished every swallow. Then he shoved two corncakes, filled with walnuts, into his mouth and seemed to swallow them whole. When he'd finished, he wiped his hands on his leggings, heaved a sigh, and looked up at Yi.

The afternoon gleam that streamed down from the smoke hole lanced the thick blue wood smoke. As he lifted a hand to wipe his mouth, the sunlit smoke curled around it. He looked nervous, perhaps even afraid. As well, he should.

It had only been through her good graces that he had not been murdered when he'd appeared at the gates demanding to speak with her. After all, he came from a village that had just betrayed their nation.

Yi ran a hand through her graying black hair. She had seen forty-eight summers pass, but she'd never witnessed a winter like this. The wrinkles that cut around her mouth and across her forehead deepened when she glared at him.

"I need to know every detail of the battle."

"I'll be happy to answer any question you have, Matron."

Yi considered her words, before asking, "At some point, matrons Zateri, Kwahseti, and Gwinodje decided to fight against Chief Atotarho. Was it after they'd received news of the former High Matron's journey to the afterlife?"

He nodded. "Yes. In the middle of the battle, Atotarho dispatched a messenger to Matron Zateri, asking her to move her forces into position around Bur Oak and Yellowtail villages to prepare to attack. At the same time, he informed her that her grandmother was walking the Path of Souls, and told her the former High Matron had named Kelek to succeed her."

Zateri must have known it couldn't be true. Like every other matron in the Wolf Clan, she would have suspected foul play on Atotarho's part.

"Were matrons Kwahseti and Gwinodje present when the news came?"

"Yes, Matron." He nodded and respectfully bowed his head.

Yi resumed her pacing. Gods, how would she have felt if she'd just learned that her entire clan, thousands of people, had been stripped of their rightful place in the nation? A place their mothers, grandmothers, and great-great-great grandmothers had struggled for generations to achieve? The sacrifices their clan had made for the good of the People of the Hills were legendary. She would have been outraged. As, of course, she *had* been. But she'd been sitting here at home in her warm longhouse, not out on a battlefield watching her kin shed their blood for a nation that had betrayed them.

If it were true that the Wolf Clan's rightful place in the nation had been stolen through treachery while its warriors were dying on the field of battle...clan members would demand that the Law of Retribution be fulfilled.

"Have Zateri, Kwahseti, and Gwinodje set themselves on the path of retribution?"

"I have no knowledge of any official statement to that effect, Matron. However, our former High Matron told Matron Zateri's daughter, Kahn-Tineta, that she planned to appoint Zateri to succeed her. So..."

When he hesitated, she ordered, "So...what?"

"Well, there is talk that Atotarho knew this and had our former High Matron murdered before she could appoint Zateri. Rumors say that Kelek and the Bear Clan were accomplices. If it proves to be true, we have the right to retribution."

Yi's face slackened. Murder was the worst crime. It placed an absolute obligation on the relatives of the dead to avenge the murder. They could demand reparations, exotic trade goods, finely tanned beaver robes and food. They could also claim the life of the murderer, or the life of another member of his clan, including the new High Matron's life. Such a blood feud would devastate both clans and tear what was left of the Hills People apart.

"Tell me about the storm."

The messenger's head jerked up. "How do you know of it?"

"Hundreds of our warriors have been flooding in for days. It's all they can speak of. That and the fact that Zateri and her friends apparently managed to create an alliance between three nations, or portions of three nations."

Awe filled his sparkling eyes. "Then you already know—"

"I wish to hear every detail, Skanawati."

"Yes, Matron, forgive me." He took a breath and let it out haltingly. "Gods, Matron, the storm... it was...enormous. It came boiling over the eastern hills like the wrath of the ancestors. I—"

"What was happening in the battle before the storm?"

The warrior seemed to refocus his thoughts. "The Flint People had just joined the fight on Matron Zateri's side. The fighting was ferocious. When it started to look as though we had the upper hand, Chief Atotarho dragged Zateri's daughter from his war lodge—"

"*What?*" Her heart seemed to stop. "I've heard nothing of this! Atotarho had Zateri's last surviving daughter?"

Skanawati swallowed hard. "Yes. Actually, though, I said that incorrectly, Matron. The Bluebird Witch, Ohsinoh, dragged little Kahn-Tineta from the chief's lodge, where the chief had apparently been keeping her in case he needed—"

"To use her against Zateri and Hiyawento?" she said in shock. "Are you suggesting that Chief Atotarho was working with...with the most evil witch in the land?"

"He was, Matron. Clearly."

Yi stalked before the fire while blood rushed in her ears. "We wondered what happened to the girl. The day the former High Matron died, Kahn-Tineta and her cousin, Pedeza, vanished. We looked everywhere for them." She suddenly felt very weary. "All right. Finish telling me about the storm."

He nodded. "First, Matron, I should tell you that I was there. I was fighting not more than ten paces from Hiyawento when it happened. I saw these things with my own eyes."

"Go on."

"Chief Atotarho shouted at Hiyawento, 'You dare to defy me! I should kill your daughter before your eyes! I will kill her if your forces do not surrender and pledge themselves to me.'" Skanawati paused to take a breath. "Truly, Matron, Hiyawento looked like he was dying inside. He told Atotarho he didn't have the authority to order such a thing, that only the matrons could approve—"

"I know that. Continue."

"Atotarho told him to get the authority, and as Hiyawento trotted across the battlefield for the matrons' camp to the south, War Chief Sindak ordered your forces to disengage, to back away"— *Your forces, not our forces. How can I ever repair this?*—"then Ohsinoh hissed something to Sky Messenger, something I couldn't hear, but the words affected him like stilettos plunged into his heart. He staggered. Then Sindak said, 'Chief, end this battle. You're asking your warriors to murder their cousins!' He—"

"Sindak was right. It should have never happened."

"Yes, well, then Sky Messenger said, as you just did, 'Sindak's right. Chief, clear the battlefield so we can talk to one another. Please, just give me fifty heartbeats.' Atotarho laughed, Matron. He laughed out loud and told Sky Messenger that he'd always been a coward." Skanawati's eyes went huge, as though seeing it again. In a reverent voice, he continued, "That's when Sky Messenger stepped away and lifted his hands to Elder Brother Sun. He shouted across the battlefield, 'This war must end! We're killing Great Grandmother Earth!'"

Skanawati halted. He started breathing hard. "Matron, it was..."

He shook his head, as though he still couldn't believe what he'd seen.

She waited.

He blinked, and his eyes returned to her. "There was a strange far-off rushing sound. We all turned to the east, and people started asking so many questions, the battlefield hummed. Then, and I swear to you this is true, this is how it happened."

"Tell me."

"It—it was though the mist was suddenly sucked away. The sunlight was so bright and sparkling, it hurt. The rushing started growing louder and louder, then a black wall boiled over the forest and swelled upward into the sky. It rose so high it blotted out Elder Brother Sun's face. As it flooded toward us, the roar shook the ground. It sounded like a monstrous growling creature straight out of the old stories. We all broke and ran, trying to find any shelter we could."

She clenched her fists at her sides. "I heard that Sky Messenger did not run."

"That's true, Matron. He—he grabbed Kahn-Tineta and held her in his arms as he turned to face the storm. It was madness. We all knew he'd be killed. Trees were exploding as the storm came on. Branches, leaves, and whole trunks blasted upward into the spinning darkness."

Skanawati seemed lost in memories again.

"And then what happened?"

He jerked at the sound of her voice. "Oh"—he licked his lips—"sorry. The storm...I swear. I swear to you...the storm parted and mist, like clouds, formed on Sky Messenger's cape. It looked like he was wearing a cape of white clouds and riding the winds of destruction. Just like the old stories about the human False Face who will come at the End time to save us."

He stopped.

Yi stared into his dazzled eyes, and even she felt awestruck. She let out the breath she'd unwittingly been holding. Could it be true? Stories had been running up and down the trails for over a moon, carrying bits and pieces of Sky Messenger's Dream. Supposedly, he'd Dreamed the end of the world. Zateri had tried hard to get all the Hills matrons together to hear the story from Sky Messenger himself. They had refused. Yi had wanted to, but...so many others were against it. Now, much too late, she wished she had listened.

"Skanawati, I wish you to take a message back to Matron Kwahseti."

He rose to his feet, and his dusty cape swayed around him.

"Tell Kwahseti that I will do what I can, but she must promise me that while I am working on the clan's behalf, her warriors will not lift a hand against their relatives."

Skanawati spread his arms. "Matron Zateri has already given that instruction, Matron. If attacked by your forces, we will defend ourselves, but we will make no hostile moves toward our relatives unless provoked."

Respect for Zateri swelled in Yi's chest. *She must be considering reunification.* "Tell your matrons I need time. I must find witnesses. There are always witnesses. I will send messengers as necessary to keep her informed of what's happening here." Yi stabbed a finger at him. "Now, go."

He bowed. "Yes, Matron."

Skanawati left in a hurry, ducking through the entry curtains. She heard his feet pound away.

Yi's thoughts raced, trying to figure out how in the world she could...

To her right, the leather curtain parted again. Light flashed, illuminating the thick smoke in the house. Matron Inawa stepped inside.

Inawa had seen fifty summers pass and had plump cheeks and a red nose. Gray-streaked black hair hung limply over her shoulders. She fixed Yi with a look that stilled the blood in her veins.

"So," Inawa said, "you received a messenger, too. Mine came from Gwinodje. Yours?"

"From Kwahseti."

Inawa walked forward and stood beside Yi, warming her hands over the fire. Inawa's gaze moved up and down the longhouse, noting the positions of those standing close by, before she quietly said, "Tomorrow, with your agreement, I will send word to the other villages. We must call a council meeting of the Wolf Clan matrons to inform them of this news. There are only four of us now."

"Of course, I agree. You are next in line after Zateri." Yi stared at the finely woven mats around the fire. Light danced in the herringbone patterns.

Inawa leaned closer to her to whisper, "It is one little girl's voice against the Chief's voice, but if the former High Matron really did name Zateri as her successor—"

"One little girl's voice won't be enough, Inawa. Someone saw something, or overheard a conversation, or was part of a conversation. We must find the witness. After our meeting, the village matrons, Ganon and Edot, must return to Turtleback Village and Hilltop Village and start asking questions—and you and I must do the same here. There had to be someone nearby in the Wolf Clan longhouse when the High Matron died. Someone heard something that day."

Inawa's gaze locked with Yi's. "If Kelek catches

wind of our questions, we may not survive long enough to bring the issue before the Ruling Council. If we're wrong, the Bear Clan will charge us with treason and declare a blood oath against us."

"As we will them if this is true."

Yi's gaze drifted down the length of the longhouse, meeting the eyes of those who watched them. Even though they'd kept their voices very low, people with good ears had at least caught words, maybe a phrase here or there. Just as people had that fateful day when Tila died and Kelek became the High Matron.

Softly, she said, "Who should we select as our messengers? They must be absolutely loyal to the Wolf Clan."

19

High above Gonda, pink Cloud People continued to glide slowly across the glacial blue sky. Their rich colors stood in stark contrast to those of Bur Oak Village, still cloaked in the iron-gray shadows before dawn. Snow outlined every undulation in the bark walls of the longhouses, and frost sheathed the palisade poles like a fine glitter of quartz crystals. Throughout the plaza, people moved as though their shoulders were weighted with lead. The feel of doom pervaded the morning.

Gonda folded his arms. He stood two paces away from where Jigonsaseh, Kittle, and Sindak engaged in a quiet debate outside the council house. The meeting of the Ruling Council had begun two hands of time ago, long before dawn, and just concluded. People were filtering back across the village, heading to the warmth of their own chambers. There had been no panicked shouting or fists shaken, no accusations that they'd made a mistake staying here rather than abandoning the village and moving on...though they would come. Instead, the last remnant of the once great Standing Stone nation had discussed their possible annihilation with a degree of dignity and logic that stunned Gonda.

Kittle tucked shoulder-length black hair behind one ear and gave Sindak a poignant look. "Tell me what Atotarho wants. You should know. You're his former war chief."

Sindak calmly replied, "Only he can see the tracks of his own souls, Matron, but I fear he is utterly mad. I think his soul was stolen by his witch sister many summers ago."

Gonda was an outsider from a destroyed village, a refugee who'd thrown himself upon the mercy of Bur Oak Village. He really had no right to comment unless asked a direct question by the matrons, but it was hard to keep his mouth closed. For many summers, he had served as a deputy war chief, then as the Speaker for the Warriors of White Dog Village. It didn't matter that his village no longer existed, the need to participate in decision-making persisted.

"But surely he plans to attack us this morning. Tell me—"

"I'm not sure of that," Sindak replied uncomfortably.

"What are you talking about?" Kittle gestured wildly to the world beyond the palisades. "His forces are on the move, getting into position around us."

Jigonsaseh's arm muscles bulged through her white cape. In the lavender gleam, the silver threads in her short black hair glinted. "I think Sindak is right, Kittle."

"About what?" Kittle demanded to know. "He's told us nothing!"

Sindak clamped his jaw. "High Matron, if I had to guess, I would say Chief Atotarho is not planning to attack today."

"How can you say that? He's—"

"Because, Kittle," Jigonsaseh interrupted, "he's not moving his warriors into attack positions. From what I can tell, they are moving into areas where there's better protection from the wind, off the hilltops, and down into the valley, closer to water, near the ponds and creeks."

Kittle ran a hand through her shoulder-length black hair. Her large dark eyes had a strained tightness. "Which means what?"

Sindak answered, "Maybe he's giving you time to truly panic."

"*Truly* panic? Truly? That's an interesting

choice of words." She glanced at him like he was a fool.

Jigonsaseh shifted, and the black bear paws encircling the bottom of her white cape seemed to be bounding away. At twelve hands tall, she looked down upon everyone else in the circle. Blessed gods, she was still beautiful. Even at thirty-nine summers, with silver threads streaking her black hair, the sight of her oval face, jet black eyes, and full lips went straight to Gonda's soft spots—and he was married to another, a good woman named Pawen. But he'd been wed to Jigonsaseh for twelve summers. He couldn't help the way he felt. A part of him would always love her.

Gonda tugged his red-painted leather cape more tightly around him.

The frosty wind pricked his bones. He tried to force his attention away from their debate and to the happenings in the plaza.

No one had really slept last night, but those who'd gone to bed at all had arisen many hands of time ago. As had the enemy. Out beyond the plaza, murmuring echoes of unknown forces moved across the hills, and the musty scent of old leaves, kicked by thousands of feet, wafted in on the wind.

Kittle was right. *Truly* panic was an odd choice of words, since Gonda doubted it was possible for them to be more panicked. Thousands of dead bodies lay rotting everywhere they looked. The stench was growing. This was a special kind of panic, however, not the frantic grouse-with-its-head-chopped-off kind. No, this was the sort of panic the end of the world was made from. A certainty felt in the bones. A knowledge that everything a person cherished was about to be taken from him, and there was little he could do about it.

It would be easier if Atotarho would just attack.

Gonda glanced away when two litters emerged from beneath the door curtain of the Deer Clan longhouse. Upon them lay the bodies of those who'd died during the night. Thirty or so mourners followed the litters. Their cries blended eerily with the cynical amusement of the warriors on the catwalks, men and women who could see the enemy surrounding the village, and were preparing for their own deaths the only way they knew how, with morbid jokes.

Gonda turned to the west. Just over the rim of the palisade, Grandmother Moon shone like an oblate silver pendant. Most of the noise came from that direction. Large war parties on the move resembled massive wolf packs. They yipped and growled. The effect was a combination of the clatter of weapons' belts, arrows rattling in quivers, laughter, and feet puncturing crusted snow. It made the hair stand up on the back of Gonda's neck.

As well, the dawn smelled like resin. It was a subtle, but terrifying scent, known to every warrior. Bur Oak Village was virtually helpless, Atotarho's victory a near certainty. His army was eager for the kill, sweating in anticipation, and the vile stench of their emotions filled the air.

"Gonda," Kittle called. "Please assist us."

He lurched forward, covering the distance in two bounds. "Yes, High Matron? How may I help?"

Kittle shoved windblown hair away from her dark eyes. "What is your opinion of Atotarho's intentions? What does he want? What can we give him to convince him to leave in peace?"

Sindak vented a low close-mouthed laugh, and shook his head at the inane notion, which drew a lethal glare from Kittle.

"Would you rather answer first, Sindak?" she asked curtly.

"You already know my opinion, High Matron. I'd rather hear Gonda's ideas."

"Then endeavor to hold your tongue."

Sindak suppressed a grim smile. "Yes, High Matron. My apologies."

Gonda glanced around the circle. Expressions were hard and unyielding. Sweat beaded the curve of Sindak's hooked nose. Kittle's chest rose and fell in swift breaths. Only Jigonsaseh appeared to be in utter control of her senses.

He turned to her. "My former wife, I think there's only one thing Atotarho really wants. And I suspect you know it, too."

"Maybe, but tell me anyway."

"He wants our son."

Jigonsaseh held his gaze, then nodded. "You mean because of the Human False Face prophecies?"

"Yes. For most of Atotarho's life, his people believed him to be the prophesied Spirit-Man who would don the cape of clouds at the end of time and save the world. I remember, twelve summers ago, when he told us it had never been an easy title to bear."

"And now that Sky Messenger's vision is sweeping up and down the trails, and he sees his own people applying that title to Sky Messenger, he's desperate to—"

"I'd like to say something," Kittle broke in. Jigonsaseh gracefully yielded to the High Matron. "If Sky Messenger is the only thing Atotarho really wants, all he has to do is hunt him down and kill him. He doesn't have to destroy the entire Standing Stone nation. Yet, here he is, massed outside the last bastion of the Standing Stone People, a village filled largely with starving elders and children. Why?"

Sindak waited while Gonda, Jigonsaseh, and Kittle stared at each other, then he said, "Because

Sky Messenger isn't all he wants." He dipped his head apologetically to Gonda. "I mean no disrespect, Gonda. You are right that Atotarho is obsessed with achieving Sky Messenger's death, but he wants a lot more than that. He wants to rule all five nations south of Skanodario Lake."

"Well, that's never going to happen," Kittle blustered. "He's an evil cannibal sorcerer. No one will agree to submit to his rule. He'll have to enslave us to do it."

As though to affirm her suggestion, the yips and growls of the huge army moving across the valley outside penetrated the palisades, and the warriors on the catwalk muttered darkly. Several nocked bows. Others reached uneasily to dip cups of water from the pots hanging from the palisade wall, getting one last drink while they had a chance.

Jigonsaseh's eyes suddenly cut to Sindak. "If that is his intention, we are no good to him dead. He needs us alive to work the fields, to build new longhouses, to repair his vast new territory and help to guard it."

Sindak nodded. "A few of you, at least."

"Does that mean he plans to negotiate? Is that why he didn't attack last night?"

"Well"—Sindak's head waffled—"you know as well as I do that night attacks are unwise. In the darkness, it's hard to tell your own warriors from the enemy's. Too many accidents happen. The only thing night is good for is sneaking warriors closer to their targets. As to whether he plans to negotiate your surrender..." He shrugged. "If so, why didn't he send a messenger to you yesterday?"

Gonda's souls sifted the information, trying to think like his enemy, and a feeling of impending disaster seeped through his veins. "Maybe he plans to wait until we're desperate enough to give him everything he wants. When our food and water run out, when our warriors have no more arrows to let fly..."

He let the conclusion hang.

"Anything he wants?" Kittle asked. "Including Sky Messenger's dead body?"

"Or live body. He probably thinks Sky Messenger is still in this village."

The litter bearers reached the inner palisade gate, and the warriors on duty obediently checked with the second palisade guards to confirm it was safe to exit, then swung the gates open. The guards had been instructed to allow the dead to be transported beyond the walls, for as long as it was safe to do so, to keep the plaza from becoming filled with rotting corpses.

Gonda watched the middle palisade gates swing open. As the litter bearers moved toward the exterior gates, he returned his attention to Sindak. "You realize, don't you, that in the end, Atotarho will also demand that we turn over you and your warriors?"

Sindak gave him a level stare. "I do."

"Well." Kittle exhaled the word. "I give you my oath, we won't do that."

Sindak smiled faintly, but it didn't reach his eyes. "That's nice to hear. However, High Matron, there will come a time in the struggle when the circumstances will require that you make a choice between my people and your own villagers. I assure you, it won't be hard."

Kittle's eyes flashed in indignation. "If you were intelligent enough to allow us to adopt you into the Standing Stone nation, that choice would cease to exist. You would *be* my villagers." Her eyes blazed. "And in the future, do not presume to tell me what I will or will not do, or your next sight will be from high up on my longhouse wall." Meaning she'd keep his severed head for a trophy.

A breath of icy wind swept the plaza, swirling up snow, and sending it gusting about.

Jigonsaseh clutched her white cape beneath her chin. "With respect, Kittle, adopting Sindak and his people may change their status in our own nation, but it will also obliterate their status in the eyes of the Hills nation. Right now, though they have opted to fight on our side, the Hills nation may reunite and the new Ruling Council may forgive them. Especially if there are other Hills matrons and chiefs who think Atotarho is insane—"

"And there are," Sindak said.

"However, if Sindak and his people become sons and daughters of the Standing Stone nation, it's treason. A death penalty."

Kittle cocked her head slightly, as though seeing an opening to Sindak's vitals. In a soft, deadly voice, she said, "I want to know the names of every matron and chief who thinks Atotarho is insane. If we can win them to our side—"

"I'll give them to you."

Sindak and Kittle stared at each other.

As the exterior palisade gates groaned open on damp leather hinges, the litter bearers trotted outside. Elder Brother Sun was still below the horizon, but a yellow halo arched into the eastern sky. The shadows of the hills scalloped the valley, and the dismantled ruin of Yellowtail Village glowed sadly, its palisade missing in too many places to count. The last two rings of palisades remained upright only because the gaps were held together by the catwalk. Through one of the gaps, Gonda spied movement, low to the ground, probably dogs hunting the ruins of the refugee shelters that had been built between the rings. Piles of debris cluttered the bent pole skeletons, which leaned precariously. Many of the ruins would collapse in the next strong wind.

Sindak turned to Kittle with an expression of guarded annoyance. "High Matron, if I may, I'd like to..."

A roar went up from the catwalk and warriors began running just as screams erupted outside.

Kittle said, "What..."

Litter bearers and mourners shoved one another as they scrambled to make it back inside the palisade gates ahead of a hail of falling arrows.

"I'm a fool!" Gonda cursed himself, and yelled, "Move! They're shooting from Yellowtail Village!"

As though part of a synchronized dance, Jigonsaseh, Gonda, and Sindak drew their war clubs simultaneously and ran to defend the gates.

20

Before Baji opened her eyes, she was conscious of the slight, steady rhythm of Sky Messenger's breathing and the feel of his ribs pressed against her back. His arms were around her, holding her.

A sensation of contentment possessed her.

When the morning breeze eddied, crackles sounded two paces away, and cedar smoke, rich and sweet, filled the air. Sky Messenger must have carried her to a bed beside the fire—though she didn't remember—and added branches throughout the night to keep her warm.

She inhaled a deep breath and let it out slowly.

The almost soundless shift of paws told her that Gitchi sat on his haunches nearby, his yellow eyes on the forest, guarding them, as he had always done.

When she opened her eyes and smiled at the old white-faced wolf, Gitchi's tail thumped the ground. He leaned down, licked her forehead, and vigilantly took up his duties again, glancing only briefly at the falcons that wheeled in the sky.

Sunlight streamed through the deep brown hickory branches above her. Where it landed, the forest floor steamed. Already much of yesterday's snow had melted into shining pools. Had they slept so long? It must be at least two hands of time past dawn.

Gently, so as not to wake Sky Messenger, she tilted her head to look out across the vista. They slept upon a rocky high point overlooking a broad river valley. The largest boulders below appeared tiny and distant, like the dream of her own death that had tormented her for half the night...*falling, with him, bright light, can't get air...*

For a while, as the forest became luminescent, she lay there in Sky Messenger's warm arms, watching the bone-white winter light being born—light licked clean by the invisible Spirit predators that hunted the rolling land.

She eased one hand up to touch her head wound. The swelling had diminished by half, but pain continued to throb through her skull.

Sky Messenger must have felt her move. He tightened his arms around her, drawing her slender body more securely against his, and whispered, "How are you feeling?"

"Better today. I...for the past few days...I've been waking...with my heart thundering, and I wonder if my heart is bursting...or if I'm just dying of loneliness."

She rolled to her back to look at him. Every line of his round face told her how much he cherished waking this way. His brown eyes shone. A small, fragile smile turned his lips, as though he was afraid to be happy, for fear that she would vanish. Last summer, during the brief alliance between the Flint and Standing Stone nations, they'd awakened this way every morning.

"I'm here, Baji. You're not alone now."

He tenderly pressed his lips to hers, then pulled aside the wealth of her long hair and studied the wound behind her right ear. "The wound looks better. Thank the Spirits you're a fighter. Last night, I was giving you poor odds."

"Fortunately, no one who knows me would ever count me out."

He smiled. "True. However, we must be careful. I don't think we should run the trail for a few days. Walking will be good enough until you're feeling stronger."

"I thought you were in a hurry to get to the country of the People of the Landing?"

"That was before I knew you were hurt."

The statement worried her. She did not wish, in any way, to detain or sway him from his mission. If coming here had...

He sat up and looked down, just staring into her eyes, as though what he saw there went straight to his heart. The blanket coiled around his waist. Like all warriors on the war trail, he'd slept in his cape. It hung crookedly about him.

Baji touched his short black hair. "Did you cut it for Tutelo's husband?"

It was dangerous to say the name of the dead too soon after they'd been lost, or it might draw their souls back to earth, and they'd never again be able to find their way to the afterlife.

"He was a good man."

"I'm sure he was. Tutelo wouldn't have loved him otherwise."

Sky Messenger petted the long waves of her hair that spread over the blanket. "I'll build up the fire and get breakfast made. Why don't you lie here and stay warm."

"For a little while."

He rose, pulled his soot-smudged cape straight, and tugged the blanket up to Baji's chin.

She rolled to her side to watch him.

Branches clacked as he pulled them from the woodpile and tossed them onto the coals, then he knelt and blew upon them until flames leaped through the fresh tinder. The delicious tang of cedar smoke rose. Cedars were sacred trees. Their smoke healed and purified. She breathed it in, letting it work its magic on her wounded body.

Images from the dream she'd been having when she woke flitted behind her eyes.

She'd been with Cord, walking down the trail, looking for her own body among hundreds of dead Flint warriors. She'd rounded a bend and seen herself lying face-down, covered with a thin blanket of snow. She'd lived for a while. As her strength had waned, her feet and hands had dug troughs in the ground, kicking, clawing to get away. Afterward, the victorious Hills warriors had stolen her jewelry and weapons. Even her cape had been stripped off, probably to be carried home to a beloved wife back in Atotarho Village. In the process, her limbs had been left akimbo. Cord had let out a cry and rushed to her side. *"Gods, someone help me! I think she's alive!"* Cord had dragged her into his arms and clutched her tightly against him. What a curious sensation that had been. She'd understood that she no longer inhabited that body, but somehow, it was all right.

She'd had such dreams before. All warriors did. It was the afterlife soul's way of preparing for the inevitable, but the dreams had never before been so vivid, so lifelike. The tears in Cord's eyes still broke her heart.

Gitchi softly nosed her hand, as though to bring her back to this camp on the rocky hilltop.

"I'm here, Gitchi," she whispered. "Everything's all right."

Gitchi curled his bushy gray tail over his forefeet, and his yellow eyes studied her for a long moment, before returning to the valley below.

Save for the popping and snapping of the fire, a vast silence had imprisoned the morning. Down the hill in the trees, fifty paces away, she saw the corpse of the man she'd killed last night. Shadows darkened the spot, preserving the snow where he lay. His lips had shrunken back over his gums, revealing the rotted teeth in his gaping mouth. Where Gitchi had ripped out his throat, an ocean of frozen blood spread across the snow.

Looking at him gave her a strange, otherworldly sensation.

It was as though a desolation lay upon the world, lifeless, its presence so cold and indifferent it possessed not even a hint of sadness. Rather, it seemed to be watching her with the infallible eyes of eternity...and waiting. Though she had no idea what the desolation waited for.

Baji propped herself up on one elbow, then gingerly shoved to a sitting position. Her headache pounded for ten heartbeats, making her nauseous, and then it slacked off to a constant, but bearable ache.

She staggered to her feet and walked over to slump down beside the fire. When she extended her frozen hands to the warmth, it struck her as odd that they didn't immediately tingle, as they always did on cold winter mornings like this. She rubbed them together to get the blood going.

Sky Messenger frowned at her. When she'd risen, he'd been in the process of twisting a pot of tea down into the hot coals. He finished, moved the tripod with the cook pot to the edge of the flames, and rose to his feet. "I don't want you to get cold."

He walked over, retrieved their blankets, and draped them snugly around her shoulders.

His breath frosted when he said, "You must stay warm, Baji. You know as well as I do that head wounds have curious effects. Do you recall what happened to young Janoh?"

"Janoh?" She had to search her memory. "Blessed Ancestors, I do."

"So do I. After he was clubbed in the head, he seemed fine. He joked as never before. For two days he made everyone laugh out loud. His only complaint was that he couldn't feel his feet striking the earth."

"I remember. He told everyone that he'd learned to fly and grew angry when anyone insisted he was still running, but just didn't know it."

Sky Messenger gave her a grave nod. "Then, on the third day, he fell over dead right in the middle of the trail. It happened so fast, the warriors on the trail behind him had no idea what had happened."

"Until later, you mean, when we all understood that his soul *had been* flying. It had leaked from his cracked skull and been hovering close to his body."

Sky Messenger pointed a stern finger at her. "I'm taking no chances with your head wound."

"Don't want me to learn to fly, eh?"

"No."

He drew open the laces on his belt pouch and pulled out a bag of jerky. As he crumbled the dried meat into the cook pot hanging from the tripod, he said, "In fact, if you get light-headed, or lose feeling in your hands or feet, or have any other unusual symptoms, I expect you to tell me. Agreed?"

She pursed her lips in silent chastisement. "Of course. I'm not as dimwitted as you think."

"When you're thinking properly, no."

He reached out to stroke her throat, and a strange shimmer lit the air, as though the light itself had fluoresced, leaving all living things aglow, softening sight and sound. Sky Messenger's tanned face had a golden glitter.

Baji's heartbeat slowed, barely there. Time seemed to linger, stretching like a bobcat on a warm summer afternoon.

In a tone that was at once hurt and half-angry,

he said, "I'm glad you're here. Don't ever leave me again, Baji. I couldn't bear it."

"I won't."

He stroked her throat again, then turned away, and drew two wooden cups and spoons from his pack. After he'd placed them beside the fire, he said, "Hiyawento is going to meet us."

"Really? Where?" The news gladdened her heart.

"On the trail to the east of Shookas Village, but it'll probably be a few days. First, he needs to lead his warriors to Canassatego Village. Coldspring Village, Riverbank Village, and Canassatego Village decided to combine into one village."

"To protect each other?"

"Yes."

Baji squinted at the mossy patterns on the rocks that thrust up here and there around camp. "I pray they make it. We didn't."

The words affected her like a knife, cutting a dark pathway inside her. She could see it—the tunnel twisted down toward an inner chamber where her soul awaited deliverance from the tormented sense of isolation. It persisted even with Sky Messenger so close she could reach out and touch him.

When he sat down and put an arm around her, the dark tunnel evaporated like fog in warm sunlight. "Tell me everything. Where did Atotarho ambush you?"

"On the main trail to Flint country. Do you recall the narrow defile that leads up over the crest of the hill and plunges down into that stubby second-growth country near the Seagull Shallows?"

"Near the Rocky Meadows?"

"Yes."

"Blessed gods, did they hit you as you came over the hill out of the defile?"

"No," she said solemnly, "on the far side of the valley. Just as our war party was climbing up the steep slope through the rocky ledges, I...I should have seen them. I don't know why I didn't."

"Probably because Atotarho's warriors were under penalty of death if they even breathed until you were in position. Sometimes, there's nothing you can do, Baji." He hugged her.

Guilt made her throat ache. "It was...bizarre. Father and I were talking about Shago-niyoh when the attack came. Did you know that Cord saw him the night the old woman died?"

Sky Messenger jerked around to stare at her. "He never told me that."

"Nor me." Baji fumbled with her fingers, squeezing them in her lap as dread filtered through her. "Father had just asked me if I'd ever seen Shagoniyoh again, and I'd said no. Not even when I knew you were speaking with him. I used to try to see something, anything, moving around you, or hear his voice. I never did."

"Until a few days ago, you mean."

"Yes."

One memory from the battle repeated behind her eyes: Cord, bleeding badly, rising to his feet with his war club in his fist, suddenly right beside her.

"I wish I...maybe if I'd..."

Her voice trailed away, and Sky Messenger seemed to sense that scenes of the battle tormented her. *Hundreds of warriors stretched out like ants, climbing the steep incline...glitters in the sunlit air in front of the pines...*

"Stop blaming yourself," he ordered. "Cord didn't see them, either, and he was one of the greatest war chiefs your people have ever known. Did Dzadi see them and call a warning? What about your scouts?"

"No. No one saw them. But...hundreds died, Sky Messenger. Hundreds."

"How many warriors did Atotarho have?"

"Two thousand, maybe three. I didn't have time to get a good count. We were outnumbered at least four to one, and completely surrounded. Father was wounded, shot through the right side." Her hands clenched to fists. "Gods, I pray he's all right."

Sky Messenger's brow furrowed. He picked up

one of the wooden spoons and used it to stir the cook pot. The scent of smoked venison jerky wafted up with the steam. "How did you escape?"

She shook her head. "I don't know. Truly. I heard your voice, and I—"

"My voice?" he said in surprise.

"Yes, you cried, 'Baji, get down!' and I leaped without thinking, just dove out of the way." She lightly massaged the wound behind her ear. "That's why I received a glancing blow rather than a crushed skull."

As Sky Messenger listened, the nostrils of his slender nose flared in and out, and the lines around his wide mouth went hard. He must be fighting the battle in his mind, trying to see what she had seen.

"And then?"

Baji struggled to remember. "I don't remember anything else."

"You were completely surrounded. You were hurt. Cord was injured. You must have fought back or run."

"Probably both...but I recall none of it."

Gitchi must have heard the tension in her voice. He trotted over and lay down at Baji's side. As he propped his big muzzle in her lap, he looked up at her with loving yellow eyes—as though he thought she needed comforting. She petted his soft back.

Sky Messenger said, "What's the next thing you remember after you escaped?"

Out in the trees, two deer slipped through the shadows, a buck and a doe. Their thick winter coats had a pearlescent ash-colored sheen. Quietly, she said, "There's dinner."

Sky Messenger turned. "I have plenty of food in my pack. Let them go. I'd rather hear your story."

The doe lifted her head at his voice and sniffed the air, startled that she hadn't scented them before, then she followed the buck onto the trail, and their hooves kicked up snow as they bounded away, heading down into the sunlit valley far below.

"Odd that they didn't scent us, or Gitchi, or the campfire."

"The wind must have been wrong."

Sky Messenger squinted down the trail for several long moments, before he repeated, "What's the next thing you remember?"

Her head had started to pound again, and with it, nausea welled. She put a hand to her belly. "I don't remember a place as much as a feeling of pure panic. I knew I had to find you, to protect you. The need was overwhelming." She hesitated and watched the steam rising from the teapot. Behind her eyes she glimpsed trees passing, enormous chestnuts, hills in front of her that seemed to roll on forever. "Then I found myself running. That's the next thing I recall. Running as hard as I could...at the very edge of my endurance, my lungs bursting. I think I must have collapsed or fainted. I woke up in the middle of the night...on this trail." Nausea tickled the back of her throat. She squeezed her eyes closed, trying to force it away.

Softly, he said, "All right. That's enough for now."

"I think I need to eat something."

"I'll fill your bowl this instant."

As he went about filling their bowls and dipping cups of tea, Baji continued stroking Gitchi's thick fur. Why had she only told him about Shagoniyoh finding her on the trail, and not the details of their conversation?

Because I'm afraid to.

21

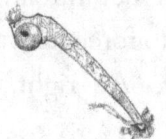

As High Matron Kittle stalked in front of her fire in the Deer Clan longhouse, her many shell rings and bracelets clicked musically. Even through the walls and the three rings of palisades, she could hear the enemy calling taunts from the catwalks of Yellowtail Village. All day long, both sides had been urinating off the palisades, yelling, shaking their penises at each other, and firing arrows smeared with feces. A combination of terror and indignation tormented her. She'd barely looked at the four women who sat around her fire, drinking cups of rosehip tea. Kittle had been an utter fool. She should have listened to Jigonsaseh. Because she hadn't, innocent people had died.

The Deer Clan longhouse was smaller than the longhouses in other nations, stretching only five hundred hands long. Twenty-five fires burned down the central aisle. People stood around each blaze, their faces firelit, engaged in barely audible conversations that mostly dealt with the probable extinction of the Standing Stone nation. The hum of voices carried the low, dire quality of defeat.

Since the attack, people had begun looking longingly at the corn, bean, squash, and sunflower plants that draped from the roof poles. Kittle wondered how long it would be before desperate parents started stealing them to feed their hungry children. She'd ordered all baskets of food and water pots kept in a single storehouse under heavy guard, but had not had time yet to pull down the whole plants from the roof poles. She must attend to that immediately.

Kittle swung around to glare at the other matrons. "Well? The enemy has just stuffed our kirtles down our throats. What are we going to do about it?"

She folded her arms over her knee-length dress, and waited for someone to answer. Instead, the matrons fell into a soft discussion, which Kittle found annoying. At least one of them should have shouted or raged. She wished they would. It would help relieve her tension.

Jigonsaseh of the Bear Clan sat across the fire, her smooth oval face impassive, the silver in her black hair shimmering in the firelight. To Jigonsaseh's left, Matron Dehot of the Wolf Clan hunched. She'd seen forty-five summers and had a gaunt face and black-streaked gray hair. White wolf tracks decorated her blue cape. Beside her, Matron Sihata of the Hawk Clan fiddled with her white hair, twisting it nervously. She'd seen sixty summers. Her deeply wrinkled face resembled a shriveled plum. To Jigonsaseh's right sat Matron Daga, formerly of White Dog Village, now a refugee. Her toothless mouth kept trembling, as though she couldn't keep it still.

Fear glittered in the eyes of each one, except Jigonsaseh's. Her large dark eyes were as calm as obsidian—hard and translucent. Warfare was something she understood better than any of them, and Kittle was heartily glad to have her on the Ruling Council.

Kittle irritably braced her legs. She hadn't eaten all day—as a symbol—and felt light-headed. Her hunger was exacerbated by the sweet scent of cornmeal mush that filled the air. She'd ordered rations cut by half. No one was happy about it. She looked down the length of the house, surveying haunted expressions.

Finally, Dehot leaned forward. "High Matron, I would speak." Her short, black-streaked gray hair fell around her gaunt face.

"Please do."

Dehot respectfully dipped her head to Sihata,

begging forbearance that she'd asked to speak first. It was generally accepted that Sihata's sixty summers gave her that right. Sihata gestured for Dehot to go on.

Dehot straightened her blue cape. "We all have different ideas, High Matron. Personally, I think we should send a messenger to Chief Atotarho telling him we agree to surrender if he will grant us the right to—"

"Surrender, Dehot?" Kittle's fists clenched. "Have you no confidence at all in our warriors?"

"You know I do, Kittle. But I am also a practical person. What good are three hundred trained warriors and a bunch of children with toy bows against perhaps two thousand? Even if we can trust War Chief Sindak, his group only adds another forty-one trained warriors. I do not see the utility in sacrificing our people in a futile cause."

Kittle started to respond, but Matron Daga said, "You're a coward, Dehot. You always have been. We should fight until our last breaths! When we surrender, Atotarho will murder our warriors anyway, and then he'll take the rest of us as slaves."

Dehot tartly replied, "He'll take the children and young women. Atotarho makes a point of killing all the warriors and elders of any village he conquers. So—"

In a very quiet voice, Matron Sihata broke in,

"May I speak, High Matron?" She was sweating. White hair stuck wetly to her wrinkled cheeks.

"Yes."

Sihata shifted to face Daga. Both snowy-haired and wrinkled, they would be twins were it not for Sihata's bulbous nose. "I agree with Kittle and Daga that we should fight for as long as we can before we are forced to surrender—though, like Daga, I have no illusions about our victory."

A particularly fierce gust of wind shivered the longhouse's repaired walls, and ash swirled in the firelight.

"So," Kittle said in a hard-edged voice, "one of you wishes to surrender now, and two of you wish to surrender after we've been defeated. Is there anyone else here, besides me, who thinks we can win?"

The entire length of the longhouse went silent. Every person strained to hear. Her question must seem pure foolishness, yet she knew each wanted to believe, and belief was often the difference between survival and death.

Jigonsaseh's eyes narrowed.

Kittle stared at her. Jigonsaseh always waited until the elder matrons spoke before she addressed the matrons' council, but tonight, she seemed to need time to process every other opinion before opening her mouth.

"Jigonsaseh?" Kittle prompted. "Have you anything to say?"

Jigonsaseh slowly lifted her gaze from the fire, and her eyes locked with Kittle's. "I respectfully suggest that we cease focusing on the end, and start at the beginning."

"What do you mean?" Dehot asked.

Jigonsaseh extended her arm toward the longhouse entry where the curtain swayed in the night wind. "Let me tell you what's going on in the hearts of your warriors on the catwalks. They don't care how much food and water we have, or whether we will surrender or win. Each is concentrated on just one thing. Surviving for the next one hand of time. And that, matrons, is what should concern us."

"Are you saying we shouldn't plan in case we are defeated?" Dehot asked.

Jigonsaseh raised her voice. "Defeat is *impossible,* Dehot."

There was a stunned moment where people throughout the longhouse just blinked and shuffled their feet. Somewhere in the middle of the house, a dog's tail thumped the floor.

Dehot, incredulous, said, "Why? Because you expect Sky Messenger to save us? I believe his vision, too, but—"

"No, Matron," Jigonsaseh slowly replied, "because we are going to kill our enemies."

The power and conviction in Jigonsaseh's voice

rang through the longhouse. Jigonsaseh had been one of the greatest war chiefs of the Standing Stone nation. Though she had not been a war chief in many summers, people still trusted her.

Conversations eddied like waves up and down the length of the house, people repeating her words to elders who couldn't hear very well, questions washing back. A general cacophony rose, people murmuring, *"Jigonsaseh has a plan...She's in charge of our warriors...She's never lost a battle in her life!"*

Kittle lifted her chin and stared down her straight nose at Jigonsaseh. "Explain."

Dehot, Sihata, and Daga turned to Jigonsaseh, awaiting her next words. Jigonsaseh looked around the circle, meeting each elder's eyes, then scanned the listeners in the longhouse, and at last, looked back at Kittle. When she wanted to, Jigonsaseh's gaze could pierce like an arrow to the heart—as it did now.

"War Chief Deru has informed me that there may be five hundred enemy warriors in Yellowtail Village. They've already started repairing the palisades and longhouses, which means they plan to stay."

"To use it as a stronghold from which to attack us?"

"Yes. They won't allow us to venture beyond our gates for food or water. While they repair Yellowtail Village, however, they'll probably conserve their arrows. They'll kill anyone who tries to go outside, and entertain themselves by firing a few random shots at our cat-calling warriors. Once they've secured their defenses, though, they'll start launching volleys of arrows into Bur Oak Village, probably flaming arrows into our longhouses. That will force us to use what little water we have to put out the fires. We must kill them before they can do that."

More murmurs echoed through the house, questioning voices. Speculations were running rampant.

"How?"

Jigonsaseh replied, "We're going to burn down Yellowtail Village with as many of them inside as we can. If we plan it correctly, we can kill all five hun—"

"Burn down Yellowtail Village?" Sihata asked in a frail, elderly voice. "How will we accomplish that? They watch our gates like falcons. Any warriors we send out will be killed instantly."

"Not if we select the right warriors," Kittle said as her thoughts raced.

Dehot leaned toward Jigonsaseh and placed a clawlike hand upon her arm. "Who? If Sky Messenger were here, perhaps the Faces of the Forest might protect him long enough for him to—"

"Sindak and Gonda have volunteered for the task. They are the right people."

Kittle unfolded her arms. Like everyone else in the circle, she gaped at Jigonsaseh, who gazed back stoically. Kittle had to admit that she liked Sindak, but trust him? That was quite another thing.

Dehot said, "Gonda, of course, but War Chief Sindak? What makes you think he will fire the village instead of traipsing right over there and spilling every detail of our defenses?"

Kittle suddenly felt shaky. Everything might depend upon this, and Jigonsaseh wanted to send Sindak, rather than a group of their own loyal warriors? She went to the fire and sat down in her usual place, on a fire-warmed deer hide. As she dipped her cup into the teapot sunk into the coals at the edge of the flames, she said, "Let us all think about this for a time."

"Sindak is here because he was chosen by Power," Jigonsaseh said.

Dehot laughed. "Is that your opinion? Are you certain enough that you would risk everything—"

"I am," Jigonsaseh interrupted. She stared unblinking at Dehot, and her eyes narrowed.

Kittle took a drink of tea to give herself time to consider the ramifications of what would happen if Sindak betrayed them.

Daga said, "Only two days ago, he *apparently* betrayed Atotarho. If he would betray his own people, why wouldn't he betray us even more easily —perhaps for a price?"

Dehot nodded vigorously. "I think he's unreliable. We need—"

"We need Sindak," Jigonsaseh countered. "He's not here by accident."

Kittle said, "Please explain why you think he's necessary for the assault."

The jeering and obscene calls coming from outside were growing louder. Something thumped the wall right behind Kittle. She spun around to see an arrow lodged in the bark wall just above her sleeping bench. The warriors had been exchanging shots all day, but this was the first one that had skewered her bedding hides. She hoped it wasn't one of the arrows smeared with feces.

She turned back and gave Jigonsaseh a "hurry, will you?" look. "Explain, please."

"First, Sindak knows the weaknesses of every warrior occupying Yellowtail Village. He knows if they tend to aim left or right, if they have vision problems, who their wives and husbands are, the names of their children and what frightens them. More important, Sindak was a greatly beloved war chief. I believe that if he's spotted, his warriors might hesitate for an instant before letting fly, and often, that is enough time to kill an opponent."

Sihata twisted her clawlike hands in her lap. "That makes sense to me. There will certainly be no hesitation if they see one of our warriors."

"No," Kittle answered. "There won't. Dehot?

Daga? What do you think of Matron Jigonsaseh's explanation?"

Dehot had her head down, thinking, staring at the glowing branches in the fire. "Well, I am not convinced. But perhaps it is an opportunity."

"An opportunity?"

"Yes. Why not give Atotarho's former war chief the chance to prove he's loyal to us? Frankly, if he does not survive, it will be an insignificant loss."

"But what if he reveals the details of our defenses?" Daga asked.

Kittle said, "Well, what could he tell them? That we only have three days of water left? They'll know that soon enough anyway."

"But they don't know we only have three hundred trained warriors. If he tells Ato—"

Jigonsaseh said, "Atotarho doesn't care. We could have one thousand left, and it would make no difference. He knows he greatly outnumbers us. He thinks he's invincible. And that's why we're going to kill him." Hadui flung aside the door curtain at the opposite end of the house and battered his way through the fires, shoving sparks and smoke in front of him. As it gushed over the matrons' council meeting, the women closed their eyes and turned away. Kittle waited until Hadui had whipped aside the curtain to her left, and sailed outside into the darkness before she drew up her knees and propped her teacup atop them. Steam curled into the warm air before her.

Kittle forced confidence into her voice, though she didn't feel it. "I am satisfied with Matron Jigonsaseh's suggested course of action. Are there any other questions?"

Dehot shook her head. Sihata stared at the hands in her lap, and Daga wiped her nose on her sleeve.

Kittle gave Jigonsaseh a firm nod. "Make your plan. I'll find a way to push it through the Ruling Council."

Jigonsaseh's mouth tightened. "I will speak with our warriors."

"Do it soon. If we don't get rain or snow, we have three days until our water is gone."

The people who'd been listening to the meeting began to filter back to their chambers. Without their bodies to block the light of twenty fires, it fluttered unhindered, coating the walls and roof, turning them liquid.

Kittle softly asked, "After the water's gone... how long?"

Without a shred of emotion, Jigonsaseh said, "Another three days. Probably."

Kittle swirled the tea in her cup, and took a long drink. "That's when the riots will start."

"Then we'd best start killing Atotarho's warriors."

22

Matron Buckshen slowly ambled across the sunlit plaza of Wild River Village. Feeling her way with her black walnut walking stick, she placed her moccasins with care. She had seen sixty summers pass. Thin gray hair fell around her wrinkled face, framing her white-filmed eyes. Half-blind, she had to stare hard at things to make them out, but over the past five summers, she'd discovered that if she just took her time, she could do it.

She stopped and used her walking stick to poke at something on the ground.

Five heartbeats later, a little boy rushed up, panting. "I'm sorry, Matron. We're playing hoop-and-stick, and the hoop got away from us."

Buckshen smiled and reached out to find his head, which she then patted. "Are you winning?"

"Not yet, Matron. Pibbig has a stronger arm than I do."

"Well, just keep practicing. Someday, you'll be the best lance thrower in Wild River Village."

The boy laughed, picked up the hoop, and charged back to the game.

Buckshen concentrated and could see what looked like three boys racing across the plaza after the rolling hoop. It made her chuckle.

Propping her walking stick, she took another step and continued across the plaza. The day was cold, but the sunlight felt warm on her face. Many people filled the plaza, most working. The constant *thump-thump-thump* of women using mallets to pound corn in hollowed-out logs beat the air, and to her right, she heard the *click-clack* of men knapping stone tools with an antler tine. Happy voices carried.

As she neared the Turtle Clan longhouse, she paused to look around. Four longhouses hemmed the plaza of Wild River Village, creating a rough square inside the palisade. Three hundred hands long, each longhouse had white birch bark walls. As the afternoon cooled, heading toward evening, Elder Brother Sun slipped lower in the sky, and his light sheathed the longhouses with a rich gleam. Through her filmed eyes, they resembled enormous blurry creatures carved from pure amber.

She heaved a sigh. With the plague and

attacks, they'd had a terrible summer. Many people she'd loved were gone. But for the first time in many summers, the Flint People had plenty of food to carry them through the long winter ahead. The corn bins were full to bursting. They'd buried beans, squash, goose and duck eggs, in large pits to keep them from freezing, and every house had hundreds of bags of dried raspberries, cherries, persimmons, and plums, not to mention the chestnuts, walnuts, and pecans they'd harvested last moon. If they didn't get raided, they'd have a joyous winter of storytelling and weaving baskets.

Just as she started walking again, surprised voices rose from the palisade. Warriors hurried along the catwalk, staring down at something outside the village gates.

"*Blessed gods!*" a man shouted. "It's Kanika! He was with Chief Cord's war party. Open the gates!"

Buckshen carefully shuffled around to peer at the crowd gathering in front of the gates, waiting for the guards to remove the locking planks and shove them open. People sprinted past her.

She focused on the gates and saw them swing open. The crowd rushed out, and a din of concerned voices erupted.

More people raced by her. "What's happening? Someone, come tell me what's happening?"

"I'll be right back with the news, Matron!" a man yelled as he galloped by at full speed.

Buckshen fiddled with her walking stick, trying to be calm as cries rent the air, and she thought she saw a man being carried across the plaza. "What happened? Is he hurt?"

A tall man dashed toward her. Her hazy vision couldn't make out his face. He stopped, breathing hard. "Matron, it's Kanika. Chief Cord sent him ahead. He's been running flat out for two days and nights to get here. He's fevered and raving—"

"Where is Chief Cord and his war party?"

The man seemed to straighten up, and his fists clenched at his sides. "They were attacked by the Hills People, Matron, less than one day's run from Bur Oak Village."

She weakly reached out to clasp his arm, to keep her knees from buckling. "The war party contained over six hundred. How many did we lose?"

"I—I'm not sure, Matron. I think Kanika said four hundred in the ambush. I don't know how many were lost in the battle the day before—"

"Four hundred? Dear gods. Where is Chief Cord?"

"He was wounded badly. The survivors of the attack are hauling him home on a litter, as well as many other wounded warriors. They can't travel very fast. They're probably two days away. You should also know that Kanika was spouting gibberish. Apparently, he and the other survivors hid in the forest near the Hills camp and heard the new war chief, Negano, telling his warriors that they were heading back to Bur Oak Village to destroy the Standing Stone nation once and for all."

"What else?"

"Something strange, garbled. About a miracle happening during the Bur Oak battle. Apparently, Sky Messenger's Dream is coming true. Kanika said the Prophet stretched out his hand, and Elder Brother Sun brought a great storm that swept the Hills warriors from the battlefield. But he was raving, Matron. It may just be his fevered imaginings."

Buckshen's trembling fingers squeezed his arm. "Find the other matrons. Tell them to meet me in the council house. We will wish to question Kanika as soon as he's rested and eaten. Hurry."

23

Hiyawento stopped on the crest of a hill to look down across the rolling hills. The smoky air clawed at the back of his throat. Afternoon sunlight enameled an endless vista of charred trees and scorched earth. As he pulled his water bag from his belt, and took a long drink, his gaze narrowed. The forest fire had been intense. It must have burned through almost one moon ago, for the ash had washed down every crevice and drainage, streaking the vista like deformed onyx roots. Agweron Village sat in the heart of the blackened chaos. From this distance, the longhouses resembled heaps of burnt splinters.

Towa finally caught up and stood beside him, breathing hard, staring across the charred country. He'd seen thirty-two summers pass. Though his long hair had not yet surrendered to silver, lines carved the corners of his eyes and cut half-moons around his mouth. "Dear gods, this happened after I was last here."

Hiyawento handed him the water bag and waited while Towa gulped several swallows down his parched throat. When Towa lowered the bag, Hiyawento said, "I heard the mysterious fever that ravaged the land last autumn hit the Landing villages especially hard."

"It did. When I was here, the longhouses were half empty. There were so many orphans the clan mothers seemed overwhelmed. But surely they wouldn't have set fire to their own country to rid it of the evil Spirits that brought the fever? They must have been attacked by Mountain People, and the fires spread into the forest."

Hiyawento rested his hand on his belted war club. The quartzite cobble felt cold beneath his palm. "Why do you think it was Mountain People?"

Towa exhaled hard and looked at Hiyawento. "I passed through the Mountain People villages first, and they were much worse off than the Landing villages."

"In what way?"

"They were so sick they hadn't been able to harvest their fields. Most of their crops had withered and were eaten by animals. They were starving. They had nothing to Trade, not even a single kernel of corn. War Chief Yenda had just been named Chief of Wenisa Village. After he underwent the Requickening ritual, he flew into a tirade, blaming the Landing People for the fever and every other misfortune."

"I heard he'd been made chief. So he's Chief Wenisa now?"

"Yes. I left as soon as I could, praying I'd make it to the Landing villages while they were still standing."

"And you found them sick, too?"

Towa's mouth twisted. "Yes. Sick and desperate. Several people offered to Trade me their only blankets for what little food I carried in my pack. I refused the blankets and gave them everything I had, but it wasn't much. Blessed Ancestors, it was a terrible sight."

In the distance, Hiyawento could make out the vague form of the next Landing village, Shookas Village, the principal village of the Landing nation. The intact log palisade stood out in stark contrast to the blackened hills. He wondered what they would find there.

Wind Woman gusted over the hilltop, flapping Hiyawento's cape around his legs. "Sky Messenger would have headed straight to Shookas Village. If all went well, he should arrive tomorrow."

"Then we should hurry. If we get there before

him, and there's any elder left to speak with, we can prepare the way for him."

Towa clapped Hiyawento on the shoulder, and broke into a shambling trot, heading down the hill through stark blackened trees that seemed to go on forever.

24

"It will take just a few moments," Zateri said. "Kwahseti and Gwinodje are lodging in the Snipe Clan longhouse. It's all the way across the village."

"Matron Yi told me to wait, so it doesn't matter how long it takes, but I thank you for informing me."

Of average height, handsome, and somewhat boyish, Hikatoo had a reputation for being a fine singer. Zateri recalled the richness of his deep voice last summer at the green corn ceremony. He'd seen perhaps thirty summers, and spent the past three as one of her father's personal guards. She found it curious that Yi would choose this man as her messenger. He wasn't Wolf Clan, and though he was known as a reliable and courteous man, Zateri was certain to distrust him...which she did. He kept toying with his left arm, cradling it against his belly, then lowering it, only to pull it across his belly again.

"I heard you were wounded at the White Dog Village battle," Zateri said.

"It's nothing, Matron. The arrow skewered my upper arm. It's healing cleanly."

"I'm glad. We have lost far too many good warriors already."

He gave her a half-smile, perhaps wondering at her usage of the word "we."

Zateri looked away. The Wolf Clan longhouse in Canassatego Village had suffered during the recent attack. Charred holes gaped in the roof. Hastily covered with slabs of bark, none quite fit. Twilight seeped around the edges, creating a patchwork of luminous ovals. As many people as possible had been crowded into the forty chambers, so that the longhouse seemed to be bursting at the seams with humanity. Twenty fires glittered down the central aisle. People stood shoulder-to-shoulder in the warmth.

"May I dip you a cup of tea, Hikatoo?"

"That's kind of you. I would appreciate it, Matron. Thank you."

The sweet fragrance of dried cherries wafted around Zateri's flat face as she dipped a cup of tea from the soot-coated pot hanging on the tripod at the edge of the flames, and handed it to Hikatoo.

She thought his buckskin cape had black snipes painted across the middle, but the soot of countless campfires obscured the designs. "You are Snipe Clan, aren't you?"

He bowed slightly. "I am, Matron."

"I know it must have been a dangerous trip, and you had no idea what sort of reception you would receive when you arrived here. Thank you for taking the risk."

"Since my injury, I am not of much use in the fighting, so I go where my elders send me, Matron." Hikatoo sipped the cherry tea, and a smile came to his lips. "This is wonderful. We've eaten all the dried cherries at Atotarho Village. This is a special treat."

"On our way here, we passed a grove with a few cherries still clinging to the branches. We grabbed as many as we could before we had to..."

Conversations broke out as people cleared a path through the longhouse for Kwahseti and Gwinodje, who hurried past without a word to anyone, heading straight as arrows for Zateri's chamber in the center of the Wolf longhouse. Windblown gray hair spiked up around Kwahseti's face. Gwinodje looked very short and thin, striding beside her. Her heart-shaped face had reddened in the cold air as she'd crossed the plaza. Both wore half-frightened expressions.

When they reached Zateri's fire, Kwahseti

shoved gray locks away from her catlike nose, and eyed Hikatoo severely. "Who sent you?"

Hikatoo bowed to her. "Matrons Yi and Inawa."

Suspiciously, Gwinodje asked, "You are not Wolf Clan. Why would they send you?"

Hikatoo's boyish face fell into stern lines. He spread his feet. "Matrons Yi and Inawa wish you to know that they have found witnesses." He took a deep breath and calmly met each of their gazes in turn, before continuing, "And I am one of them."

25

Dusk came as a mournful solace to the long day. Tired, her headache pounding, Baji listened to the meltwater pouring from the roof of the rock shelter where they'd made camp. It drummed outside, sounding like the clattering hooves of panicked white-tailed deer.

Baji propped herself on her elbows in the warm nest of blankets, and her long hair scattered like black silk over Sky Messenger's chest and arm.

"I think Trade is the answer," Sky Messenger said. He had his fingers laced beneath his head. His eyes focused on the soot that blackened the roof above them. Many campfires had burned in this shelter, though they had not built one. In the heart of Hills country, they couldn't risk being seen. "Trade is peace."

"Trade?" Baji asked. "Why?"

The rock shelter stretched two body-lengths across and a single body-length wide, but rose five body-lengths over their heads. Like a dark gray eye-socket, it seemed to peer out into the densely forested hollow that surrounded them. Leafless cottonwoods and quaking aspens crowded near the mouth of the rock shelter. The location was, for the most part, windless. As a result, old autumn leaves clustered at the bases of the trees, contrasting sharply with the white bark of the aspens. The musty scent of moldering vegetation seemed concentrated in the rock shelter.

"The most important reason is that it's the answer to food shortages. If one village has a good summer and stockpiles lots of crops, it will be beneficial for them to be able to Trade that surplus for other goods they need—say Spirit plants, buffalo hides from the west, salt, dried seafood, pots."

Baji paused as she thought about it. Where he lay at the foot of their blankets, Gitchi shifted to prop his white muzzle on his forepaws. His yellow eyes fixed intently on the world outside, concentrating on seeing through the waterfall of runoff and beyond the shining rivulets that poured down the hillside into the aspens.

"That sounds good, but the truth is no one will be willing to Trade food unless they are certain they're safe. It's the grouse and the egg. Which comes first? Peace or Trade? We all hoard food because we expect to be raided. If we keep our surpluses hidden in a variety of locations, we know we can still feed our peoples through the winter even if half is stolen."

As the brightest campfires of the dead appeared in the sky outside, their gleam played through the waterfalls and flickered over the rock shelter like cast handfuls of silver dust. Sky Messenger turned his head to look up at her, and his round face bleached to pale gray. The flicker danced in his short black hair.

"Baji, we can't go on like this. You know we can't. We're all starving."

"Not all of us. This winter, the Flint People have food."

"But only because you were ravaged by the plague that decimated your country. If half your population hadn't perished, you'd be just as desperate for food as everyone else."

"True."

"We are all weakening. Even the Hills People." His wide mouth tensed. She could see his teeth grinding beneath the thin veneer of his cheek. "Every time Atotarho wipes out a village and enslaves the women and children, it compounds his problems. Next year, there will be one less village growing food he can steal, and more slaves mean more mouths to feed."

"That's not how he thinks of it. To him, more women and children mean more people to cultivate, plant, and harvest the crops—and more warriors to guard the Hills nation."

Gray mist rolled in the low places outside, seeping down the hills toward the dark hollows below. She could just barely see the starlike points of enemy villages visible through the dense weave of trees.

Sky Messenger said, "More women also mean more babies, and while in the end that will mean more workers and warriors, in the short term, infants drain their mothers' strength, and the slave women must be fed more to keep the babies healthy."

Gitchi lifted his big head, as though he'd seen something beyond the wall of water. Baji and Sky Messenger went still, listening, their glances moving from Gitchi to the darkening forest outside. Finally, two buck deer stepped out of the cottonwoods and stared at the rock shelter. The largest, his massive antlers shining in the glow, lifted his chin to sniff the air. He had one front hoof lifted. He took a tentative step toward the shelter, as though waiting for something. When his expectations did not materialize, both bucks trotted away into the striped forest shadows.

Gitchi slowly rested his muzzle on his forepaws again, and heaved a sigh.

Softly, Sky Messenger said, "No matter what it costs me, I have to convince the other nations to join our peace alliance."

Baji stiffened. "Even if it costs your life? If they kill you, it won't help any of us. And what of your vision?"

She felt his shoulder move beneath her hair, tugging it. "That's simple. If I'm killed, it means my vision was false. It will come as a shock to me, of course, but—"

Baji chuckled, unexpectedly amused. She leaned down and kissed his forehead. "I don't see how that's possible."

The reflected light flickered in his dark eyes. "I worry. Sometimes."

"Not often, I hope."

"No. Not often." He pulled a hand from behind his head and stroked her long hair where it draped his chest. "How are you feeling? How's your head?"

"Healing. Too slowly for my tastes, but better today. Tomorrow, I'll be able to run."

As his gaze moved across the undulations in the roof, he absently replied, "We'll see."

For a time, Baji let herself drown in the soothing feel of his hand stroking her hair. Contented, she contemplated his Dream. Cord had said: *Believing is the doorway to believing.*

Despite her best efforts, she could not escape

the doubts and fears of the skinny, tormented girl she'd been at twelve summers. Believing was a hard thing. Life had taught her that. She'd grown up, become a strong woman and discovered her talents and purpose in life—yet that little girl continued to cry inside her. At odd times, especially when she felt safe and warm, pitiful sobs seeped from the invisible internal world where the girl lived. For a long time, those sobs had startled her. She did not understand, and probably never would, why that little girl never grew up. Did her twelve-year-old soul live solely to remind her to stay vigilant, that life could go terribly wrong at any instant? And what was that soul? Obviously it wasn't her afterlife soul. Was it the soul that remained with the body forever? She found the notion odd and unsettling. It frightened her to think of that scared girl locked forever in her deteriorating bones.

When Sky Messenger spoke again, his voice was soft. "What are you thinking? Every muscle in your body has gone taut."

"Has it?" she asked in surprise and consciously willed her shoulders to relax. "I hadn't realized."

"You were thinking about the old woman, weren't you?"

She gave him a bitter smile. "Strange, isn't it? That each of us can tell when the other is remembering those awful moons?"

A particularly fierce gust of wind surged over

the hill above them, and old leaves showered down through the hollow, piling against the bases of the cottonwoods and aspens. Gitchi's ears pricked as he surveyed them.

"Not so strange, perhaps," he said. "We had to protect ourselves. We watched each other so closely, our senses were still tuned to the slightest shift in each other's posture. There are times when I'll be watching Tutelo combing her daughter's hair, and she'll hesitate for a split instant, and I know she's back at Bog Willow Village."

"Do you ever ask her to make sure you're right?"

"I don't have to. I know. As I knew what you were thinking just now."

The old woman's shadow seemed to hover over Baji again, blotting the starlight as wrinkled hands reached down to drag her to her feet and shove her into the arms of waiting men. Men who had paid a lot for the privilege.

Baji's muscles clenched again. As her frosted breath rose toward the Sky World, she struggled to understand why she couldn't let go of those memories. The sickening throb of her heart choked her. She swallowed. Then swallowed again, forcing the memory away. A tremendous sadness came upon her.

Sky Messenger reached over to clasp her hand hard. "Stop thinking about it." A savage glitter lit his eyes. "She doesn't deserve your attention."

"No. She doesn't." But her veins felt as if glassy flakes of obsidian rushed through them. She couldn't move or breathe without pain.

His grip tightened, crushing her hand. "You're here with me. You're safe."

"Not if you break my thumb. How will I draw back my bow?"

The ghost of his smile warmed. He brought her hand to his mouth and pressed warm lips to her thumb. Changing the subject, he said, "Anyway, I need you to help me think about the People of the Landing."

"You mean how to approach them about peace?"

"Yes. Tomorrow, if we survive crossing through Hills territory, we should reach the border of the People of the Landing. Soon after, we will reach their villages."

"Have you determined which village you will visit first?"

He stroked her palm while he contemplated the question. "Shookas Village. High Matron Weyra has a reputation for fairness and intelligence. At least among my People. What do the Flint People say about her?"

Baji shrugged. "Among my People, she's known as Slow Thinker."

"That doesn't sound very flattering."

"Well, she's called that because apparently, she never makes rash decisions. She ponders matters for a long while, discussing every possible permutation with the clans, before bringing an issue before the Ruling Council. I've heard it can take weeks for any major decision to be agreed upon. Keep that in your heart, lest you hope to have a decision the same day you speak with her."

"I don't."

Baji watched him. "And what will you tell High Matron Weyra? You should begin with your Dream."

"I will. Then I'll explain that our alliance already includes three nations—"

"Be specific. Say it includes the Standing Stone nation, the Flint People, plus three Hills villages."

He frowned. "You're right. Yes. Then I will present the benefits of our alliance—"

"Explain them to me."

His mouth quirked, and he gave her a crooked smile. "I haven't really figured them all out yet."

"Don't you think you'd better?"

He heaved a breath. Moments later, he said, "Well...mutual defense, for one thing. We will also redistribute food to needy villages...and expand our Trade networks, as we spoke about earlier."

Baji toyed with his hair. "May I question you as I believe High Matron Weyra will?"

He rolled to his side, braced his elbow, and propped his head on his hand. "I would welcome it." His breath frosted in the cold air.

As more of the campfires of the dead blazed to life outside, the prismatic reflections through the runoff streaming from the roof strengthened, swathing the rock shelter with what appeared to be a thousand silverfish swimming through a Stardust ocean.

"Weyra will first note that you have no food to redistribute, and even after you tell her that the Flint nation will contribute to the cause, she'll say it won't be enough. How will you respond?"

He drew her hand to his heart and held it there. "I'll say she's right. This winter. However, next autumn, the alliance will pool its harvests, so that we all have enough."

"Providing the crops are good."

"That is a given."

"And providing you can talk them into it, which won't be easy."

"I still have to promise her that we can."

"Yes, you do."

He frowned. "What else will she say?"

"Next, she'll tell you that the members of your pitiful alliance are too far away to help protect Landing villages from the Mountain People raiders. The Mountain People are their closest and most dangerous enemies."

His elbow shifted upon the folds of woven fox hide blankets. "If we create a war party and station it on the border between the Mountain and Landing peoples, they can block raids into Landing country."

"Who will compose such a war party?"

"Warriors from every nation."

"That's idealistic. How will you feed so many warriors?"

He gave Baji a lockjawed glare, as though he wished she hadn't asked that. After ten heartbeats, he answered, "I suppose every member of the alliance will have to provide for its own warriors."

"Which means they won't send warriors to serve in the war party."

"Maybe. Maybe not. What else?"

"That's all I can think of for now."

"Think they'll kill us on sight?"

Her grip tightened on his hand. "That's what I'd do."

"Well," he replied reasonably, "if they do, we won't have to solve all of these hard problems for High Matron Weyra."

Baji lay for a moment, not certain what to say. It was the first time he'd ever sounded so casual about his own life. She didn't like it. She released his hand and rearranged herself into a cross-legged position at his side, looking down at him. Her long hair fell forward in a black torrent. "Do not ever speak to me so offhandedly about your death again, or I'll—"

"Beat me to death to spite me?"

"Don't joke."

He laughed softly and forcefully took her hand again, though she tried to pull it away. "Let me hold it. Until your head wound is better, it's one of the few things I can touch."

She smiled and yielded. As he stroked her fingers, she said, "I think you need to remember the lessons Wakdanek taught you."

"Wakdanek? The Dawnland Healer? There isn't a day that goes by that I don't think about him." His deep voice turned soft, like cattail down against the skin. "He told me that everything in the world is related. People, animals, trees, stones, the Faces of the Forest, the Cloud People. We are all One. I remember Wakdanek telling Sindak that every time he placed his fingers upon a branch, the tree recognized him, and that if he listened, he could hear the tree calling his name, trying to reach across the gulf that separated them to touch his heart."

"What did Sindak say?"

"He said that was usually when the first blow landed."

Baji chuckled. "That sounds like Sindak."

"Yes." Sky Messenger seemed to be lost in memories, smiling sadly. He caressed her hand.

"Wakdanek also said that because all things are related, we must name our enemies carefully, because killing the enemy has only one outcome: We kill a part of our own soul. And by doing so, we cripple the world itself."

Baji laced her fingers with his and squeezed hard to get his full attention. When his gaze focused on her, she asked, "Do you believe him?"

"With all my heart."

"Then you must carry his words with you when you enter Shookas Village."

He stroked her hair. "I will. Thank you for helping me, Baji."

In a quiet voice, she answered, "That's why I'm here."

26

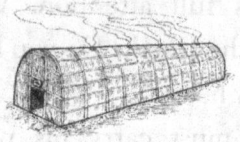

The scent of hickory smoke filled the council house in Atotarho Village. A round structure forty paces across, it had been constructed of log saplings and roofed with elm bark. Six rings of wooden benches encircled the central fire. High Matron Kelek restlessly paced from one side of the house to the other, moving through the flickering firelight like a lone ghost.

Hadui buffeted the walls, rushing between the bark slabs and banging the sacred False Face masks that hung around the house. On occasion, he whistled or whimpered through their contorted mouths.

Kelek drew her long buckskin cape closed beneath her wrinkled chin and tried to keep her eyes off the large mask that hung to her left. The old stories said it had been created by Hadui himself. Called *He-of-Divided-Body,* the mask seemed to be trying to get her attention—its shell-inlaid eye sockets flashed, while a soft eerie hooting erupted from its mouth. *He-of-Divided-Body* was a Powerful Spirit. During the Creation, Hadui had traveled to a place where lay the body of a freshly dead human, and exclaimed, "Come, you who are my brother," then he'd bent down and divided the corpse in half. Taking up one half of the cold flesh, he'd conjoined it with half of his own Spirit body, and the two halves had become one. As a result, one-half of the mask's head was covered with white human hair and the other half glistened with Hadui's coal-black hair. *He-of-Divided-Body* was a creature of life and death, human and supernatural, of death and Requickening. One half of his face was red, the other black. He had chosen to live forever on the earth in the forests, so that he could help human beings in time of need.

Kelek refused to face him. Instead, she turned her attention to the door, watching for Little Matron Adusha. Adusha led the Bear Clan in Turtleback Village. Scouts had seen her hurrying up the southern trail with two guards. Kelek had ordered that she be escorted to the council house when she arrived, but that had been more than one-half hand of time ago. What was taking so long?

He-of-Divided-Body let out a long, shrill wail

that chilled Kelek's blood. As though to emphasize his words, he shuddered violently, battering the wall. She looked around. Every mask seemed to be rocking back and forth, as if ready to leap from the walls and pounce upon her elderly body in punishment for her crimes.

"I did what I had to," she hissed at them. "It was my duty to increase the Power of the Bear Clan! Any matron would have..."

The flapping door curtain was shoved aside, and as Adusha entered the council house, her plain moosehide cape whipped about her red leggings. Sweat plastered her short black hair to her round face, accentuating the width of her flat nose and the thinness of her lips. A short woman, she had a husky voice. "I apologize for being late, High Matron."

She strode forward with her guards. The man to her left was tall and muscular. Kelek didn't know him, but he was Wolf Clan. Yi's lineage. Red paw prints encircled the bottom of his black cape. The man to Adusha's right was Hikatoo. Of average height, handsome in a boyish way, he had seen thirty summers. Kelek knew his grandmother well. Snipe Clan. For several summers, Hikatoo had been one of Atotarho's personal guards.

"Your messenger said to expect you at noon," Kelek called irritably.

"Yes, well, I've never seen Hadui this violent.

He's ripping whole trees from the ground and casting them across the trails that lead into Atotarho Village. It's as though he's trying to block off the village to isolate you, High Matron. We were forced to veer around many such obstacles."

Kelek stiffened, frowning at the comment.

Adusha stopped less than a pace from Kelek. "I assume you know Hikatoo." She extended a hand to the guard on her left. "This is War Chief Tajan from Hilltop Village."

Kelek's gaze slowly examined the man. "Yi's lineage."

"I am, yes." The man's dark eyes had an eerie gleam.

This isn't right. Adusha is a Bear Clan matron from Turtleback Village. She should have Bear Clan guards.

"I hope things are well in Hilltop Village, War Chief. It is not usual for—"

"No, but nothing is *usual*, is it?" Adusha folded her arms tightly beneath her heavy moosehide cape. "Things are not well in the world outside Atotarho Village, Kelek."

"I assume you're referring to the war."

"I'm referring to the fact that Hilltop and Turtleback villages are buzzing with the news that on her deathbed, our former High Matron told Zateri's daughter she planned to name Zateri to replace her when she was gone."

Kelek lifted her chin to stare down her nose in disdain. "It's a rumor, nothing more."

Tajan's piercing gaze was like a hot lance thrust into Kelek's vitals.

Kelek waved a hand. "Come, come, you don't believe it, do you? Zateri probably told her daughter to say it in the hopes of ousting the Bear Clan."

Adusha shook her head gravely, and the War Chief shifted to prop his hand on his belted war club. At the strange, threatening gesture, Kelek bristled and straightened.

"Your behavior is outrageous. What is the meaning of this?"

Adusha softly said, "Turtleback Village and Hilltop Village received messengers. Both villages called council meetings so everyone could hear the story from the messenger himself. The man who came to Turtleback Village repeated the girl's story perfectly, and it was filled with so many small details that no child could have made them up. They could only have come from our former High Matron."

Kelek swallowed hard. No messenger had come to her, but she knew the story. Already, four separate versions were circulating around Atotarho Village. "So...Turtleback Village believes it?"

"Every person outside of the Bear Clan believes it."

She glanced at the guards who nodded slightly. "And the Bear Clan? What's being said by our own relatives?"

Adusha's folded arms tightened, bulging beneath her cape. After Coldspring, Riverbank, and Canassatego villages split away, there were only three villages left in the true Hills nation: Turtleback Village, Hilltop Village, and Atotarho Village. No matter the cost, they had to remain united.

"I think most of our relatives believe it, too."

Kelek started pacing again to release some of her anxiety. "War Chief Tajan? What is the opinion of Hilltop Village?"

"Our village council believes Zateri is the rightful High Matron," he responded bluntly.

Kelek snorted. "And just how do they speculate that I became High Matron if not through the words of our former High Matron? Is the Bear Clan being accused of wrongdoing?"

Adusha unfolded her arms and lowered them to her sides where she clenched her fists. "Not the Bear Clan. Just you, Kelek. It is being whispered that you conspired with Chief Atotarho to deny Zateri her rightful place—"

"Other than a child's word, what evidence is there to support this claim?"

Hikatoo's eyes narrowed, as though he knew something.

Adusha said, "Some people—the kind ones who love you—say that Atotarho lied to you when he told you that our former High Matron had named you to succeed her, and you unwittingly accepted the position without further verification. After all, we were headed off to war with the Standing Stone villages. There was no time, and someone had to lead the nation."

Kelek hesitated. "And what is being said by those who do not love me?"

Adusha stared at her. "They say you so coveted the position that you were the one who approached Atotarho. That you offered him—"

"I most certainly did not!"

"No? Well, those who have ears find it odd that as soon as you ascended to the High Matronship, you announced the marriage of your granddaughter to Atotarho." She cocked her head in a distasteful accusatory manner. "Is it true that you agreed to link Atotarho to the Bear Clan so he could remain as chief?"

"Stop looking at me like that," Kelek ordered. "It is impudent. I am the High Matron!"

Adusha's glare dimmed only slightly. "High Matron, these are perilous times. Our nation is split down the middle, and Hills People are killing other Hills People. I am under orders to discover the truth. The other leaders of the Bear Clan are deeply worried that these rumors are true."

Kelek's knees felt slightly weak. In a dignified manner, she eased down to the bench beside the fire and straightened her buckskin cape around her. As she primly laced her hand in her lap, she said, "Go on. I need to hear every word."

"Our elders fear that you worked with Atotarho to kill the former High Matron—"

"How dare they! I did not!"

"Kelek, please listen. There is another reason I am here. I was in the Wolf Clan longhouse the day our former high matron died. I saw something."

"What?"

"I, along with five other people, saw Zateri's daughter, Kahn-Tineta, leave the former High Matron's chamber with her cousin Pedeza. Immediately afterward, we saw a man come into the longhouse and enter the former High Matron's chamber. His face was heavily painted with black and white stripes. None of us recognized him, but we heard later that many people had seen the evil witch, Ohsinoh, speaking with Chief Atotarho that day, and he'd had his face painted with black and white stripes. The man left the High Matron's chamber in less than thirty heartbeats. When we went to speak with her, to seek her guidance, we found her dead. She still had the corner of one of her bedding hides pressed over her nose and mouth. No one can prove she was smothered, but we all suspected it."

"If so, I had nothing to do with it. I loved her! She had served our nation well for more than thirty summers!"

"Right now the story is being whispered through the entire nation. If it can be shown that you were involved in her murder, the Wolf Clan will swear blood feuds against every member of the Bear Clan. Isn't that right, War Chief Tajan?"

He nodded once. "My clan elders have assured me that we will."

Adusha continued, "If this happens, it will split the Hills People yet again. The Wolf Clan greatly outnumbers us. One by one, they will hunt the Bear Clan down, even if it takes generations. The other Bear Clan elders fear that our clan may not survive."

Legends spoke of many clans that had been wiped out by blood feuds. The tragic stories were told around the winter fires so that every child knew the possible outcome of a blood feud initiated as a result of the Law of Retribution.

After thirty heartbeats, the blood surging in Kelek's veins began to slow, and she could think again. Had she been so desperate for her clan to rule the nation that she'd brought it to the brink of destruction?

She'd thought her clan would be jubilant. And they had been...for a time. She felt Adusha watching her with eagle eyes, as though waiting for

Kelek to lie so that she could give War Chief Tajan the order to strike a deadly blow.

Surely that's why he's here. He's Wolf Clan. Under the Law of Retribution, it is his right, the right of his clan.

"The village councils of Hilltop and Turtleback respectfully ask to hear your version of how it happened, High Matron. I will carry the story back for their consideration."

Kelek swore the ground beneath her feet shifted, as though Great Grandmother Earth was preparing to suck her down into the depths of darkness.

Her mouth had gone bone dry. She licked her lips nervously. "It's a simple tale, Adusha. The night before our former High Matron died, Chief Atotarho came to me. It was the middle of the night. He was alone. He told me he'd just been with the High Matron, and that she'd named me to succeed her." *Does my face show the truth?* "However, since he had no ties to the Bear Clan, he knew we would probably choose to replace him as Chief. He made me an offer. He said that if I would grant permission for him to marry my granddaughter, and work on his behalf with our clan so that he could retain his position, he would assure that by next spring, the People of the Hills would be the only nation left standing south of Skanodario Lake.

He guaranteed that we would have conquered and adopted everyone else."

She paused to swallow and study their expressions. She couldn't tell whether they believed her or not.

Adusha's voice was low. "How did you think he could accomplish such a thing? Our Ruling Council would surely have refused—"

"Don't you see? If he could, the People of the Hills would become the most powerful nation in the world. Think of what we could do! We could send out armies to conquer the Algonquin and Cherokee to the south, and the Islander's Confederacy to the north. Our armies could sweep westward like locusts, taking whatever we wished. We would be wealthy beyond our wildest dreams! Our children would never be hungry or frightened again." *And I would become a legend. The greatest High Matron in the history of the People.* She extended a translucent parchment-like hand to Adusha. "Isn't that worth allowing him to retain his position? Of course, if he'd failed, we would have been forced to replace him with someone else, but I felt certain—"

"Certain?" Adusha's voice was terse. "Are you telling me that you betrayed us so our nation could make war on distant Peoples we don't even know?"

War Chief Tajan had his gaze on her.

Curiosity filled his dark eyes. Hikatoo's mouth had tightened into a white bloodless line.

"Betrayed who? The Wolf Clan? I didn't betray them. Atotarho assured me that our former high matron had named me to replace her."

Adusha stared at Kelek for a long time. "Please tell your story, Hikatoo."

Kelek's panicked gaze jerked to the Snipe Clan warrior, and her heart thundered.

"I only heard a few words of the chief's conversation with Matron Kelek. As she says, he did go to her. One hand of time earlier, however, I was standing right outside the Wolf Clan longhouse, barely three paces from where the Chief spoke with the former High Matron in her chamber. Though the longhouse wall hid many of their words, all of his personal guards, me included, heard the former High Matron when she raised her voice to tell the Chief, *'You are unfit to rule this nation, but the council cannot afford to remove you on the eve of battle.'*" He paused to take a deep breath and glared at Kelek. "One hand of time later, he ordered us to accompany him to the Bear Clan longhouse so he could speak with Matron Kelek. He stood under the porch until she appeared. The chief began their conversation by saying, *'I have a proposition I think you will appreciate.'* After that, I only caught certain words. But we were all worried by what had happened that day, so later that night, we discussed what each of us had heard. Between the five of us, we filled in much of the conversation."

Kelek felt slightly faint. She gritted her teeth and lifted her chin, trying to glower. "You were standing twenty paces away. What could you have heard?"

Hikatoo's dark gaze did not waver. "You told the chief that in exchange for his saying the former high matron had named you to succeed her, you would marry him to your granddaughter, and you assured him that he would retain his position as Chief."

Adusha's head tilted in an unpleasant accusatory manner. After ten heartbeats of waiting for Kelek to deny it, she lifted her arm and pointed a finger at Kelek's chest. "When I said you had betrayed us, I didn't mean the Wolf Clan, Kelek. I meant the nation. Your own words make it clear that you conspired with Atotarho to circumvent the wisdom of the Ruling Council. That alone is treason, *High Matron*." She said the words with contempt. "And once the rest of the story has spread across the entire nation, the Bear Clan will be spat upon and hunted down like dogs. Our clan will be extinct."

Kelek rose to her feet, shaking with a combination of indignation and fear. "Tell your village councils that I demand they appear before me to discuss this issue in person. This *pieced-together* conversation is pure fabrication! I refuse to stand here any longer being maligned by a cowardly warrior and an insignificant *Little Matron!*"

A cold smile came to Adusha's thin lips. "I will tell them. In the meantime, we have heard that Atotarho requested you to send two thousand warriors to join him in the destruction of the Standing Stone nation."

"Yes. I'd planned to bring the issue before the Ruling Council tomor—"

"Take no action until you've heard from our village councils."

Kelek stiffened. "But he needs those warriors."

Adusha didn't deign to respond. She turned on her heel and stalked toward the door with her guards behind her.

When they'd gone, Kelek stared at the wind-whipped curtain. The sacred False Faces on the walls rattled and hooted shrilly, crying out to each other. Her shaking knees finally gave way. She sank down to the bench and dropped her head in her hands.

AUTHORS' NOTE

Some of the Peacemaker stories say that in the end, Atotarho submitted to Hiyawento and let him comb the snakes from his hair. When Hiyawento had finished, the evil cannibal-sorcerer transformed before his eyes. The Chief's lost soul returned, his crooked body straightened out, and his heart turned toward reason and compassion. For the rest of his life, Atotarho was a good and just leader who dedicated himself to implementing Dekanawida's message of peace. The Great Council Fire of the League of the Haudenosaunee is still safely kept in the land of the Onondaga.

A LOOK AT BOOK EIGHT:
ECLIPSE DANCER

In the thrilling conclusion to the acclaimed *People of the Longhouse* series, *Eclipse Dancer,* takes readers on a journey through ancient America, where the fate of the Iroquois nations hangs in the balance.

The relentless Atotarho wage a devastating war across the land. As villages fall to his ruthless army, the prophet Dekanawida foresees an impending great darkness. With time running out, he calls upon his loyal friends, Baji and Hiyawento, to join him in a final, desperate battle. The stakes are high, and the sacrifices are immense.

Will their mission of peace succeed in time to save their loved ones?

With their unparalleled expertise in North American prehistory, Kathleen and W. Michael Gear weave an epic adventure about the founding of the League of the Iroquois and the origins of American democracy.

Dive into this epic saga and witness the gripping finale.

AVAILABLE OCTOBER 2024

ABOUT W. MICHAEL GEAR

W. Michael Gear is a *New York Times, USA Today,* and international bestselling author of sixty novels. With close to eighteen million copies of his books in print worldwide; his work has been translated into twenty-nine languages.

Gear has been inducted into the Western Writers Hall of Fame and the Colorado Authors' Hall of Fame—as well as won the Owen Wister Award, the Golden Spur Award, and the International Book Award for both Science Fiction and Action Suspense Fiction. He is also the recipient of the Frank Waters Award for lifetime contributions to Western writing.

Gear's work, inspired by anthropology and archaeology, is multilayered and has been called compelling, insidiously realistic, and masterful. Currently, he lives in northwestern Wyoming with his award-winning wife and co-author, Kathleen O'Neal Gear, and a charming sheltie named, Jake.

ABOUT KATHLEEN O'NEAL GEAR

Kathleen O'Neal Gear is a *New York Times* bestselling author of fifty-seven books and a national award-winning archaeologist. The U.S. Department of the Interior has awarded her two Special Achievement awards for outstanding management of America's cultural resources.

In 2015 the United States Congress honored her with a Certificate of Special Congressional Recognition, and the California State Legislature passed Joint Member Resolution #117 saying, "The contributions of Kathleen O'Neal Gear to the fields of history, archaeology, and writing have been invaluable..."

In 2021 she received the Owen Wister Award for lifetime contributions to western literature, and in 2023 received the Frank Waters Award for "a body of work representing excellence in writing and storytelling that embodies the spirit of the American West."

GLOSSARY

Flying Heads—Just heads with no bodies that thrash wildly through the forests. These fearsome creatures have long trailing hair and great paws like a bear's.

Gaha—The soft wind. She is spoken of as Elder Sister Gaha.

Gahai—Spectral lights that guide sorcerers as they fly through the air on their evil journeys. Sometimes gahai lead their masters to victims, other times to places where they can find charms.

Hadui—A violent wind.

Hanehwa—Skin-beings. Witches sometimes skin their victims, enchant their skins, and force them to do their bidding. Hanehwa warn witches of danger by giving three shouts.

Hatho—The Frost Spirit.

Haudenosaunee—The People of the Longhouse, called "Iroquois" by the French.

Ohwachira—The basic family unit. An ohwachira is a kinship group that traces its descent from a common female ancestor. The ohwachira bestows chieftainship titles, and holds the names of the great people of the past. It bestows those names by raising up the souls of the dead and requickening them in the bodies of newly elected chiefs, adoptees, or other people. In the same way, if a new chief disappoints the ohwachira, after consultation with the clan, it can take back the name, remove the soul, and depose the chief. It is also the sisterhood of ohwachiras that decides when to go to war and when to make peace.

Otkon—One of the two halves of Spirit Power that inhabit the world. The other is Uki. Don't think of these as good and evil, however. Both powers share equally in light and dark. Otkon and Uki form a unified spiritual universe that must be kept in balance. Otkon has a trickster-like character. It's unpredictable and can be either beneficial or harmful to human beings. It's half of the day lasts from noon to midnight. Otkon is often associated with the Evil-Minded One, the hero twin also known as Flint.

People of the Flint—The Mohawk nation. However, the word *Mohawk* is an Algonquian term meaning "flesh eaters." They call themselves the Kanienkahaka, or Ganienkeh, meaning "People of the Flint."

People of the Hills—The Onondaga nation. The word *Onondaga* is an anglicized version of their name for themselves, *Onundagaono,* which means "People of the Hills."

People of the Landing—The Cayuga nation. Including People of the Landing, several other possible derivations have been offered for the word *Cayuga,* including "People of the Place Where Locusts Were Taken Out," "People of the Mucky Land," and "People of the Place Where Boats Are Taken Out."

People of the Mountain—The Seneca nation. They call themselves the *Onondowahgah.* Their name can also be translated as "People of the Great Hill."

People of the Standing Stone—The Oneida nation. The word *Oneida* may be a rather poor Anglicization of their name for themselves, *Onayotekaono,* meaning "Granite People," or "People of the Standing Stone."

Requickening Ceremony—The raising up of souls for the purpose of placing them in other bodies, such as those of adoptees. This concept does not exactly correspond to the eastern religions' concept of reincarnation. For example, there's no idea of karma to be accounted for. Being reborn is neither punishment, nor reward. Instead, there is a strong concept of duty to the People. Only strong souls were requickened, usually within the same maternal lineage. The ceremony was performed in the hopes of easing grief and restoring the spiritual strength of the clans, but a returning soul also had an obligation to help the People in times of crises. Many "Keepings" of the Peacemaker story say that Dekanawida was the returned soul of Tarenyawagon—also Tarachiawagon, the culture hero also known as Sapling, the Good-Minded One, who served as the Creator. Those same traditions identify Atotarho as Sapling's troublesome younger brother, Flint—Tawiscaro/Tawiscaron—who was called the Evil-Minded One. Jigonsaseh, similarly, was sometimes identified as the returned soul of Sky Woman's daughter, the Lynx.

Uki—One of the two halves of Spirit Power that inhabit the world—see *Otkon*. Uki is never harmful to human beings. It's half of the day lasts from midnight to noon. Uki is often associated with the Good-Minded One, the hero twin also known as Sapling, or Tarenyawagon.

SELECTED BIBLIOGRAPHY

Bruchac, Joseph. *Iroquois Stories: Heroes and Heroines, Monsters and Magic*. Freedom, CA: The Crossing Press, 1985.

Calloway, Colin G. *The Western Abenakis of Vermont, 1600-1800*. Norman: University of Oklahoma Press, 1990.

Converse, Harriet Maxwell. "Origin of the Wampum Belt" and "The Legendary Origin of Wampum." In *Myths and Legends of New York State Iroquois*, New York State Museum Bulletin 125, edited by Arthur Caswell Parker, 138-145 and 187-190. Albany: University of the State of New York, 1908.

Custer, Jay F. *Delaware Prehistoric Archaeology: An Ecological Approach*. Cranberry, NJ: Associated University Presses, 1984.

Dye, David H. *War Paths, Peace Paths: An Archaeology of Cooperation and Conflict in Native Eastern North America*. Lanham, MD: Altamira Press, 2009.

Ellis, Chris J., and Neal Ferris, eds. *The Archaeology of Southern Ontario to A.D. 1650*. London, Ontario, Canada: Occasional Papers of the London Chapter, OAS Number 5, 1990.

Elm, Demus, and Harvey Antone. *The Oneida Creation Story*. Lincoln: University of Nebraska, 2000.

Engelbrecht, William E. *Iroquoia: The Development of a Native World*. Syracuse University Press, 2003.

Fagan, Brian M. *Ancient North America: The Archaeology of a Continent*. 4th ed. London: Thames and Hudson Press, 2005.

Fenton, William N. *The False Faces of the Iroquois*. Norman: University of Oklahoma Press, 1987.

—. *The Iroquois Eagle Dance: An Offshoot of the Calumet Dance.* Syracuse: Syracuse University Press, 1991.

—. *The Roll Call of the Iroquois Chiefs. A Study of a Pneumonic Cane from the Six Nations Reserve.* Cranbook Institute of Science, Bulletin No. 30, 1950.

Foster, Steven, and James A. Duke. *Eastern/Central Medicinal Plants.* The Peterson Guides Series. Boston: Houghton Mifflin Company, 1990.

Hart, John P., and Christina B. Rieth, eds. *Northeast Subsistence-Settlement Change: A.D. 700-1300,* New York State Museum Bulletin 496. Albany: University of the State of New York, 2002.

Heckewelder, John. *History, Manners, and Customs of the Indian Nations Who Once Inhabited Pennsylvania and the Neighboring States.* New York: Arno Press, 1971.

Herrick, James W. *Iroquois Medical Botany.* Syracuse: Syracuse University Press, 1995.

Hewitt, J. N. B. "The Iroquoian Concept of the Soul." *Journal of American Folklore,* 8 (1895): 107-116.

—. "Orenda and a Definition of Religion." *American Anthropologist,* N.S., 4 (1902): 33-46.

—. "Status of Woman in Iroquois Polity before 1784." In *Annual Report of the Board of Regents,* 475-488. Washington, D.C.: Smithsonian Institution, 1933.

—. "Wampum." In *Handbook of North American Indians North of Mexico,* 904-909. New York: Rowman and Littlefield, 1965.

Jemison, Pete. "Mother of Nations: The Peace Queen, a Neglected Tradition." *Akwe:kon* 5 (1988): 68-70.

Jennings, Francis. *The Ambiguous Iroquois Empire.* New York: W. W. Norton, 1984.

Jennings, Francis, ed. *The History and Culture of Iroquois Diplomacy.* Syracuse University Press, 1995.

Johansen, Bruce Elliot, and Barbara Alice Mann. *Encyclopedia* of the Haudenosaunee (Iroquois Confederacy). Westport, CT: Greenwood Press, 2000.

Kapches, Mima. "Intra-Longhouse Spatial Analysis." *Pennsylvania Archaeologist*, 49, No. 4 (December 1979): 24-29.

Kurath, Gertrude P. *Iroquois Music and Dance: Ceremonial Arts of Two Seneca Longhouses*. Smithsonian Institution, Bureau of American Ethnology, Bulletin 187. Washington, D.C.: U.S. Government Printing Office, 1964.

Levine, Mary Ann, Kenneth E. Sassaman, and Michael S. Nassaney, eds. *The Archaeological Northeast*. Westport, CT: Bergin and Garvey, 1999.

Mann, Barbara A., and Jerry L. Fields. "The Fire at Onondaga: Wampum as Proto-writing." *Akwesasne Notes* (1995): 40-48.

--. *Iroquoian Women: Gantowisas of the Haudenosaunee League*. New York: Peter Lang, 2000.

--. "A Sign in the Sky: Dating the League of the Haudenosaunee." The Wampum Chronicles, www.wampumchronicles.com/signinthesky.html.

Martin, Calvin. *Keepers of the Game: Indian-Animal Relationships and the Fur Trade*. Berkeley: University of California Press, 1978.

Mensforth, Robert P. "Human Trophy Taking in Eastern North America During the Archaic Period: The Relationship to Warfare and Social Complexity." Chap. 9 in *The Taking and Displaying of Human Body Parts as Trophies by Amerindians*, edited by Richard J. Chacon and David Dye. New York: Springer, 2007.

Miroff, Laurie E., and Timothy D. Knapp. *Iroquoian Archaeology and Analytic Scale*. Knoxville: University of Tennessee Press, 2009.

Morgan, Lewis Henry. *League of the Iroquois*. New York: Corinth Books, 1962.

Mullen, Grant J., and Robert D. Hoppa. "Rogers Ossuary (AgHb-131): An Early Ontario Iroquois Burial Feature from Brantford Township." *The Canadian Journal of Archaeology/ Journal Canadien d'Archeologie* 16, (1992).

Murray, David. *Forked Tongues: Speech, Writing, and Representation in North American Indian Texts*. Bloomington: Indiana University Press, 1991.

O'Callaghan, E. B., ed. *The Documentary History of the State of New York*. 4 vols. Albany: Weed, Parsons and Co., 1849-1851.

Parker, Arthur C. *Iroquois Uses of Maize and Other Food Plants*, New York State Museum Bulletin 144. Albany: University of the State of New York, 1910.

--. *Seneca Myths and Folk Tales*. Lincoln: University of Nebraska Press, 1989.

--, writing as Gawasco Wanneh. *An Analytical History of the Seneca Indians*, 1926. Researches and Transactions of the New York State Archeological Association, Lewis H. Morgan Chapter. New York: Kraus Reprint Co., 1970.

Parker, Arthur C. ed. *Myths and Legends of the New York State Iroquois*, New York State Museum Bulletin 125, 138-145 and 187-190. Albany: University of the State of New York, 1908.

Richter, Daniel. *The Ordeal of the Longhouse: The People of the Iroquois League in the Era of European Colonization*. Chapel Hill: University of North Carolina Press, 1992.

Scheiber, Laura L., and Mark D. Mitchell, eds. *Across a Great Divide: Continuity and Change in Native North American Societies, 1400-1900*. Tucson: University of Arizona Press, 2010.

Slotkin, J. S., and Karl Schmitt. "Studies of Wampum." *American Anthropologist* 51 (1949): 223-236.

Snow, Dean. *The Archaeology of New England*. New York: Academic Press, 1980.

--. *The Iroquois*. Oxford: Blackwell, 1996.

Snyderman, George S. "The Function of Wampum in Iroquois

Religion." *Proceedings of the American Philosophical Society* (1961): 571-608.

Spittal, W. G. *Iroquois Women: An Anthology.* Ohsweken, ON: Iroqrafts, Ltd., 1990.

Talbot, Francis Xavier. *Saint Among the Hurons: The Life of Jean De Brebeuf.* New York: Harper and Brothers, 1949.

Tehanetorens. *Wampum Belts of the Iroquois.* Summertown, TN: Book Publishing Company, 1999.

Tooker, Elizabeth, ed. *Iroquois Culture, History, and Prehistory.* Albany: University of the State of New York, 1967.

Trigger, Bruce. *The Children of Aataentsic: A History of the Huron People to 1660.* Montreal: McGill-Queen's University Press, 1987.

Trigger, Bruce, ed. *Handbook of North American Indians, Vol. 15: Northeast.* Washington, D.C.: Smithsonian Institution Press, 1978.

Tuck, James A. *Onondaga Iroquois Prehistory: A Study in Settlement Archaeology.* Syracuse: Syracuse University Press, 1971.

Wallace, Anthony F. C. *The Death and Rebirth of the Seneca.* New York: Vintage Books, 1972.

Walthall, John A., and Thomas E. Emerson, eds. *Calumet and Fleur-de-Lys: Archaeology of the Indian and French Contact in the Midcontinent.* Washington, D.C.: Smithsonian Institution Press, 1992.

Weer, Paul. *Preliminary Notes on the Iroquoian Family.* Prehistory Research Series. Indianapolis: Indiana Historical Society, 1937.

Whitehead, Ruth Holmes. *Stories from the Six Worlds: Micmac Legends.* Halifax: Nimbus Publishing, 1988.

Williamson, Ronald F., and Susan Pfeiffer. *Bones of the Ancestors: The Archaeology and Osteobiography of the Moatfield Ossuary.* Gatineau, Quebec: Canadian Museum of Civilization, 2003.

PRAISE FOR THE PEACEMAKER'S TALE SERIES

"Extraordinary...The Gears colorfully integrate authentic archaeological and anthropological details with a captivating story replete with romance, intrigue, mayhem, and a nail-biting climax."

— *LIBRARY JOURNAL*

"Authentic detail, believable action and perceptive insights into connections between past and present help make these novels into significant contributions to our understanding of who we are and where we came from."

— *THE BEACON*

"So well researched and evocative one can almost smell the drying pine needles, and feel the heat and choking dust raised by the stampeding of thousands of warriors."

— *RAPPORT*

Printed in the USA
CPSIA information can be obtained
at www.ICGtesting.com
LVHW031512200924
791666LV00016B/319